Praise for *Very Well*

In her novel Very Well, Chana beautifully points to something that spoke deeply to me, her gentle touch left me feeling seen, uplifted, and embraced. I laughed, cried, and felt so much during the reading! I love how Chana balances a captivating story and sprinkles it with common sense and great suggestions. I highly recommend this book!

                                        Natasha Swerdloff, Owner of The Principles Institute, and co-author of *Coming Home: Uncovering The Foundations Of Psychological Well-Being*

Very Well is a must read for anyone who feels hijacked by their hormones or their body. Chana truly understands and clearly articulates what many women go through and she presents a transformational way of viewing health and wellbeing. The deeper truths touched upon in this entertaining novel will help you see any and all experience in a fresh, new way. I will be recommending Very Well to my clients and to all of the women in my life!

                                        Dr. Amy Johnson, Ph.D., author *of The Little Book of Big Change: The No-Willpower Approach to Breaking Any Habit and Just a Thought: A No-Willpower Approach to End Self-Doubt and Make Peace with Your Mind*

If you're a woman looking to learn how best to support your mental and physical health, look no further. This inspiring novel provides readers with an in-depth look at the Three Principles as described by the late Sydney Banks and the mind-body connection, and how this understanding can help alleviate any of the common, women's health-related issues and improve overall well-being.

Through her captivating narratives, Chana delves into a range of themes in the book - from hormone levels and circadian rhythms to psychological issues such as depression, stress, and trauma. She shares her wealth of knowledge in an accessible way that's easy to understand - making it a great resource for anyone interested in improving their health from an exploration of their innate well-being.

Chana's passionate writing and storytelling make it an enjoyable and informative read. But most importantly, reading this book and deepening your understanding of the principles behind our experiences can transform your life!

Highly recommended! I'm already planning to give out copies of the book to my female clients.

Dr. Rani Bora, Holistic Psychiatrist, Mental Wealth Coach, and author of *How To Turn Stress On Its Head*.

Such an interesting book that opens with the seemingly simple premise of a woman and her two daughters, but as we move through it, we see that as always there is more to it than that.

As a menopause coach, I'm always open to different viewpoints about what's really causing the symptoms that women experience that are generally associated with our hormones being out of balance, so Chana hit the nail right on the head here for me. I love the way she weaves so many helpful facts into a fictional story leaving the reader unknowingly educated by the time she's finished reading.

Chana interweaves the story with interesting information to show that despite all being on the same journey, not every woman experiences it or reacts to any challenges she encounters in the same way. A great story about real women's issues written for real women with the most wonderful ending!

Vikki Ede, Nutritional Therapist, Natural Menopause Specialist, CEO and Owner of Soothe Your, and founder of the Menopause Support Group

Chana has written a fascinating book that deeply understands the experience of women. She leads the reader to see through the fog of their feelings to a deeper place of truth. One where drugs and surgeries are a last, rather than a first resort. One where they get to explore their rich and uniquely feminine gifts. Seeing what others might term as the "downside" of being a woman, Chana shows us that it is all in fact part of the Masterplan of perfection. The mysterious world of hormones is explained in a way that I can understand and has prepared me for what is to come. Her bold voice and willingness to say what others shy away from is a guide for us all.

Chayelle Rose, Mentor and coach,
'Expanding bandwidth for Mum's worldwide'

As someone who suffered significantly from PMS and who could pretty much guarantee a major marital fight once a month, I wish I had read Chana's book Very Well in my twenties so I could have understood my experience better, recognized there was nothing wrong with me, not felt alone in my suffering, and most importantly, known there was hope.

I have always believed in holistic health modalities and food as medicine, but in this area of my life, they didn't seem to help. The novel Very Well would have helped me understand the impact of trauma on my physiology and stress hormones and shown me there was a way to heal.

Fortunately, I came across the teachings of Sydney Banks and experienced firsthand improvements in my health in time for me to experience a graceful peri and post-menopause. So even though the story Chana shares is fiction, the healing available is real.

Chana's book is a timely reminder about the impact of stress on health and debunks disempowering myths around chemical and hormonal imbalances. She highlights the importance of understanding the health in the feedback of our bodies and the resilience and capacity we all have to heal.

The story also includes eye-opening non-fictional revelations about the underpinnings of psychoanalysis and introduced me to the influential figure of Bertha Pappenheim, whose good works have not received the acclaim they deserve, unlike the pseudo-science of analysis. Fortunately, Chana addresses this imbalance in Very Well!

Rohini Ross M.A. LMFT, Co-Founder of The
Rewilders and the Rewilding Love podcast

In this groundbreaking novel, Chana Studley successfully challenges the patriarchal narrative surrounding female hormones through her delightful storytelling abilities. As women, we have become better at talking about mental health, but we still shy away from discussing periods, miscarriages, postpartum mental health, endometriosis, and menopause. This results in a lack of vital understanding for women, particularly as those processes are inextricably connected to our mental health. Chana, however, introduces her readers to a simple yet profound understanding that ultimately guides us repeatedly back to our own wisdom and well-being.

A must read - informative, funny, moving and wise. This is a book to buy, read, digest then buy again for your friends and family. After all, life is a journey we take together, don't we?

Jacquie Forde Nurse, Midwife, Women's Life and Business Coach

Praise for Chana Studley's previous novels

The Myth of Low Self Esteem

Chana Studley has written a powerful novel about how we can use the power of our mind to heal us from the negative messages that cause us to feel anxious, enraged, and depressed. Her book provides hope to people who have been diagnosed with various disorders, showing how, by letting go of their self-limiting inner narratives, they live a life of unlimited joy and inner peace. I heartily recommend this book to those who want to free themselves of negative mental constructs.

> Dr. Miriam Adahan, Ph.D., Teacher,
> author, and spiritual guide

Painless

Painless has the potential to awaken fresh hope to the millions of people worldwide who spend the majority of every day enveloped and overwhelmed by their experience of pain. This state when left unabated often results in permanent disability and all too often in suicide. Chana does this with a clarity and certainty that would make Candace Pert Ph.D., the late pioneer in the oneness of the body-mind phenomenon, proud.

> Dr. William F. Pettit Jr., M.D., Retired
> Psychiatrist, now full-time student and mentor of
> the 3 Principles, with fifty-plus years of clinical and
> teaching experience and past recipient of Board
> Certification in Psychosomatic Medicine

Very Well

A novel about hormones, women, and why Freud was wrong

Chana Studley

Very Well
Copyright © 2023 Chana Studley
First printing 2023

All rights reserved. No part of this publication may be reproduced, distributed, or transmitted in any form or by any means, including photocopying, recording, or other electronic or mechanical methods, without the prior written permission of the author, except in the case of brief quotations embodied in critical reviews and certain other noncommercial uses permitted by copyright law. For permission requests, write to the author at the address below.

Very Well is a work of fiction. The information and opinions in this novel should not be regarded as a substitute for professional medical advice. The author cannot be held responsible for any loss, claim, or damage arising out of the misuse of the suggestions made or failure to take professional medical advice. If you have a medical problem or concern, please seek professional medical advice. The characters in this book are fictional, and any resemblance to actual persons, living or dead, is purely coincidental.

Cover design by Chana Studley
Photograph of Bertha Pappenheim used by Courtesy of the Leo Baeck Institute, New York.
Back cover photograph by Andrea Brownstein
Editing and formatting by Heather Osborne

ISBN: 9798375047744

Chana Studley www.chanastudley.com

Contents

Foreword	i
1. Pacific Palisades	1
2. Mar Vista	10
3. Century City	26
4. Los Angeles	38
5. The Venice Canals	52
6. Santa Monica	64
7. Brentwood	83
8. February	94
9. March	105
10. San Diego Morning	114
11. San Diego Afternoon	133
12. April	147
13. May	159
14. June	172
15. July	184
16. August	197
17. September	212
18. October	228
19. November	240
20. December	256
21. January	270
22. February, March, and April	283
23. Beverly Hills	296
Acknowledgments	311
About the Author	313
Resources	314

Foreword

Chana Studley is a pioneer in looking at the connection between pain, chronic conditions, and state of mind. She brings her wisdom and insight into this book by explaining the connection between Thought and Suffering. Courageously, she takes on the myths surrounding women, hormones, and mental health. She writes about this in an engaging story with characters that will seem familiar to all. Everyone who is female or knows a female will relate to the story. Chana also weaves into the story the history of how medicine and psychiatry have looked at women as mentally ill as a result of their reactions to hormone changes and have been treated as if they have a disease that needs to be managed.

The most beautiful thing about this book is that Chana is able to provide hope to women who have been suffering in silence by not just discussing this topic in a way that doesn't pathologize what is happening to women, but also by sharing her understanding of the 3 Principles of Mind, Thought, and Consciousness and how they work to create experience in people. Chana merges this fresh paradigm in psychology and psychiatry into the story in a manner that is very simple and easy to understand. The reader will awaken to how these Principles work through the characters and see the potential for change and empowerment.

The book engages the reader to look at this topic through new eyes, and I believe it will bring relief to many women who suffer needlessly from their own thinking about what is happening in their bodies. I know that I will share this book with my clients, as well as friends and family. I think it will give women permission to get the help they need without feeling like they are going crazy and thus get relief from their needless suffering.

Christine J. Heath, LMFT, CSAC
Hawaii Counseling and Education Center, Inc.

1
Pacific Palisades

Helen Vargus stepped onto the escalator heading up to the cosmetics department of Neiman Marcus, Beverly Hills. She had just finished her Wednesday morning coffee break. As the ground floor slowly came into view, she became acutely aware of an eerie silence. The busy upscale department store was totally empty. Twenty minutes earlier, when Helen had left her post in Women's Shoes, it had been full of noisy and demanding customers. The high-end store, which was always bustling with shoppers, staff, and the occasional movie star, was as still as an abandoned church!

Where was everyone?

Her heart sped up. Was she dreaming? Did she forget something? Had she entered the twilight zone? She took a deep breath as she spun around and saw a young man flat on his back lying in a crushed glass display case, bleeding from his head and hands! He looked dazed but immediately jumped up and ran frantically between the cosmetic counters and out of the front door onto Wilshire Boulevard. Helen wasn't sure why, but she instinctively ran after him as he knocked over displays in his desperate effort to escape. As she reached the front entrance, a security guard stopped her. She was about to put her hand in blood the thief had left behind on the chrome handle of the large glass door!

"Let him go, clean this up, and welcome those customers." The guard called for backup as he ran off into the busy traffic of Beverly Hills.

Helen grabbed a bunch of Kleenex from the L'Oreal counter next to her and wiped up the bloody handprint as some unsuspecting patrons came in. As she turned around, the rest of the staff and customers were getting to their feet, and within seconds, it was all weirdly back to normal.

"What .... *what happened*?" Helen exclaimed to another plainclothes security guard who came rushing up.

"A shoplifter was trying to get away with a Rolex from the Men's department on the top floor. Just as William from Men's Shoes approached him, the idiot thief jumped over the safety glass and fell down four flights, crashing on and off each glass banister next to the escalator until he landed in that Judith Leiber display case! We all thought a bomb had gone off! Didn't you hear the screaming or the explosion as he hit the glass?"

"No! I was down in the break room, and I came up to find him on the floor by my feet!"

Very Well

For the next few days, the story was the buzz of every conversation in the store. Everyone had their version of what happened, yet no one outside the staff would ever hear about it. It wasn't good press for the store and with such high-end clientele to protect, the story soon disappeared along with the broken display case.

Life in Women's Shoes soon returned to its regular routine and Helen was back to serving affluent ladies of all shapes and sizes with their designer footwear needs, desires, and devotions. Most of her customers were "ladies who lunch," women who lived in Beverly Hills, Pacific Palisades, or Malibu with husbands who had become thick around the waist. They would come in on Monday and try on the latest Badgley Mischka or Manolo Blahnik shoes and put them on layaway. On Tuesday or Wednesday they would come back, this time with their girlfriend, to have lunch in the downstairs restaurant or drinks in the bar in the Men's department and then purchase their latest obsession. On Thursday or Friday, they would return the shoes because their husband didn't like them or they didn't match that new Michael Kors or Vivienne Westood outfit they had bought at Barneys, and the following week, the ceremony would start all over again. These faithful devotees of designer fashion were regular worshipers at the store whilst movie stars, famous musicians, sports personalities, and other celebrities, past and present, were an almost daily delight. Some of the faithful were known to preorder the latest designs without even seeing them; their desire to *have* was all-consuming. Helen's role as high priestess of Women's Shoes was often entertaining, and the commission much appreciated.

This hadn't always been her life. In the previous decade, Helen had been one of those women who "lunch," a happily married housewife and mother. Not quite so devoted to fashion, but she had enjoyed shopping as a minor pastime with her affluent friends. Her two girls were seniors in high school when her husband Gary died in a car accident. He'd had a heart attack at the wheel of his Mercedes and hit a wall in the underground parking lot of his Century City consultancy offices. Helen, devastated with grief and dealing with the shock of losing her husband, then had to deal with the shock of discovering they were now completely broke.

Gary Vargus was the grandson of immigrants. His grandparents had emigrated from Guatemala to harvest crops in the fields of Ventura County. Their son, Gary's father, had done well in school, bought an apartment that he rented out while his family lived in one room, and went to night school to become a lawyer. He worked hard and bought another apartment and eventually the whole building. Gary had taken over after finishing law school, and had made it into a very successful real estate business. It was the American dream. Gary had just invested heavily in a property deal that was going to make millions, but on his death the other investors pulled out, leaving Helen with massive debts.

Very Well

The house in the Palisades had to be sold. Helen's SUV, the timeshare in Hawaii, and the retirement plan all went to pay off what he owed. The girls would have to put themselves through college. Helen had to suffer the indignity of putting her life into a few boxes and moving to a small apartment in Mar Vista, a Los Angeles neighborhood that was, well, between all the others. She needed to work now, so with limited experience and after much rejection, she landed herself a job in a budget shoe store in the Westside Pavilion mall.

"Does this mean you won't be here when I get home from school?" Kara had asked.

Helen sensed at the time that her youngest daughter had been relieved at the thought of having some freedom but nervous to be alone in a new apartment and a strange neighborhood. "Yes, honey, and I'll have to work some weekends, but hey, we will all have new shoes!"

For the next few years, Helen worked her way up to a select boutique on Montana Avenue as the "shoe consultant," and then a "Shoe Dog" as it was affectionately called at the cathedral of all fashion worshipers, Neiman Marcus, Beverly Hills.

Helen's eldest daughter, Lily, had now finished high school and was in college on the East Coast. Kara had one more year before she would head that way too. As soon as Lily was gone, Kara had taken over their room for herself in their little two-bedroom, unremarkable apartment in Mar Vista.

"Mom, I'm putting all Lily's crap in her closet. I hate her

stupid posters, I hate her stupid books, and I don't see why I should have to look at them! And if she doesn't like it she can stay in New York, which is where her stupid stuff should be!"

Helen had just nodded. She knew Kara's hostility at Lily's lingering presence would pass. They had often struggled to get along, but deep down, they all knew it was Kara's hormones speaking. The girls looked so much alike that they were often thought to be twins, "Irish twins" someone had once called them. It would have made sense if they had Helen's blonde features, but they had dark hair and olive skin like their father. Helen had dressed them alike when they were young, but as they got older, their personalities were turning out very different.

Lily was the intense, quiet one. Serious and analytical, she went off to study marketing. Her sister had once suggested that she was so up in her head that her brain probably wouldn't notice if her body went the other way. Kara, only eleven months younger, was the passionate one, feeling her way in the world through her emotions–helping, caring deeply, and always seeking to understand. She had a tough time struggling with the ups and downs of teenage insecurity and angst. Each month she would hide away, suffering the anguish of her hormonal tornado, doing her best to ride the tsunami of emotions with as little damage to herself and her relationships as best she could. There were howling tirades at Helen and Lily; the slamming of doors and screams of "*Nobody understands!*" were common, only to be replaced by deep mood swings and punishing sulks the

Very Well

rest of the month.

Helen had often been worried for her. She took her to the family doctor for help, but the only help they could offer was a diagnosis of PMDD[1] and medication. It had gotten worse when her father died as Kara struggled through the stress of her exams, desperately trying to stay afloat of her grief and hormones.

Both girls had the usual monthly highs and lows–cramps, acne, and anxiety–but Kara's were off the charts. Helen was almost glad that the girls had had to share a room so that Kara had someone there when she was at her worst. She always said that she would never hurt herself, but it was very distressing for Helen to know those thoughts were there. Lily had done her best to tolerate her sister's endless crying and lashing out, but there were many volatile fights and the occasional scratch as hair was pulled and claws came out. They had tried many types of therapy, but neither Helen nor Kara wanted her to go on medication. As time went by, they had managed to work out some things that helped to bring a little relief.

Eating was one. Kara would get so distressed that she would lose interest in food, but then lack of good nutrition added to the nightmare. So they learned together that whether she wanted to eat or not, she would feel better if she did. Helen did her best to make as much healthy food as possible, like veggie burritos or a burger without the fries, something protein-heavy, as opposed to the ice cream cake

---

[1] Premenstrual Dysphoric Disorder.

they both really wanted. They knew something was better than nothing, so if the shot of serotonin came in a smoothie, that was okay too. Those late-night runs in their PJs to the smoothie store on Santa Monica Boulevard were some of the best nights they had together.

"Why is this happening to me, Mom? It's so not fair." Kara had asked her on one of those nights as she took the lid off her banana protein smoothie to get to the last drop, desperately trying not to cry again.

Helen had parked the car outside their apartment building as they returned home and turned to her daughter. "I don't know, honey. I wish I could make it all go away for you. All I know is you are incredibly brave and that I love you very much."

Helen spent many hours just holding her daughter as she scaled the walls of her anxious, sometimes suicidal thinking. Kara would often refuse any help when in the midst of the tornado, but afterward, she would always thank her mom for talking her off the ledge. Other things they discovered that helped were working out, keeping busy, and supplements from a very understanding naturopathic doctor. By the time Lily left for college and Kara had their room to herself, things felt a bit more under control. She didn't feel great, but the tools and techniques she had learned enabled her to tough it out, deal with her grief, and survive each month.

Lily seemed to be getting by in college. Helen was suspicious she was burying the grief about her father, but there were regular phone calls, and she was making new friends and enjoying her courses. Helen trusted she would let her know if anything was wrong.

"You sound like you are doing well, sweetheart?" Helen tried not to be too obvious but called once a week to hear her latest news and let her know she was missed.

"I guess."

"We can't wait to see you for winter break! Kara has made the place look so nice and is really looking forward to you coming home for the week."

"I doubt that very much." Lily had been on the receiving end of Kara's hormonal outbursts so often that Helen couldn't blame her for feeling like her sister didn't want her to come home.

"Oh, honey, you know Kara doesn't mean it. She can't control what's happening to her."

Lily sighed. "I know, Mom. Look, I have to go. Love you."

"Love you too."

So life shifted. Together, they got through their grief and the now predictable tidal wave of Kara's hormones.

2
Mar Vista

Helen had woken up at 4 am in a sweat. She turned over with the frustrating thought that maybe she was coming down with a fever. She decided to ignore it and went back to sleep. The next day at work the head of her department had reorganized the shoe stockroom again. Helen had a good laugh with Kim from Display that one day they would get so lost in the maze of shelves of shoes. In the evening, she watched a terrible movie on TV with Kara, then sleepily made her way to bed.

The following night Helen woke up at 3 am, hot and sweaty. The fleeting thought that she was getting sick wandered through her mind again as she rolled over and went back to sleep.

Helen had a good laugh with Kim the next day about how the manager wanted to rearrange the stockroom,

Very Well

again.

"One of these days, we're never going to find our way out and they'll have to send in a search party!" she quipped, sending Kim into giggles.

The evening progressed as normal. She and Kara had dinner and watched some TV before heading off to bed. That night, she was awoken again by a hot sweat. Squinting at the alarm clock by her bed, Helen noted the time–three in the morning. Maybe she was getting sick after all. She'd see how she felt in the morning and wearily closed her eyes once more.

The next morning was Helen's day off. She leisurely ate breakfast, went to meet some old friends for lunch, and later she cooked a nice healthy meal for herself and Kara. Her daughter was in between hormonal nightmares and so they were both enjoying the few days of quiet before the next storm touched down.

Helen awoke in a sweat for the fourth night in a row! The heat from her chest was so intense that she threw off the bedclothes. *That's so weird! I keep getting sweats every night, but I'm not sick during the day .... just sweaty at ... night? Noooo! No, NO, this can't be happening*! Half asleep, Helen was in shock. *Night sweats?! I'm too young for this! NO! I'm only 45!!* Weirdly she fell back asleep almost immediately, but this time, it was the first thing on her mind when she woke up.

Helen was a little anxious as she arrived at work. She knew nothing about menopause; she didn't have sisters and her mother had never said a thing about it. She remembered her mother being very forgetful later in life before she passed away, but "The Change," as that generation called it, had never been mentioned.

"Hey, question for you."

"Yes, honey?" replied Julie, one of the more mature "Shoe Dogs," as she and Helen reboxed some of the mess in the stock room before the store opened.

"Do you ... well, do you .... you know, do you get night sweats?"

Julie laughed, "Honey, I get so hot that I have to have the fan on me all night. My husband is freezing and I'm like an oven!"

"And how long does it go on?"

"It depends. Just a few minutes, usually. Sometimes I get about three or four a night but it can go up to five or six."

Helen gasped. "Really? No, I mean, how long have they been going on?"

"Oh. Well, let's see. It's been about seven years so far."

Helen's heart sank. *Seven years of waking up in the middle of the night feeling like I have a fever, great!*

Although it had been about four years since her husband had passed and Helen had to leave her affluent life in Pacific Palisades, a couple of loyal friends had stood by her, good friends that cared about her and not what car she was driving or where she had her hair done. They had continued to do lunch, picking up the bill until Helen was back on her feet and able to support herself. They kept her up to date on the gossip from the Tennis Club and the various charity

Very Well

organizations they all liked to support.

"Do either of you get night sweats?" asked Helen cautiously one evening as they stood in line for a movie.

"No, but my older sister is having a horrible time. She's like an oven. You can just feel the heat coming off her. The sweat drips off her nose sometimes. It's dreadful!" announced Michelle as she glanced at her reflection in a store window.

Helen pulled a face.

"Me neither. Why, are you?" asked Patti curiously.

"Well, I woke up the last four nights with hot flushes. I thought I was getting sick, and then, on the fourth night, I realized I wasn't sick during the day. I can't believe it's happening."

"Will you go to the doctor?" Michelle bought her ticket, stepping aside for the other two to do the same.

"No, why? I'm not sick." Helen joined Michelle as they waited for Patti.

"No, but you don't have to suffer these days."

"It's hardly suffering, well, not yet anyway."

Michelle shrugged as the trio headed into the movie theater, and the unpleasant topic was dropped.

Over the next few days, everything went back to normal—no sweats, and no waking up. Helen forgot about it and went back to being herself. However, she started to notice a progression of symptoms. The night sweats would come for about five to seven days in a row and then stop for a month. The days in between the sweaty episodes gradually grew less until it had become a nightly thing. It was tolerable as it only kept her awake for a few minutes each night, and by morning, she had usually forgotten about it.

A year went by like this. Helen, sweating her way through the night, and Kara somehow managing to graduate high school. Her youngest daughter left for college on the East Coast to study social work, close to where Lily was finishing her master's. She was now living alone for the first time since before she was married. Helen enjoyed being an independent woman–working, having a social life, and making her own entertainment. It was on a Tuesday lunch date that Patti and Michelle had invited Helen to join them, excited to introduce her to a new friend, Ramona.

"So, Helen, we are thinking of starting a new charitable foundation, and we want you to be part of it!" announced Patti excitedly. "We want to call it 'Unsung Heroes,' you know, people who do amazing things behind the scenes and never get any credit for it."

Helen sipped her water and fanned herself as a hot flash crept over her. The AC in the restaurant was working well but she still could feel her temperature suddenly rise. "Okay, I think I've seen something like that on TV. You mean, like someone who mends their neighbor's roof?"

"Yeah, but more than that. Then they start mending all the neighbor's roofs, or whatever, and so we would raise money to buy them tools or something."

"Yeah," continued Ramona. "And we've found the most amazing kid that we want to help. She's 17, lives in Westchester, and after school, she goes to supermarkets and

Very Well

collects damaged stuff–you know, dented food cans, or past best fruit and veggies–and then she pushes or buses it all back to her parent's house, and on Sunday mornings, she opens up a food pantry for the homeless in their garage! *This girl is amazing*!"

Helen was in awe. "Wow, that's incredible! How did you find her?"

"Patti heard about her," said Michelle, patting her friend on the back.

"She's my housekeeper's niece. We want to do a fundraiser and get her a car; it'll be a graduation surprise. What do you think?" asked Patti.

"I think it's a great idea. What do we need to do?"

As they waited for the waitress to take their lunch order, the women set to work planning how they would raise the money and where to have the event. It would be a medium-sized affair, and they each offered what they could do to make it happen. Ramona had organized some similar events before so her experience was going to be invaluable.

"I think we will need a special guest. You know, like the governor or a movie star to make the presentation? That way, more people will want to show up and we get more donations," suggested Ramona.

"Wow, you are thinking big," laughed Helen.

"Well, if we are going to do this, we better do it right."

"Anyone know the governor of California?" laughed Patti.

"Actually I do," admitted Helen. "Well, not personally, but before he became governor, he was one of the investors who pulled out of my husband's real estate plan and turned my life into a disaster. That guy owes me a *big* favor." She put her coffee down and folded her arms.

"Okay, it's all settled then."

As soon as she got home, Helen looked for a number for the governor's office. That part was easy; it was a bit harder to find a number where someone would actually answer the phone. She finally got through to an assistant of sorts, explained the situation and left her information. Surprise, surprise, she got a call back the next day. A personal assistant said the governor would be honored to take part in the event and providing there were no conflicts they would confirm shortly.

That was a bit too easy, thought Helen. *Amazing what a guilty conscience will do.*

The ladies continued to work on the event, asking for donations, secretly gathering information about their unsung hero, Ayeesha, and locating a venue. The more they learned about Ayeesha, the more amazing she was. On Saturday nights, she would go to restaurants and event halls and collect leftover food and then take it to the homeless and people in need. Apparently, it had started as a school project in seventh grade and she had just kept going with it.

As the weeks went on, Patti and Michelle had taken a back seat in the organizing as they didn't seem to have as much time to dedicate to the project. Helen and Ramona excitedly took up the slack and marched forward, making flyers, checking out venues, and securing vendors. They

Very Well

managed to get a great deal on a small function room at a Santa Monica boutique hotel, and several local businesses had promised generous donations in return for advertising.

Helen had never been on the organizing end of an event like this before. She was used to showing up in heels and enjoying someone else's hard work. Who knew how many flowers were needed for table decorations or what to put in the program? There was so much to think about. Helen was a little nervous about the money. She could see how much they were spending and was concerned if there would be enough to actually buy the car for Ayeesha. She asked Ramona several times if they were covering costs and what was going towards the car, but Ramona was cool as a cucumber; she had everything under control and repeatedly told her not to worry about it. So she didn't. It was exciting working together, and as the days got closer, Helen barely noticed that she was having mischievous hot flushes during the day now as well as sweaty nights.

Ramona was doing an amazing job with the advertising and fundraising. A week before the event she already had 350 people signed up with large donations coming in. Then disaster struck. The governor's office called to say that he wouldn't be able to make it. Helen was furious!

"I might have guessed he would pull out at the last minute! That's what he's good at, the loser!"

"Now what are we going to do?!" cried Ramona. She was clearly terrified that all the donations would have to be given back.

"I don't know, I'm really sorry! I will just have to get

someone else."

"How? Do you know anyone else famous? It's got to be someone everyone knows and likes!"

Helen barely slept that night. Her mind was racing, the night sweats rolling in leaving her soaking in damp sheets. The next morning she went into work with a plan–she would ask a celebrity customer. This really wasn't allowed but she was desperate; what would Michelle and Patti think of her if she let them down and Ramona had worked so hard? All morning there weren't any sightings. Then she thought she saw Gordon Ramsey, but decided he wouldn't be the right choice, even if it was him.

"Do you have these cuties in size seven?"#Helen turned around to see Janet Jackson offering her a charming Jimmy Choo shoe. She suddenly felt very nervous. Should she dare ask?

"Here you are," replied Helen as she returned with the right size. "These are beautiful. Do you have a special occasion in mind?"

"Maybe," replied Janet leisurely. "Awards season is coming up, as you know, so I always like to be prepared. Not for an award, of course. I might be presenting something, but really I just love to be part of it all."

"These will be perfect." Helen hesitated, then took a quick glance around to see if any staff were nearby. "I'm involved in an award event, but it's nothing like the Oscars or Grammys."

Janet stood up and took a few paces to try out the new shoes. "Yeah? What are you up to?" She took a glance at

Very Well

herself in the mirror.

"Well, I am on the committee of a charity that honors Unsung Heroes. We have this 17-year-old high school girl who spends hours a week collecting food for the homeless. She's amazing, and we want to buy her a car as recognition for her incredible service."

Janet whirled around on her heels. "That's amazing! I love to hear about things like this. Can I buy a ticket, make a donation?"

Helen couldn't believe her luck! "Well, uh …. so the governor was supposed to come and make a presentation of the keys, but he had to pull out at the last minute, and now we are stuck…"

Before she could continue, Janet touched her arm and whispered, "If you need me, it would be my honor. I'm not the governor, but I bet my shoes are nicer."

Helen's stomach flipped over. "Oh my gosh, you are amazing! You have saved me and our event, I can't tell you how grateful I am!"

"Careful, I'm sure this kind of thing is frowned upon here. We don't want your boss finding out, then we'll both be in the bad books! Here is my private number. Call me in about an hour and we'll work it out." She pushed a card into Helen's hand just as a member of staff walked by. "I think I'll take these. They are divine. Be a doll and bring them to this address as soon as you can. It's on the card." She winked at Helen and left the store.

"Girl, she's got some nerve!" chuckled Dwane. "Mind you, I wouldn't mind going to visit Janet Jackson!"

"Ha, well, I am," replied Helen with a huge grin and packed up the shoes with a flourish.

"How did you manage that?!" cried Ramona with relief as Helen told her she had secured singer Janet Jackson at the last minute.

"Ah, connections. We both know Jimmy Choo... Anyway, how are we doing on money now? Are we covering our costs?"

"Don't worry about it. We are doing fine, and I just got a great deal on a car. I thought anything too big will be too much on gas and insurance for her to pay later when she is in college. This one is just perfect."

"Wow, you are doing such an amazing job. Are you sure we don't need Patti and Michelle to come and do more?"

"Nah, we are doing fine. Too many cooks just make things take longer."

"Okay. Sounds perfect. Hopefully, we have had our one hiccup for this event."

Helen's daytime hot flashes were as regular now as her night sweats. It was becoming unbearable so she decided that as soon as the event was over, she would see her doctor. There was plenty to do on the big day. It just seemed right that she and Michelle would sit at the door to take the donations, and Patti would welcome people and keep an eye out for Ayeesha. They had made a plan with Ayeesha's aunt that they were coming to this event as guests of Patti's. It was

Very Well

presented as a thank-you perk that Patti was giving to her housekeeper. Ayeesha had agreed to be her aunt's companion, and they had secretly got her whole family to dress up and hide in the wings so they could join in the celebration with her.

Ramona had done an amazing job with the decorations. It all looked stunning. Banners saying "Unsung Heroes Gala" hung over the entrance and across the stage in purple and gold. The purple and lavender table flowers were just perfect and the beautiful programs were all ready. They set up a table for registration and got busy putting up signs, making sure everything was set up just right. Helen suggested they test the microphone, but Ramona informed them she had already taken care of it.

"I will be doing all the talking, after all."

Helen was a bit taken aback by this. She realized that they hadn't discussed it; she had just presumed they would be sharing the duties. Helen's heart sank a little but Ramona had already left to talk to the hotel manager about something, so she and Michelle double-checked that they had everything ready at the registration table to welcome their guests.

At 7:00 pm the doors opened, guests began to arrive, and the evening started to buzz. In twos and threes, the ladies who lunch showed up in their designer outfits for drinks, light refreshments, and a good feeling. By 8:00 pm the room was almost full with 400 women and a sprinkling of men, all eager to see the governor of California.

Ramona took to the stage and the crowd, now sitting,

hushed in anticipation.

"Wow! It is such an honor to be addressing you tonight. I am so proud to have you here with us for the first Unsung Heroes event." Ramona gave a great introduction, and as soon as Ayeesha realized what was happening, her family rushed out to hug her and join her in the celebration. There were squeals of excitement as Patti was invited on stage to explain what it was that Ayeesha did for her community and why they wanted to support her amazing good deeds.

Helen had agreed to meet the surprise guest at the service entrance at 8:15 pm, so she left Michelle and went down just as Janet's manager messaged Helen to say they would be there in five minutes.

As she got to the door it swung open and a bodyguard in dark glasses showed Janet in.

"Which way?" he asked abruptly.

"Follow me." Helen led the way as they rushed past bemused kitchen staff and then up into the ballroom. They hovered in the darkness at the side of the stage for a few minutes as Ramona explained the change of guest of honor.

"Ladies and gentlemen, I am so sorry to tell you that Governor Campbell had to cancel at the last minute." The audience let out a groan of disapproval.

"I'm sure he had some essential state business to attend to, but don't worry, there is no need for disappointment. We are so deeply grateful for someone so special that as soon as she heard we needed help, she stepped right up! Ladies and gentlemen .... please welcome to the stage, the amazing ... Ms. Janet Jackson!"

Very Well

The crowd was stunned. Ayeesha was in shock. She started to cry as the diva of '80s and '90s pop came up to give her a hug. Janet took the microphone, motioning to the crowd to be seated.

"My friends, when I heard what an incredible young woman Ayeesha is, I had to come." She turned and looked at Ayeesha. "You are what makes us a community. You are the leaders of tomorrow, the people who will run the show and take care of us when we are all slowing down. You, my dear, are an inspiration to behold! Look at you, girl! Look what you have achieved, and I know you are going to help so many more people. You shine and you make us shine in your presence."

Patti came back onto the stage with an oversized check and a set of keys tied with a beautiful pink bow and handed them to Janet. She glanced at them and then let out a big whoop.

"Wowee girl, look what they got you!"

Ayeesha held up the big check with Janet so that photographers and family could take pictures. Then Ramona asked Ayeesha's family to come up and join them for a group photo.

Ramona took the microphone back from Janet who was hugging Ayeesha now and holding her hand. "Thanks to all of you, Ayeesha can go to college in style, and she can continue her amazing work in comfort and style." She turned to Janet. "And thank you! Thank you from the bottom of our hearts to Ms. Janet Jackson who *is* style."

The crowd rose to their feet and applauded until

everyone had left the stage. Helen thanked Janet over and over as they walked back to her waiting limo.

"Oh, my pleasure. And just make sure those Manolo Blahnik crocodile boots that I ordered are waiting for me when I come in next week! I need them for my next trip!"

"Don't you worry, size seven!"

Everyone was completely exhausted the next day so Helen waited until the following day to take the door money she had collected over to Ramona.

"That was amazing! Did you see Ayeesha's face? She was sooo cute and so surprised. It really was a special night. I can't believe Janet donated $3,000 of her own money too. We need to send her some more flowers or something as a thank you. Anyway, here is the money I collected at the door, everything is there and the printout you sent me of the prepaids, plus I've added the names and credit card info of the people who just showed up on the night. Let me know how we did!"

A few days later she emailed Ramona to make sure they had covered the costs. She was curious if there was any money left over for next year's event, but there was no reply. Helen didn't think anything of it at first as she imagined she was probably tired, and there was no real hurry. A few days later she emailed again. No answer.

That's odd, thought Helen, so she called, but Ramona didn't pick up. A week had gone by and Ramona hadn't

Very Well

answered any calls or emails, but Patti said she had spoken to her and she seemed great.

Finally, there was an email.

I don't know why you are hounding me about the money, it has nothing to do with you.

Helen gasped in shock. She reread the email several times but still couldn't understand it. So she replied:

I'm so sorry, but I don't understand. The event was a joint effort and so there shouldn't be any secrecy about the money. It has everything to do with me?! If there is a problem, we can work this out. Please send me the spreadsheets, bills, and totals as soon as possible.

A few hours later, another response came from Ramona.

Sorry, but it was my event and the finances have nothing to do with you.

3
Century City

Helen was still reeling with outrage from the emails as she called Michelle to see what on earth was happening. Her heart was pounding, blood racing to her head.

"What is she talking about?!"

"I have no idea!" replied Michelle in disbelief. "We talked the day after about what a success it was and she didn't mention anything like that. Mind you, when I mentioned doing it again next year, she did hesitate."

"Exactly! I thought we were all in this together, and if there was anything left over, it would go towards next year. What does she mean it's *her* event?"

"I guess we need to ask her."

Helen tried to call Ramona several more times but she still didn't pick up. Helen sent another email.

I'm sorry, but I really don't understand. The event

Very Well

was not yours! It was a joint effort. It was a production of our annual *Unsung Heroes* charity. Please send or show us all the accounts ASAP.

Later that day, she received a reply.

I worked really hard on that event and have paid myself. All the other bills are paid and that is the end of it.

Helen could not believe her eyes! How *dare* she? She ran to print out a copy of the spreadsheet Ramona had sent her of the prepaid names; she was desperate to know exactly how much Ramona was stealing from them. Because it was stealing! She added up the prepaid donations, multiplied them by the total number of guests that had attended, and averaged it out. Then she added up the costs of the hall, the sound guy, the car, and all the other things Ramona had listed on another page and calculated that she was pocketing about $5,000! *What?!*

"How dare she!" exclaimed Helen to Michelle. "Look, no one is debating how hard she worked. She did an amazing job, we all thanked her over and over, but if she felt she was working too hard or needed to be paid, why didn't she say something?!" Helen was fuming. "I gave her plenty of opportunities to tell me what was going on with the money!"

"Maybe she felt justified?"

"*Are you defending her*?!"

"No, not at all, but I guess she did work hard."

"So did I!" Helen was starting to have flashbacks to all the times she had gone with Ramona to check out the different venues or to talk with vendors. "So when I gave up my days off to go with her to see places, ran around putting up signs, and got there early to set up and stayed late to clean up, I was doing it for fun and for free, while she was paying herself?! *I don't believe this!*"

The next few days were painful. Helen's hot flashes were coming on fast and furious, her mind racing. She woke several times in the night with her heart pounding violently like a steam train, soaked in sweat. She typed and retyped a response to Ramona, trying to convey the right amount of shock and disgust but short of being offensive.

We both worked very hard on that event and we thanked you over and over for all your hard work. Everyone agrees you did an amazing job, but if you felt you were doing too much or that you should be paid you should have spoken up. Why didn't you talk to us about it? Just taking the money is stealing. I have estimated that you owe the charity $5,000, and we want it back, now.

I bet she is regretting sending me that printout now with the expenses on it, thought Helen, convinced Ramona would see sense and bring the money back. But she didn't. A few hours later, there was a reply.

I really don't know why you are being so

Very Well

unreasonable and mean to me. And it wasn't $5,000. Please leave me alone, I have nothing further to say about it.

Helen turned to Patti. She couldn't understand why Michelle was being so calm. Helen wanted to scream from the rooftops.

"Have you spoken to her?" demanded Helen.

"No," replied Patti, quite bemused, "but I know she just left for Hawaii with her family, so I doubt you will get any answers out of her in the next week or so."

Helen thought she was going to burst with anger. She was so distressed she didn't know what to do with herself. As the days went by, she found herself going in and out of silent rage as memories of conversations about the event with Ramona kept popping into her head at work or in the car. She contemplated taking her to small claims court, or maybe taking out a full-page ad in the *L.A. Times* saying, "Never work with this woman!" It was unbearable.

As the days went by, Helen gradually let go of the revenge ideas and decided to get practical. Okay, if she wants to call it her event, fine. *Then that means she needs to pay me for my work too!* Helen had provided the guest of honor, plus hours of work, and that was going to cost her. She sent Ramona a detailed list of her work with an invoice.

Ha! That will show her!

No.
You were a volunteer. I am not paying you anything and this is it. Stop harassing me.

Chana Studley

"Oh my gosh! *Harassing her*?! *A volunteer!* She can't have it both ways! She can't say I was volunteering, but she was working! What planet is she living on?!" cried Helen to her daughter.

"What? That's crazy!" Kara was on the phone in New York, almost as outraged as her mother.

"And another thing, she had the nerve to keep all the banners we had made. They all have the Unsung Heroes logo! They didn't say Ramona Enterprises, did they? No! We paid for those so we could use them again next year! Arghhhh!"

"Mom, I know you are upset and I agree with everything you're saying, but I think you are going to have to let this go. She's gone, the money's gone, and obsessing and overthinking it is only making you miserable."

"I know, I know. It's just so infuriating!" Helen took a deep breath. "You're right, honey, but..." She sighed. "Never mind." They chatted a little longer and Helen resolved to try to make the best of the situation.

A few weeks went by, the anger subsiding with glimpses of calm. Then it would pop back up again. It was a rollercoaster of resignation and then outrage. Snippets of conversations, examples of how Ramona could or should have spoken up just kept popping into Helen's head at weird moments. She resisted talking about it at work; it was too embarrassing. She wanted the event to remain prestigious, not to be seen as the mess it was turning out to be. The

Very Well

feelings of being cheated, betrayed, and taken advantage of were too painful. Had she been an idiot for being so trusting?

Helen was so confused. She couldn't understand why Patti and Michelle were so accepting of it. Maybe because they hadn't run around as much as she had, or maybe money wasn't such a big thing to them as it was for her? The uncomfortable feelings came and went as her thinking continued to rev up and slow down. The hot flashes were stronger than ever now, adding to the discomfort and making her daily life unbearable. It was time to make that appointment.

Helen sat across from her doctor in his Century City medical office. The panoramic view of West Los Angeles out to the ocean was eerily similar to her husband's offices a few years earlier. She told the doctor her physical symptoms–the night sweats, daytime hot flashes, how her monthly cycle was completely off now, and that she felt just awful all the time. She told him she didn't want hormone replacement pills as she had heard that they caused breast cancer.[2] Her doctor was a kind man and usually very helpful, but after listening for a few minutes and asking just a couple

---

[2] There doesn't seem to be a simple answer to whether this is true or not. The WHI study, which is the largest and most cited study, actually revealed a decrease in risk for women who took estrogen alone. Please consult your physician as we all know research can be found to support both views and there are many factors to take into account, like family history and number of pregnancies.

of questions, he started typing her up a prescription for antidepressants.

"But I'm not depressed."

"Well, you just said that you want to cry, hide in your room, and eat chocolate all the time."

"Yes, but what woman doesn't?! Look, I love my life. I'm just struggling with all the sweating and lack of sleep." Now she was getting frustrated with her doctor. "I just need something for my physical symptoms, to balance my hormones. If I'm feeling down it's because I feel like I have a fever all day and I can't think straight from lack of sleep! It's kind of hard to function like this when my hormones are all messed up."

"I know it sounds weird, but antidepressants will take all those symptoms away too."

Confusion filled Helen's mind as she wondered how antidepressants could fix the physical symptoms of menopause. Her doctor shrugged his shoulders as she voiced the question, handing her a referral to a menopause specialist.

On the way home, Helen got a sickening feeling as she imagined all the menopausal women in the world who were being shut up with antidepressants by doctors who couldn't or wouldn't listen.

"My cousin uses natural stuff," said Julie as they finished up their day in the shoe department and headed for the staff exit. "I can ask if you like, I think it's something like...yams?"

Julie came back in a few days to tell Helen that her

Very Well

cousin swore by something called bio-identical hormones and gave her the number of a hormone specialist, Dr. Bass. Helen hesitated to start spending money on quacks and herbs but was comforted by the fact that he was also an MD. The menopause specialist her doctor had recommended at the hospital hadn't helped much. She had just given her some information that Helen could have gotten off the internet, and the offer of HRT or antidepressants again. So Helen reluctantly made an appointment with Dr. Bass and decided to see what he had to say.

His office was in the back of a house in the Pico Roberston neighborhood. She guessed it was his home and began to wonder who this guy was. Why didn't he have a real office? Dr. Bass was friendly and encouraging and Helen soon got over the surroundings when she saw his medical certificates from the Berkeley School of Medicine, The American School of Naturopathy, and his State of California medical license all displayed on the wall in his office. He was younger than she had imagined but his confidence and sincerity quickly made up for it.

"First, we need to rule out anything else that could be causing these changes in temperature."

"But my doctor told me it was menopause." Helen was still a bit skeptical.

"It probably is, but we want to be thorough. There are other things that need to be ruled out. We wouldn't want to miss something, would we? He probably offered you HRT too?"

"Yes, but I told him I didn't want that, so he just offered

antidepressants."

"Right. Well, what I prescribe is BHRT which is derived from plant sources that are chemically similar to the hormones your body naturally produces. I bet your doctor didn't tell you that traditional HRT products are made from the urine of pregnant horses and other synthetic hormones?"

"What?" *Yuck*, thought Helen, and felt comforted by his professional approach but a little nervous that he might find something more serious.

"We are going to do a saliva test and a fecal test, and that will tell us if there is anything else causing your horrid symptoms, okay?"

"Not a blood test?"

"Actually, blood tests don't tell you much about hormones." He handed her the test kits. "A blood test only shows you what your hormones were like at the moment the needle went in your arm, but hormones can fluctuate throughout the day. It depends on things like stress levels, what you ate for breakfast, how much sleep you got last night, etc. Urine tests are the best way to measure hormones, and you have to do them over a few days to really get accurate information. Anyway, take care of these, and drop them off at the lab on Pico Boulevard, the address is right there. Then we can start working on getting you back to your old self."

The results came back normal, which was a relief, so Dr. Bass prescribed a bio-identical hormone cream. It came from a

Very Well

naturopathic pharmacy near Cedars-Sinai Hospital and was to be applied daily. Helen followed the directions, but it didn't help. As the weeks went by Dr. Bass upped the dose several times, but the symptoms just kept getting worse. Her hot flashes were up to every twenty minutes, and now a new symptom had developed. Just before each flash, she would get this drowning feeling, like someone had just taken out her batteries. She felt dizzy from the intense, sudden fatigue and would have to sit down before she felt like she would fall down. It was becoming impossible to function.

The brain fog was getting bad too. Simple things that Helen used to know instinctively were becoming difficult and hard work. Her mind seemed distant and slow. She had to dig deep to find the right words. Sometimes, it felt like she was having to think through molasses just to do the simplest things.

Did she have Alzheimer's? Was she going mad?

A customer would ask for a size six, she would get to the stock room and even though she had the sample shoe in her hand, Helen had to work really hard to bring the right size to mind. It was like trying to drive through thick fog in slow motion with no lights on. It felt like her brain and body were slowly melting into a pool of sweat.

Dr. Bass continued to up the dose multiple times, but it didn't help. Finally, after she had told him about her latest nightmare symptoms, he changed his mind. He hesitated and then said, "Okay, I want you to go back to your doctor, get the regular HRT and take it for three months. We need to *tame the tiger*, get your hormones under control, and then we can get back to managing them with the bio-identicals."

Helen was devastated. Why had she spent all that money just to be sent back to the regular stuff? At this point, she was so miserable that she didn't care about the possibility of breast cancer. She was desperate.

Who cares about getting cancer when you can't or don't want to live?!

Helen took a deep breath. It wasn't quite that bad yet. All she really wanted was to be able to get through the day without feeling like she was going to collapse at any moment.

As Helen sat in the waiting room to see her doctor, thoughts about Ramona popped up again. She pushed them away and focused on her daughters, then thoughts about how she was going to manage to keep working if her symptoms didn't leave would rush into her mind. What would she do for money? Her mind was like a tornado. The gusts of the thought storm were interrupted by the sound of her name being called. After a very short conversation her doctor gave her a prescription for 2 milligrams of HRT once a day, and she left for her regular pharmacy.

It was like magic. Within two days, things started to calm down. The night sweats lessened dramatically and the hot flashes started to fade away. It was such a relief. Helen hadn't slept through the night for several years at this point,

Very Well

and so the more she slept, the more she relaxed. The relief was welcome bliss.

4
Los Angeles

A couple of years had passed and Kara had graduated college. She was back from the East Coast and Helen was happy to have her home. Lily had married a wonderful young man after she'd finished her master's and was now back in L.A. too. Helen had enjoyed her time alone. She enjoyed reading and hanging out with friends and not having to clean up after everyone all the time, but she was delighted to have her girls close again. Kara and Lily seemed to be doing well considering the death of their father, putting themselves through college, and the serious life changes they had all been through. Lily was pregnant, enjoying everyone's excitement about the new baby, and Kara was enrolled in a master's program for social work at UCLA. It was a perfect fit for her, tapping into the deep reservoirs of her warm, caring heart.

Very Well

As part of her training Kara had to do 900 clinical hours and had found a placement in a women's clinic at St. John's Hospital in Santa Monica. She regularly sat in with other social workers and observed as they took case histories, made assessments, and coordinated aftercare. The hours were long, and after only a few weeks she was handed a case of her own. Helen was amazed at how well she was handling it all. The stress seemed to roll off her, and she was always able to go back each day with a good attitude and little or no frustration.

"You are amazing, my dear. I mean, how you handle all this. The customers at work drive me so nuts that sometimes I want to throw their size sixes at them!"

Kara laughed. "Oh, I'm no saint. I've just learned that they are all doing the best they can. I mean, their behavior is coming from their low moods, it's got nothing to do with me, so I don't take it personally." She picked up her books and papers and went to study at the kitchen table.

"You are a better man than me, Gunga Din!"

As the months passed, Kara began to notice that her mother's moods were still going up and down, even with the HRT. She would come home to find Helen crying in front of the TV. When she asked her why, Helen would say it was the movie or something on the news. Sometimes it was a customer or another member of staff that would set her off, or sometimes she just didn't know. Helen's moods would pass, but then they would come back like a dark storm creeping over the horizon, and the only things that would help were chocolate and bed.

The HRT was helping with the night sweats and hot flashes, and Helen's periods had stopped altogether by this point. She didn't mind; she'd never had a painful or bad time with her cycle, and the awful moods were put down to "The Change."

"It's like we've swapped places," mumbled Helen as she and Kara were watching TV one night.

"Huh?"

"Well, when you were a teenager, your hormones took you for a rollercoaster ride, and now mine are. You seem to be all chilled out and laid back these days while I'm the hormonal mess."

"I guess." Kara had been waiting for the right moment to share with her mom what had helped her understand her own battle with her moods. Maybe this was it.

"Mom..." Kara hesitated. "You know the community group I go to once a month?"

Helen nodded as she got up to put away the dishes from dinner.

"Well, the next one is a '*Back to Basics*' night. Wanna come and find out what it is that I got so interested in? It will be an intro kind of thing, so it could be really helpful. It might even be good to get out and meet some new people."

"You mean that Mind, Thought and ... Uh ..."

"Consciousness," reminded Kara as Helen tried rattling off the Three Principles that her daughter had found so fascinating.

"Maybe, I don't know. We'll see. I might go back to that alternative hormone therapy. I saw something about Mexican yams helping with hormones the other day... Now, where was that?"

While Kara had been on the East Coast finishing her undergraduate degree, she had heard about a new paradigm in psychology called the Three Principles. Not at school, but from one of her roommates. She didn't totally get it, but she was very curious. It just seemed to have more credibility, more depth than a lot of the stuff she was being taught in the classroom or had tried in L.A. Even though no one else seemed to have heard of it, it resonated with her in a deep way. The truth in what her roommate had pointed at, that *"we live in a thought-created world 100% of the time,"* seemed to have a very calming effect on her. She didn't really understand what it meant but the implication was fascinating–that you didn't have to listen to every thought that came into your head? Who knew?

When she had gotten back to L.A., she had heard about the Santa Monica Drop-in Center as a place she could direct clients. It was a kind of community center where people could come for subsidized therapy, grief counseling, 12-Step meetings, and all kinds of other support groups and classes. She had been intrigued to see that there was a monthly Three Principles Community Night and had sat in the back one time to learn more of what it was about. The meeting had been led by Deborah, a British woman who had talked about some really interesting ideas. Kara still had many questions but left feeling really peaceful. The calm feeling stayed with her for a few days. Curious, she had gone back the next month to check it out some more.

At the end of that particular meeting, she approached Deborah. "Hi, thanks for the talk tonight. I really like what you are saying, but when are you going to explain what the Three Principles are?" asked Kara cautiously, aware that she may have misunderstood something.

Deborah smiled. "I get asked that a lot, but you see, giving you a dictionary definition is not really going to help you. Talking about it intellectually will just entertain your brain. We are pointing to something quite beyond that, to something more of a feeling. After all, doesn't everyone want to feel better? This understanding really comes from insight. This is not like one of those college courses where you can study it to get a grade. It's more of a ... well, an experience ... a feeling."

There were several other women hovering next to Kara who also looked confused.

"I did have a really nice feeling last month after the talk, and it stayed with me for a few days," observed Kara.

"Great, that's it!" exclaimed Deborah. "Follow that feeling."

"I came back, is that what you mean?"

Deborah smiled. "I'm so pleased you came back, but you can follow that feeling anytime, any place. Remember how I said '*we are always feeling our thinking*?' Well, when you had that good feeling, it was because your thoughts had calmed down and you were in the moment. You were

Very Well

feeling your calm thoughts. There is no need to do anything; that calm feeling is who you really are, and it was there all the time just waiting for you to look in the right direction."

Kara hesitated. She could feel a pull to find out more; she hadn't felt that calm in years. "I saw that you do counseling work here. Would I qualify for a student discount?"

"Yes, I think so. Come and meet Bob. He's the director of this place and he can answer your questions, but I would love that. We can go a little deeper and help you see what's really on offer here."

Kara secured a discount as a student and started meeting with Deborah weekly at the SMDC. The room felt safe and cozy as they sat in the old, comfortable armchairs. After some chat about school and family, they talked about how all of our experience is really created from the inside and how our thoughts are always moving.

"So there really is no need to do anything to fix your thoughts?" inquired Kara.

"Exactly! Think of your thoughts like trains, constantly flowing in and out of a station. If a train has left the station, trying to reframe, change, or analyze is like...well, it's like dragging the train back into the station to try and work out how to make it leave. *It already left!*"

Kara started to laugh as she saw the futility of working hard to change her thoughts.

"It's actually messing with the system. Thought and moods work as a reliable system. Think about it. You can't have low, miserable, insecure thinking and be in a good mood, and you can't have joyful, abundant thinking and be in a low mood. It's just not possible."

"Yeah, I see that, but..."

Deborah smiled at Kara as she knew that most people new to these ideas had a '*Yeah, but...*'

"But what about hormones?" continued Kara.

Deborah paused. "Hmm... that's a new one. Well, hormones are made of chemicals, but we still experience their effect with the gift of Thought."

Kara pulled a face. "How can you say hormones are thinking?"

"I'm not. See if this helps. Thought and thinking are two different things."

Kara had no idea what that meant but she was intrigued.

"Thought with a capital T is one of the Three Principles that Sydney Banks[3] described after he had his enlightenment experience. It's a creative energy, and I have no idea what I'm saying right now, but it moves through our mind constantly and never stops. Like clouds or traffic or a river, it's always in motion."

Kara was fascinated.

"Thought, this creative flowing energy, can show up in many forms. We are all familiar with the thinky thoughts that say 'do the laundry' or 'go exercise.'" Deborah lifted her hands up like sock puppets and made them talk to each

---

[3] Sydney Banks (1931-2009). Teacher, philosopher and author. sydbanks.com

Very Well

other. "'*No! I don't want to!*'"

Kara laughed. She began to relax a little as Deborah continued to share.

"We are all familiar with that voice in our heads. In fact, some of my clients say they hear an English accent in their heads when they remember something I've said. Thought is always flowing, kind of like those ticker tapes you see scrolling across the screen of a TV news show. You know, like, the baseball results, the weather, and the, uh, the Dow Jones report, whatever that is."

Kara nodded in agreement.

"But I also think it can show up as images," continued Deborah. "When I worked in Hollywood doing special effects, directors and producers would ask me to make some crazy creature, and I would picture it in my mind." Deborah looked up into the air as if she was gazing at something, her eyes moving around as if working something out. "I never used to draw anything; I could just *see* how to make it."

"Yeah, but that is some really special skill that you have."

"Maybe, but you did it this morning when you got dressed. You thought about what you wanted to wear. You pictured what looked good with what and which shoes. You could sense it; you didn't need to draw it. Words didn't go through your mind about what to wear. You could just *see* it in your 'mind's eye.' And you will probably do the same tonight when you get dinner. You just know to boil the water and open the bag of pasta because you can picture the spaghetti and meatballs in your mind. You don't have to google it if you have made it before."

Kara nodded again.

"I also think it can show up as sounds, like music, for example. I mean, when Paul McCartney woke up with the tune for 'Yesterday' in his head, it was literally that–a tune made of the creative power of new Thought. He could hear it in his mind. He hadn't written anything down or played it yet, so it was made of pure Thought."

Deborah paused for a moment. "The creative power of Thought can also show up as sensations. Pain or dizziness, hunger, and the effect of hormones going up and down. They are all made of the creative energy of Thought. It's how we experience, well, everything. No exceptions. I'm not saying hormones themselves are made of Thought, but the effect they produce is experienced by us with the gift of Thought. Let me ask you a question. When you were suffering with your PMDD, how did you know that your mood had changed or that you were cramping or anxious?"

Kara had never considered it that way before. "I guess I felt it."

"Okay, but how did you know you felt it?"

"I don't know. It was miserable. I just always felt rotten. I guess…I guess it was my thinking? But that doesn't seem right. Sometimes I wasn't thinking anything, I just felt miserable."

"Sure, it was miserable. But the experience, the sensation of cramps, temperature change, and anxiety are different forms that the creative energy of Thought can take."

The Three Principles Santa Monica Group met on the first

Very Well

Tuesday of the month, and so a few months later when she felt more confident, Kara took her mother to a meeting. Helen was not at all sure about it, but agreed as she had seen such a change in her daughter. Clearly there was something here. Kara seemed calmer, able to ride the wave of hormones, and just wasn't as reactive and irritable as she used to be. She was smiling most of the time and seemed to be more flexible and easygoing. She was even enjoying her studies and meeting new people. Helen was curious about what had happened. She was very happy for her daughter, glad that she had found some peace, but hesitated at the thought of being dragged into anything too "woo-woo."

"I hope they aren't expecting me to say anything. I hate those kinds of groups that pick on you and make you talk about your feelings."

Kara turned to her and shook her head. "Don't worry, Deborah's very British. She doesn't go in for all that touchy-feely stuff."

Helen felt relieved as they sat in their seats waiting for the evening event to start. There were about 25 people of all kinds–some sitting, some talking in the back with their coffee. There was a table of books for sale and a banner at the front that said:

> *If only people could learn*
> *not to be afraid of*
> *their own experience,*
> *That alone would change the world.*
> *- Sydney Banks*

"So who's Sydney Banks?" whispered Helen as people started taking their seats. "Is he the boss?"

Kara smiled. "No, but he did put these ideas together. He passed away in 2009."

Deborah, a well-dressed woman of about Helen's age, came to the front and took a seat, smiling and welcoming everyone. She seemed relaxed and confident and very at home leading the conversation. It was very interesting, even though Helen couldn't quite understand what she was talking about. She understood that we probably spend too much time up in our heads, but how could she say everything is made of thought? Her brain fog was sadly lacking in thoughts!

There was a Q&A session towards the end. Things started to get lively as people asked some great questions. Helen enjoyed the back and forth and was impressed when Deborah would say, "I don't know," or "To quote my teacher, Dr. George Pransky, that's above my pay grade!" It was inspiring to watch how comfortable she was even when people's questions were quite personal or completely off the wall.

"Come on, I want to introduce you." As soon as it was over Kara took her mother by the arm, insisting she meet Deborah.

"This is my mother, Helen. I finally got her here!"

Helen looked confused. "You didn't have to drag me. You've never invited me before."

Deborah laughed and welcomed them both. "I'm so

Very Well

glad you came. Did you enjoy the evening?"

"Yes, very much. Can't say I understood much, though."

"That sounds about right," smiled Deborah. "I hope you will come back, and if you have any questions, Kara has my number. Maybe we can get coffee sometime?"

"Oh, uh, sure, that sounds nice." Helen wasn't sure she was ready for that, but it was very nice of her to offer.

"I need these in a size six, please."

"Of course, I'll be right back."

Helen walked the cramped aisles of the shoe stockroom, stepping over opened boxes of designer boots and pumps searching for the desired shoes, when she heard what sounded like a cry for help.

"Is anyone out there? Help! *I need help!*"

Helen looked around, but there was no one there. She hurried towards the sound of the frantic voice and realized it was coming from behind the makeshift door used by the display staff to get in and out of the large windows on Wilshire Boulevard.

"*Help!! Is anyone there?*"

Helen opened the thin door and peeked in; the smell of wet paint went straight up her nose. It was completely white with three mannequins wearing black designer outfits. At the furthest end of the window was Kim from the display team. "Quick, get in here! This Oscar de la Renta original is about to fall into wet paint, and I can't touch it. I have paint on my hands!"

"But the floor is wet!"

"I know! That's why it can't fall! Kick your shoes off. You can wash your feet later, but just get in here, *now*!"

Helen kicked off her shoes and tiptoed in the cold, wet, squishy paint to the falling mannequin.

"Oh, thank God! Now, stay here while I go and get the boys back to nail her down properly."

"What?!"

Before she knew it Helen was on her own, holding up a mannequin in the window as passing pedestrians on Wilshire Boulevard looked on, amused. The traffic was now stopped for the traffic light at North Roxbury; her audience was growing. She smiled nervously as the wig she had grabbed came unstuck and the mannequin started to fall again. Trying not to panic, Helen put her arm around the model's waist and then glanced away, trying to pretend everything was normal, that she often stood in an intimate embrace with bald women in windows. As she held on, her toes squishing in the wet paint and trying not to lose her balance, a hot flush came over her. She discreetly wiped her face on the back of the black taffeta dress, hoping no one outside could see. *What would Oscar have to say about that,* she laughed to herself.

Kim came back quickly with the display boys to secure the mannequin. Helen, relieved of her guard duty, tiptoed back out the window and sat down on the step, looking for something to wipe her feet.

"What happened to your feet?" exclaimed Dwane as he came running from the shoe department to find her. "I've

Very Well

been looking for you everywhere! Kara called. *Lily is in labor!*"

5
The Venice Canals

After nine hours of labor, Lily gave birth to a beautiful baby girl. Lily's husband Carl was beside himself with joy as the new family welcomed little Flora with love and laughter. She looked just like Lily and Kara, complete with dark hair and dark brown eyes. Finally at 4 am Kara and Helen stumbled home, happy and delighted with their new arrival.

A week after the Principles Community Night at the SMDC, Deborah had invited Helen over for a coffee. She was a little surprised and nervous about the invitation. Why was she being so friendly? Did she want something? Helen was a little cautious about jumping into a new friendship after her experience with Ramona but Kara assured her it was innocent and genuine. They sat on the deck of Deborah's home in the Venice Beach Canals overlooking

Very Well

the water. It was a quiet Wednesday evening, and the two women chatted about their lives, work, and families. Deborah was newly married to Joe who was away in Chicago for work. They had joined not just their hearts but their businesses into a management agency for sports personalities and actors. Helen felt surprisingly relaxed in her company like they had been friends for a long time, and soon forgot her apprehension.

"Kara is a lovely girl, and you have another daughter?"

"Yes, Lily. She just had a baby girl a few days ago. I can't believe I'm a grandmother! Mind you, with menopause kicking my behind, I guess it's what happens when you get older. I'm on the lowest dose of ERT[4] now, but I still get the occasional night sweat and awful mood swings."

"Yes, menopause can be tough, but how lovely to have a granddaughter to fuss over. I found vitamin B complex and magnesium a great help when I was in peri-menopause. I was told that magnesium helps with sleep, and then I was told it helps with energy during the day. I asked a nutritionist who specializes in menopause, how can it do both? How can it put you to sleep and keep you awake? She replied, 'That's the magic of magnesium.' Now I only take them occasionally and I'm fine. Try it, it might help," offered Deborah kindly.

"Thanks." Helen was enjoying the friendly chat, but

---

[4] Estrogen Replacement Therapy. For women after hysterectomy and post-menopause. This is regarded as very safe and helps with maintaining healthy bones, brain and skin.

was eager to ask some questions about the Principles. "So, I get that we are always thinking, but what about hormones? Kara tried to explain it to me, but I guess I'm a bit slow. Surely they are making our moods go up and down?"

Deborah thought for a moment, gazing out across the water. There were some ducks gliding by, and a few people out for an evening stroll. "You are not slow. This was a little tricky for me to get my head around at first." She paused to gather her thoughts. "So, the truth is, there isn't any experience that isn't made of Thought."

Helen scrunched her face in confusion, trying to grasp what Deborah was pointing to.

"Think about it for a moment. How would you know if your temperature went up or that your mood dropped?"

Helen replied with the same answer Kara had given. "I feel it?"

"Okay, and how do you know what you are feeling?"

"You...you just know."

"Right. You know because of the creative gift of Thought." Deborah reminded her of the difference between Thought and thinking and some of the different forms Thought can take in our minds. "I imagine Mozart could hear a whole orchestra in his head while Einstein's mind was full of calculations. When I see something, I see color, shape, and texture. I bet Thought showed up for Einstein as fractions, volume, and square roots in the same way it showed up as musical notes for Mozart."

"You mentioned that the other night, but it went straight over my head," laughed Helen, slightly embarrassed.

Very Well

Deborah smiled. "I was talking to a young actor earlier today, and I used the analogy of concrete. Thought is a creative energy, and there are many things we can do with it. He was only 14, but told me he wants to be an architect if the acting thing doesn't work out, so I suggested that concrete can be used in many different ways. You can make a sculpture with it, you can build a movie theater with it, or he could concrete his brother's door closed with it! This made him laugh, as I know his brother quite well. As he laughed at the idea of his brother not being able to get out of his bedroom, he lightened up a bit and started to see that all his thoughts were made of the same creative energy. They were just showing up in different forms."

"So when you say everything is made of Thought, you don't necessarily mean just different types of thinking?"

"Not at all. And just to be clear, I don't think everything is *made* of Thought, but it's how we experience everything. Hormones are chemicals and they have a job to do, independent of my thinking. Most of the time, they are doing their thing–regulating my temperature, thirst, etc.– and I have no recognition of this at all. But I experience the sensations they produce via the gift of Thought. As I said, Thought can show up in many different forms–creativity, anxiousness, joy, or boredom. It's also music, images, and now we see it is sensations, too," explained Deborah.

"I once watched a video of how Manolo Blahnik shoes are made in their factory in Vigevano, Italy," said Helen. "It got me thinking about how a piece of leather could become sneakers, high-heeled pumps, or a pair of work boots. Same material but made into different types of footwear."

"Exactly! And this creative energy we call Thought is constantly showing up in these different forms and moving through our minds. What if you didn't take those anxious thoughts seriously that come with the mood swings? What if you knew they are just…" Deborah waved her hand in the air, searching for an analogy, "…dark clouds passing through your mind, and like all storms, they will pass."

Helen was kind of getting it. She had this curious feeling that the bits she didn't get didn't matter, and her understanding would come with time. It was a strange, new experience not to feel anxious about not fully grasping something.

"I just had a funny thought," reflected Helen. "I heard this thought in my head saying, 'Why am I not as bothered about understanding all this as perfectly as I think I *should* be?'"

Both women laughed.

"But that's exactly it!" offered Deborah. "We make up rules all the time about how we think we 'should' feel and how we think we 'should' think. Look, it is a reliable system. If you are having low, miserable thoughts, you cannot be in a good mood. And if you are having happy, abundant thoughts, you cannot be in a low mood. It's just the way it works. Life literally is what you think. Can I ask you a question?"

Helen nodded.

"You have said several times that you are slow, or that you don't get it all."

Very Well

Helen stared at a spot on the floor for a moment. "Yes. I'm beginning to see how much I beat myself up. I have this fear that I'm stupid, even though I did well in college and helped my husband with his business."

"It's a story many women have. There is no truth to it, and yet, we often have these insecure thoughts. But that's all it is–insecure thinking that is passing through. It's not true, and you don't have to listen to it. I promise you, it will fade away the more you become grounded in these ideas."

"I get it!" cried Helen suddenly. "If I think I *should* feel stupid because I don't get everything, you are saying then I will feel stupid!"

"Yes! If you think you are going to feel lousy all day because you didn't get any sleep, then you probably will!"

The two women talked and laughed for a while longer until Helen realized the time.

"I have to work tomorrow, I better get going. Thank you so much. This was really nice."

"My pleasure. I hope next time you come you will meet Joe. I often travel with him, but this was just a short trip so I decided to stay home this time. Here, can I give you some Principles books to borrow? This is one of Syd's books, and this one is by my dear friend, Jack."[5]

"Thank you, I look forward to it."

Kara was waiting up; she wanted to hear all about it.

"What was her house like? Did you meet her husband?"

---

[5] See "Resources" appendix for a full list of books.

"House was very nice, and he was out of town." Helen kicked off her shoes and sat on the sofa with her daughter. "I think I'm beginning to get it. On the way home, I could hear all these insecure thoughts coming up, and I just watched them pass through. It was kind of cool."

"That's so great, Mom."

"I can see why you like it, why you calmed down. It's very soothing."

Kara was doing cartwheels on the inside, overjoyed that her mother was seeing the truth about what she had been pointing to. "Good night, Mom." She hugged her tightly before heading off to bed, delighted that she could share her newfound inner understanding with her mother.

On Helen's next day off, she called Lily to see how she was doing and if she could come over to help out with the baby. She just wanted to fuss over them both and take some gifts that she couldn't resist buying with her staff discount, but there was no answer. She guessed Lily was sleeping so she waited a few hours to call again. Still no answer. She called Carl to see what was happening.

"I hope she's sleeping!" mumbled Carl. He sounded tired and worn out. "I just left her to go to the store to get some more diapers. The baby was awake all night again last night, and Lily is really suffering."

"Oh no, *why didn't you say something*? I'm coming over."

Helen jumped in her car and drove the 20 minutes down to Manhattan Beach where Lily and Carl had bought

Very Well

a house. Carl was something big in film financing, and they had met at a movie marketing conference. Helen didn't quite understand that side of the business, but he was a really special guy. He was successful, kind, and very well-suited to Lily's way of seeing the world. Helen pulled up outside the house and rushed in. Lily was sitting on the floor of the living room, the baby in her lap, and they were both crying.

"Oh, sweetheart, what's the matter?"

Lily started bawling as her mother gave the baby to Carl. "You take Flora out in the stroller and get her to sleep. And you, my dear, come and lie down. Let's get you sorted out."

"Oh, Mom ... I can't stop crying! I don't even know why!"

"It's okay, my love. You are just tired."

"Mom?"

"Yes, sweetheart," replied Helen as she got Lily up off the floor.

"Can I have a ... a hot bath?"

"Of course you can have a hot bath, my poor thing."

"I'm leaking, and there's been some bleeding and ... and the doctor says it's all normal, but I ... oh, Mom, I didn't think it would be like this!"

Helen helped her onto the sofa and ran the hot water. Carl pushed the stroller out the front door, leaving them to it. As Lily sat in the warm bubble bath, her mother stroking her hair, Helen listened with all her heart as Lily told her about what had been happening.

"It was fine the first few days. We didn't care that we

weren't sleeping. But then I started getting so tired ... and then the thoughts started, 'You're not a good mom, you'll never be a good mom, you can't do this, Flora is suffering, she will be scarred for life.' Mom, it was awful!"

She started to sob again. "I thought it was just tiredness, but then the thoughts got louder and louder, and yesterday ... I wanted to scream at her to stop crying. The more she cried, the more scared I got that I might do something." Lily buried her face in her wet hands.

Helen was not so shocked; she knew about baby blues, but was still a little concerned for them both.

"My poor darling, why didn't you say something when I was here the other day? I can move in for a few days, and Kara can take turns. We want to help you."

"Thank you. I know you would, but my head says I shouldn't bother you, or that I am a bad mom if I can't manage on my own. I'm so ashamed."

Rather than tell her that she was being silly, Helen looked her in the eyes with all the love she had in her heart. "You are strong, and you are courageous. You *are* a good mom, you *are* doing it, and it's just your thoughts that are telling you otherwise. Just because you don't know everything yet about being a mom doesn't mean all of that stuff is true. It just means that you will learn it as you go along."

Helen gently bathed her daughter's arms. "There's no shame in not knowing it all yet. There is the wonder of what is to come ... It says in a book I'm reading right now, *'All we are is peace, love and wisdom and the power to create the*

Very Well

illusion we are not."[6]

Over the next few weeks, she, Kara, and Carl's sister all took turns to stay over and help out. Lily continued to go up and down, but she was beginning to ride the extremes of anxiety and self-doubt a little better. The love and understanding from her family were helping, although she was still very nervous about the baby, her ability as a mother, and ever getting her life back.

Helen attended a couple more Community Nights as she and Deborah became good friends. The magnesium and vitamin B complex that Deborah had suggested were really helping. She had more energy, her thinking was clearer, and her mood swings were less severe. Helen wanted to return the favor, so she invited Deborah for coffee to meet her friends, Patti and Michelle. They talked about life and relationships and, of course, the Principles.

"Last year we did a charity event together, but it didn't turn out too well. Well, the event itself was amazing and we raised a lot of money, but I had a very hard time with how it ended." Helen told Deborah about how Ramona had run off with the profits meant for the following year, and how hard it was to get it out of her mind. "She actually stole from us. Now how is that Thought?"

Patti and Michelle didn't comment but were curious to hear what Deborah would say.

"You know how we talked about separate realities, how

---

[6] Jack Pransky, *Seduced by Consciousness* (CCB Publishing, 2017).

we are all living in our own thought-created realities at the last Community Night?"

Helen nodded.

"Well, Ramona was, is living in her separate thought-created reality and you are living in yours. I bet if she told me the story, it would be quite different."

Helen could feel the old animosity bubbling back up as she put down her cappuccino. "I bet! But on what planet is it right to steal what's not yours? *And from your friends*?!"

"I'm guessing she believed that it was hers. I'm not defending her. It's not an excuse, remember, it's an explanation. Look, everyone is doing the best they can with the thinking they have in that moment."

Helen was about to get defensive again when Deborah motioned to her to slow down.

"I'm sure you ladies have watched a movie at some point and one of you loved it and one of you hated it?"

Patti and Michelle nodded, curious about where this was going.

"Well, which one of you was right?"

All three looked bemused.

"You know how we say that we all live in a thought-created world? Well, each of you were experiencing your own thoughts about the movie, not the movie itself. If it was the movie that was creating your experience, then you would all love it or all hate it."

"I get it," sighed Helen. "You mean Ramona was living in her thought-created world of how she was working so hard, and so it made sense to pay herself?" Helen was

Very Well

beginning to get it, but the other two still looked perplexed.

"It's entirely possible. Have you ever asked her?"

"I tried, but she won't answer my calls. I guess we can all rationalize anything."

"The mind creates its own reality, for sure," added Deborah as Patti and Michelle appeared quite lost.

But Helen was having an insight. A shift. She could feel the tension gradually dissipating. Very faintly, in the back of her mind, she could hear a voice saying, let go. Just let go.

Helen woke up the next morning with a strange, fresh feeling. She wasn't sure what it was at first; she just knew something was different. She explored her mind. All that anger and disgust for Ramona had...gone? All the venomous feelings she'd had about her had simply vanished. She thought about some of the things that Ramona had done but she didn't feel angry anymore. It was as if it had melted away overnight! She still thought what Ramona had done was wrong. *Very wrong*. She still believed Ramona owed them money, but the sting of the injustice no longer existed.

It was a strange sensation. It was freedom. And what was really weird was, she hadn't even worked on it to make it go away.

6
Santa Monica

Most of the Community Nights at the SMDC were general discussions, but they occasionally had topics or visiting speakers. Deborah presented one on chronic pain which was fascinating. There had been guest speakers who talked about all kinds of diverse subjects like relationships, being an entrepreneur, and losing weight. Helen started to see that the Principles were not a cure or solution for any of these things but that the problems seemed to right themselves as people gained insights into how their minds worked. As their thinking calmed down common sense seemed to kick in, and like Helen's anger with Ramona, the toxic feelings melted away. Each speaker told stories of how their pain, business, or weight problems seemed to just melt away too.

The next topic was going to be Women's Health, so Helen invited Michelle, Patti, and Lily to come. Lily was too

Very Well

nervous about bringing the baby as she was still only a couple of months old, but she was also anxious about leaving her. Being on edge seemed to be her general state of mind so Helen thought it would be good just to get her out of the house. In the end, Carl called to say she didn't want to come, it was too much for her. So Helen and Kara met up with Patti and Michelle, and they all went together.

"Are you sure about this?" asked Michelle as she looked at the large, dilapidated California-style cottage that housed the SMDC. Built in 1908, just a few blocks in from Santa Monica Beach, it had seen better days.

"Sorry it's not the Beverly Hilton but hey, maybe you ladies could raise some money to redo the roof?" retorted Helen as they drove into the parking lot.

"It's okay. It's going to be fun slumming it for a night," laughed Patti as Helen glowered at her in the rearview mirror. "Oh, get over yourself. I'm just kidding."

Helen wasn't so sure as she saw Patti and Michelle roll their eyes at each other. They made their way in and got coffee from one of the large urns in the kitchen that were kept filled by the 12-Steppers who always seemed to be in need of their caffeine.

The guest speaker was Dr. Alice Katz, a family physician from Denver. Understanding the Three Principles had helped her with her difficult menopause symptoms, and she was now helping women all over the world navigate their journey with health anxieties and life cycle issues. She was in town for a medical conference and so Deborah had asked her to come to speak to the group. The turnout was quite big, as many had heard her speak on several popular podcasts.

"Welcome, everyone! I'm so glad you are all here tonight for this very special presentation." Deborah was excited to introduce her friend and guest speaker. "Please help me welcome Dr. Alice Katz!" There was some light applause as Dr. Alice came to the front. She was tall and slim with silver gray hair pulled back in a ballerina-style bun. She had a beautiful scarf tied gently around her neck and was probably in her early 60s. She reminded Helen of Maria Callas in that classic 1950s elegance. A woman of grace and dignity.

"Thank you! What a pleasure to be with you all. So, I want to start by asking ... has anyone here heard of Bertha Pappenheim?" Everyone gave blank looks and shrugged their shoulders. "Has anyone here maybe heard of Anna O.?"

A woman on Helen's left put up her hand and offered that "Anna O." was one of Freud's most famous clients.

"Yes, well, actually she was one of his colleague's, Josef Breuer's clients, but Freud was happy to take the credit. Her real name was Bertha Pappenheim, and I want to tell you her story.

"Freud had just returned from Paris where he had been studying with the famous, or maybe I should say infamous, Dr. Jean-Martin Charcot. Charcot was a well-respected neurologist who laid the groundwork for discovering illnesses such as Lou Gehrig's disease, Parkinson's, and multiple sclerosis, but he spent most of his career studying what was then called Hysteria. He was charismatic and

Very Well

domineering and, by all accounts, ruled his hospital and clinic with a great deal of fear and ego. The name Hysteria comes from the time of Plato when physicians believed that all women's health problems were caused by the womb moving and wandering around the body, suffocating women as it moved up to the head."

The all-female audience groaned in disapproval.

"Ancient and not so ancient doctors believed that women's moods and physical anomalies were the result of their troublesome and out of control wombs and were therefore diagnosed with the 'disease' of Hysteria. The variety of symptoms were so wide, ranging from mood swings and suicidal ideation to outright convulsions and paralysis, that no one could ever give a discrete definition of the so-called disease, and yet, as women, we have been told that we are sick and broken, malfunctioning, and generally lacking something ever since. In turn, we have inherited the idea that being a woman means there is something wrong with us. Later, with the advent of anesthetics, surgeries were conducted to remove the wandering uterus in order to 'cure' us of this 'disease.'

"Anna O. or Bertha, to use her real name, had become very ill while looking after her father. She had a strange collection of symptoms, including a rigid paralysis in her right arm, a squint, lapses of consciousness, and an inability to speak her native German while still being fluent in English. She would hallucinate, have long periods of 'absence,' and became very aggressive and defiant. Breuer diagnosed her with Hysteria, and Freud encouraged him to try to cure her with his new treatment idea, Analysis. Many women like Bertha were diagnosed with Hysteria when really it was either prolonged stress or trauma, mood swings created by their monthly cycle or menopause, or they, in fact, had a neurological problem like epilepsy, as was possible in Bertha's case.

"Men with symptoms such as epilepsy or stress-related physical issues would have been given medical treatment, but women were often told that they were malingering[7] or exaggerating or just crazy, and when they really didn't know what to do with us, we were burned at the stake or sent away."

The crowd was lapping it up.

"The male body was seen as perfect, and women's bodies were regarded as male bodies, but...messier. Imperfect. Inferior. Broken and in need of repair. This early pathologizing of natural female cycles and the medicalizing of the trauma that women often experienced in their limited and contained lives, like rape and incest, is a legacy that we still endure today. Now, I'm not here to give you an angry feminist rant about the inequality of women's lives, although I do think it is important that we know where the practices and attitudes that direct our modern medical treatment come from. But, ladies, I am here to tell you that you are not sick and you are not broken!"

There was a general feeling of approval and agreement

---

[7] Faking illness in order to escape duty or work. People who had psychosomatic complaints were often referred to as malingering.

in the room as she continued.

"I am a family physician, trained at a top modern school of medicine, so you would think that I would have a bit more of an understanding of how women's bodies work, and I do, but was I prepared for the *experience* of menopause? No! Like many women of a certain age, I started to get irregular periods, then night sweats. I was led to believe, like I'm sure many of you were, that it would be a graceful transition, 'The Change' as our mothers called it. We would glow for a while and then it would be over. But it wasn't.

"As some really ugly and debilitating symptoms became part of my daily life, I started to research and was struck by how the language and message in both medical textbooks and women's magazines is still that our bodies are malfunctioning, that our hormones are in chaos, and that we need fixing. Hold on a minute, I thought to myself, why would I need fixing if my body is doing something natural and normal? Why is it being called a disease? And why, when for thousands of years women have negotiated these physical life transitions without medication, am I now being told I need it?

"So here are some facts: 1 in 20 women suffer PMDD[8], 1 in 8 women suffer PPD[9], and 8 out of 10 women struggle with menopause.[10] As I read the research, I started to

---

[8] Premenstrual Dysphoric Disorder https://faq.iapmd.org/
[9] Postpartum Depression https://www.cdc.gov
[10] Menopause https://www.nhs.uk

question the role stress plays in creating these statistics. Are the levels of stress that we live with today causing our hormones to 'be out of whack,' or are we too stressed to deal with the natural changes we all experience in our female life cycles? This is what I want to talk about tonight. Are the numbers of women who need antidepressants to deal with PMS, postpartum depression, and menopause climbing higher and higher because we are more stressed than our mother's generation, or are we more stressed because we are told there is something wrong with us and that we are broken and malfunctioning?"

Helen was fascinated. This was exactly what she had come to hear. She took a glance around the room; everyone was enthralled.

"So let's establish some facts about how our female bodies evolve. Puberty is the change from being a girl to becoming a woman. Our bodies change and we start menstruating, or menarche[11] as doctors call it. I don't know about you guys, but I had a real shock. My mother had told me that it would happen, so I was kind of prepared. I was 14 and got on with it, but was terrified when it happened again a month later! I thought I was dying! You see, I thought it just happened once and then you were done, you were a woman! Boy, was I shocked *and* disappointed!"

Everyone let out that knowing laugh.

"So our monthly cycle begins and lasts for about 40

---

[11] Menarche is the first menstrual cycle, or first menstrual bleeding, in females.

Very Well

years. Most of us experience some mood swings, physical discomfort, and tension during the monthly cycle as our hormones naturally fluctuate.

"Pregnancy and childbirth can be a huge upheaval to our hormones, but remember, it's also natural and normal. It's your body's way of equipping you with what you need. Perimenopause is the time between regular menstruation and menopause and can last from two to twelve years. Forty-five to fifty-five is the typical age range when this happens. Menopause marks the end of the reproductive years in a woman's life. Monthly periods stop as the result of the declining reproductive hormones estrogen and progesterone that were produced by the ovaries. And here is something I find that most women do not know. Menopause lasts just one day."

Everyone looked confused.

"That's right. Menopause is the 365th consecutive day that you have not had any period. The day you have gone a whole year without any bleeding is the day you have reached menopause, and the day after, you are now post-menopause."

Dr. Alice took a pause as several audience members put up their hands to ask questions.

"I'm so happy to take questions, but I would like to finish this presentation part first, and then we can get into the discussion. Many of you, I know, have been offered medications when you have shown up at the doctor's office in desperation–birth control pills and coils, antidepressants, and HRT, whether it was for PMDD, postpartum, or menopause. What is interesting to me as a family physician is that we are taught to send our patients to specialists with specific training to discuss treatments and medications for things like asthma or diabetes. But it's fascinating, if not frightening, that when it is our reproductive cycle, serious addictive psychiatric drugs are offered after just a few minutes of general consultation!"

Helen had always wondered why her family doctor, who was excellent in all other respects, had offered her a powerful psychiatric drug so nonchalantly.[12]

"Back in the dark distant '70s and '80s, when we were going through puberty, we weren't offered psychiatric or hormonal medications for all those natural but very uncomfortable teenage changes, so have you ever wondered why these other transitions in life require it now? I could get into how the pharmaceutical companies educate and pressure doctors to prescribe these medicines, or that they fund the research that says they are the best solution to your hormonal 'diseases,' but what I want you to know is that after menopause, your hormone levels return to that of your prepubescent self. That's right. You are on a journey through your whole life, a life cycle of health and wellness, to come full circle.

"So what I want to talk about next is how we can

---

[12] Family doctors prescribe over half the antidepressants in the US. They are not fully trained in this area and often do not give full disclosure of the facts about side effects and detox or follow-up. https://www.reuters.com/article/us-drugs-mental-idUSTRE58T0NE20090930

Very Well

navigate this journey from a place of wellbeing and spend life in health and freedom, rather than exhausted, anxious, and medicated. Now that we have understood a little more about our biology, let's look at the nonmedical, non-stressful way to travel this journey more peacefully."

Dr. Alice smiled, taking a sip of water before she continued. "I know many of you have heard Deborah and other speakers talk about the Three Principles of Innate Health. Is there anyone here tonight who is new to these ideas?"

Patti and Michelle cautiously put their hands up, along with a handful of other women.

"Great! That gives me a chance to go back to some basics that all of us need to look at regularly. We all have innate wellbeing and these principles of wellbeing are how we all experience life."

Dr. Alice gave a wonderful introduction to the Three Principles understanding of how experience is created. Helen felt like she just got something a little deeper. She could see how each person has their own way of describing the Principles in action and caught a glimpse of the sheer breadth of its impact. She was beginning to understand how her mood, how her state of mind affected everything. How being in a low mood just made everything seem more awful, even if it wasn't.

"So what I want you to see is that, yes, there are real physical effects caused by hormonal changes, and for some of us, that can be quite a lot. You are not imagining it. But then there is our thinking about it. And this is what we are actually experiencing. Here is an insight that changed things for me. When I had a hot flash I would tense up, the thoughts about how it wasn't fair and how am I going to get through the day would flood my mind and speed up everything. But then I remember a patient saying she thought of her hot flashes as a cleansing. I got goosebumps! I felt a release, a...a relaxing of my ideas about them.

"Since then I have not had a bad reaction to my hot flashes. In fact, I hardly get any now, and if I do, they just don't bother me anymore. Not because I reframed my thoughts or worked on not reacting, but because of an insight, a shift in my thinking that created a whole new experience of what was happening to me physically. I did not have to work on it or remember any affirmations or reprogram anything. It just shifted. Ladies, this is the amazing power of insight."

Dr. Alice smiled warmly at the audience. "Let's look now at what that means from an understanding of the Three Principles. As Deborah has said before, symptoms are Thought in physical form. That doesn't mean Thought created them, but this is the form it has taken in this moment. In the next moment it may take the form of emotion, hunger or inspiration. Thought is fluid, always moving, creating our experience.[13]

"During my time as a family physician, I have had many, many women come to me for a wide range of female reproductive issues and I would prescribe a combination of

---

[13] Chana Studley, *Painless* (Amazon.com, 2020).

treatments, including birth control pills, coils and HRT; therapy; diet; exercise; reducing caffeine, alcohol, and sugar; adding vitamins; and multiple ways to deal with stress. But I was always fascinated when, quite soon, these same patients were back in my office and nothing had really changed. At some point, they had given in to the sugar or booze or they had stopped going to the exercise class or the therapy sessions, and the mood swings had come back along with the bloating, brain fog, anxiety, and for some, thoughts of suicide. As I began to understand the Three Principles more, I started to see that any program of personal change that was dependent on us showing up is often doomed to failure, and here's why."

Dr. Alice took a few paces and looked out at her audience. "All the treatments and programs I was suggesting required willpower. Pills alone won't do it, and so if getting better requires willpower to persevere with lifestyle changes, like diet and exercise, then sooner or later, we are going to flake. How many times have you said, I'll start the diet after the holidays, or just one more bite? No matter how good or expensive that personal trainer is, if we don't show up at the gym, they can't help us. All those stress-reducing techniques seem so good in the video but when your kids are fighting or your boss is yelling, well, we just don't have the time or patience to journal or meditate, or we do it obsessively in a panic to fix ourselves, innocently creating more stress. Deep down, we know we are limited. We are human, and there is a limit to our strength, our patience, and our 'show-upness,' and when we are in a low mood, it just ain't happening."

"As I looked closer, I started to see that when real change does happen it's because of insight, a sight from within. That's how a smoker of 40 years can just stop and never smoke again, or people can lose 50 pounds after a lifetime of failed diets. They had a shift in their thinking and suddenly, it doesn't make sense to keep doing the bad habit, harmful behavior, or overreacting to life's stresses anymore. The main cause of death for women isn't cancer, it's heart disease. Women actually have more heart attacks than men.[14] And the common start for arthritis, dementia, diabetes, cancer, and heart disease...is stress."

The room was quiet, just the faint sound of voices coming from the parking lot as the late-night Grief Support Group regulars gathered outside.

"So hormone fluctuations like pain and bloating are real, but our response to them is made of our thoughts, just like our response to hunger or bad news. The lower our mood, the more reactive we will be. And the more we overreact negatively, the more danger messages get sent to the brain and then the more rotten we feel. I have seen many patients come into the ER thinking they have had a heart attack, when really it was a panic attack. But the most heartbreaking patients are women asking, *begging* me to refer them for surgery. They are so desperate and confused

---

[14] Heart attacks are generally more severe in women than in men because they don't show up as dramatically. In the first year after a heart attack, women are more than 50% more likely to die than men. In the first six years after a heart attack, women are almost twice as likely to have a second heart attack.

Very Well

with what's happening to them physically that they have thought themselves into just one way out. *'Cut it out of me!'* they scream."

Dr. Alice pointed at her belly. "It's like we have gone back 100 years to the time of Freud and Charcot, where surgery to remove that uterus seemed the only answer.

"So what happened to Bertha Pappenheim, otherwise known as 'Anna O.,' the woman who was said to have been one of the first patients to be cured by psychoanalysis? Well, it was actually Bertha who named it the 'talking cure' until Breuer's wife reportedly complained about the amount of time her husband was spending with this intelligent and charismatic young woman. At his wife's urging, and after seeing Bertha daily for two years, he abruptly stopped her treatment. Bertha, distraught at this sudden and unexplained rejection, became even worse and ended up in a hospital in Switzerland where she languished. Freud went on to tell the world of the triumph of psychoanalysis, that Anna O. was cured, but in reality, Bertha was left to suffer.

"I am proud to say that she soon got well. Not only that, but she went on to become a pioneering social worker, author, and political activist for children and women's rights at a time when Germany and the Nazis were preparing for war. She founded an orphanage, traveled internationally in support of women's rights and the banning of forced prostitution, which today we call sex trafficking. For a single Jewish woman in 1920s and '30s Germany, who had spent much of her early life in illness and isolation, this was nothing short of heroic! But who has heard of Bertha

Pappenheim? Not many, but we've all heard of Dr. Freud, a man who had the insane notion that women have *penis envy*!!"

The female crowd fell about laughing and started to clap.

"So, in honor of Bertha, I would like to open up the meeting for questions. Who would like to start?"

There were already hands shooting up as Helen looked around the room. A woman in a sparkly sweater went first.

"Thank you for the medical information, that was very useful, but how can changing your thoughts cure a medical problem like hormones that are out of balance, for example?"

Dr. Alice smiled. "Two things. First, no one is talking about changing thoughts; that would be pointless, as every thought you ever had has already moved on. The nature of thought is to move, so that would be like trying to control clouds. Could you see that? And secondly, the majority of us have normal hormonal fluctuations, so therefore they are not a medical problem, and definitely not a disease. If you are concerned there is something abnormal, please get it checked by your doctor, but it's part of the normal cycle of a woman's life for hormones to fluctuate. And finally, these ideas we are sharing can completely change your experience of it."

Another woman asked, "I have terrible brain fog; just getting here was a major effort. The other day, I found a jar of mayonnaise in the freezer! What was I thinking?"

Everyone laughed, nodding their heads.

Very Well

"I'm curious how what you are talking about is going to help me with this. I'm terrified it's just going to get worse, that I'm going mad or I have Alzheimer's or something!"

Dr. Alice smiled sympathetically. "Yes, I had similar experiences, and it is frightening when you don't know what is happening. But that fear is a large part of what is keeping the brain fog going. The more stress messages that arrive in the brain, the more the brain believes we are in danger and keeps us on high alert, which is exhausting. At some point, it has tipped from being hyper-alert into 'fog.' The way out is to let it all calm down and not react to it. Lack of sleep and bad nutrition are often big contributors to brain fog, and these are happening because our minds are so busy. Stay in this conversation, and you will see how slowing down internally leads to eating better and sleeping more."

Kara put her hand up. "I just wanted to share that in my teens I used to have terrible monthly mood swings. I would cry all the time, hide in my room, and I was so hostile to my poor mother and sister. I couldn't concentrate and was struggling in school. I was losing all my friends, and by the time I graduated I just felt dreadful all the time. I barely made it through college, but when I came across this understanding, and with help from Deborah, my life completely changed. I am calm, my mood swings have melted away, and all my other symptoms just seem to have disappeared. The stress of being stressed all the time was fueling the physical reactions, and now, well, I can still get some ups and downs, but they just don't bother me anymore. Ask my mom; she's right here!"

Helen gave a little wave and felt very proud of her courageous daughter. Other women asked more questions, and Dr. Alice gave more fascinating answers. There was a real buzz in the air as the evening came to a close. Kara and Helen stood in line to thank Deborah and Dr. Alice for such a wonderful evening before they made their way out to the car.

Michelle was very chatty on the way home. She reported on the many things she had noticed; how there were no men, how stupid or smart everyone seemed, and how many women clearly hadn't looked in the mirror before leaving the house, but Patti was strangely quiet. She thanked Helen for an interesting evening but didn't say much else. As Helen and Kara continued home, they talked excitedly about what they had heard and the insights they were both having.

"So many women are suffering," lamented Helen. "I wish we could do more to help."

"Why don't you?" asked Kara enthusiastically.

"Like what? More community nights?"

"Well, yes, but what about something more direct or more…I don't know, something…something more helpful?"

Helen woke up the next morning with an idea right at the front of her mind. It bounded around her head like an excited puppy begging to go out for a walk. She couldn't wait to tell her daughter.

"*A hotline!*"

Very Well

"Huh?" Kara was still half asleep as she slouched into the kitchen in her PJs to get her morning coffee.

"A hotline for women in hormonal distress!"

"Isn't there something like that already...the ah...the Samaritans or some–"

"Yes, yes, they do amazing stuff, but this would be dedicated to women and the stress that comes specifically with changes in their life cycles!"

Kara nodded her approval.

"We could offer them guidance and point them back to their own wellbeing! Look how it helped you and me!" Helen was practically bouncing around the kitchen by this point.

Grogginess quickly vanished from Kara's face. "Wait a second. *We*?"

"I can't do this on my own. I have no idea how."

Kara stood up and stretched. "Mom, I love it. It's a great idea, but I'm studying all the hours God sends, and I have to do my clinical hours." She picked up her coffee cup. "Get Lily to help you. It would be good for her. You'll work it out and you will be amazing." She yawned and shuffled off to get ready for class.

Helen's mind was on fire as she drove to work, thinking of all the things she needed to do to make this happen.

Julie laughed at Helen's idea as they put out the newly arrived footwear on display at Neiman Marcus. "What's so funny? This is serious stuff!"

"Hotline!" exclaimed Julie as she handed Helen some

Ferragamo pumps. "Get it? Hot flashes, hot sweats, it's a *hotline*! Everyone is too *hot*!"

Helen burst out laughing. She was about to throw a shoe at Julie but then remembered where she was. So instead she enjoyed the good feelings and the excitement of a new project and thanked her friend for making her laugh.

7
Brentwood

Helen was so excited to tell Deborah about her idea.

"That's fantastic! Oh my gosh, you could help so many women."

"Sure, but where do I start? I have no idea how to do this."

"Okay, well, I suggest you start small. You will need a new phone and a dedicated phone number and...and put up some flyers? Later you can do things like Facebook groups and Zoom support groups. I would start with local people so that you can get to know them, what they need, and see what really helps. I'm happy to help, but between my coaching work for Joe's business, volunteering at the SMDC, and the community nights I can't promise much right now."

After her experience with Ramona, Helen was a little

cautious about working with friends. She totally trusted Deborah, but she had learned the hard way to have everything up front, so going slowly on her own, with support from Deborah, felt right.

"I'd be happy to mentor you with handling the hotline. My first volunteer job was on a women's crisis hotline in London. But my first suggestion is to learn a lot more about hormones and women's health. I'm sure Dr. Alice will be supportive. I have some books that I think you should take a look at too."

So Helen had a plan–get a new phone with a new number, make some flyers, and start reading.

A couple of days later, Kara brought home some interesting books from Deborah including a massive one, *Why Freud was Wrong* by Richard Webster.[15] There was a note.

Helen,
Would love to hear your feedback on this!
Love, Deborah x

"Does she think I'm going to read all that?!" Helen lifted the enormous book and dropped it back down on the table with a loud thump.

"I don't know. Maybe she thought you might find it interesting?" offered Kara. "I think knowing more about the

---

[15] Richard Webster, *Why Freud was Wrong* (Orwell Press, 1995).

Very Well

history of women's health is going to help a lot. Dr. Alice was pretty down on Freud and seemed to blame him for a lot of our misunderstandings." She flipped through some of the pages. "Ooh, this stuff looks fascinating!" mused Kara, and then left her mother to it.

Helen took the book to bed with her and suddenly felt overwhelmed. Her thoughts about possible calls, women crying, and her not having answers started to spin around in her head. The responsibility of it all made her feel quite uncomfortable. Then she realized that no one was actually pressuring her to do any of this. In fact, no one was demanding anything of her, as no one even knew anything about what she was doing. She had created this project herself! It wasn't even a thing yet; it was just an idea made of thoughts. The only pressure she was experiencing was coming from her own thinking!

Helen laughed to herself and automatically popped out of the rotten feeling. It occurred to her that the pressure was probably coming from thoughts of failure, making a mistake, or what people would think of her. Those thoughts had been hanging out in the back of her mind all day, but they were so quiet that she hadn't even noticed them in the excitement until their heavy feeling got her attention. *Wow*, thought Helen, *this is how it works!* As soon as she recognized them for what they were, just some anxious thoughts, they vanished. Just like Syd Banks had promised in the books Deborah had lent her. It is a reliable system. No work needed–just recognition and then it's automatically followed by fresh new thoughts and a good feeling.

Amazing, thought Helen excitedly.

She took a look at the Freud book but could not believe what she was reading.

"Oh my gosh," cried Kara the next morning as her mother started to tell her about just *how wrong Freud was*! "I knew he had some strange ideas, like we are all dark beasts at our core and that we all want to have sex with our parents, but really?" She pulled a face as Helen read to her some of the things she had highlighted.

"Listen to this. Both Freud and Breuer claimed they had cured Anna O. with psychoanalysis, 'the symptom was permanently removed,' and 'in this way, the whole illness was brought to a close,'[16] but there is clear evidence, written records that she was admitted to some Swiss sanitarium in a desperate state after they stopped working with her. How is that permanent? Apparently, Carl Jung saw through the pretense! Look, he wrote, 'So much spoken about an example of brilliant therapeutic success, was, in reality, nothing of the kind ...There was no cure at all.'[17] Oh my gosh, psychoanalysis is based on a lie!"

Helen read out more examples of the proof that Anna, or rather Bertha, was admitted to a hospital after her psychoanalysis finished with a severe addiction to morphine and seriously ill. "This Webster guy is pointing out tons of

---

[16] Sigmund Freud and Josef Breuer, *Studies on Hysteria* (1895), SE2 pp.40-41; PF3 p. 95.
[17] Webster, *Why Freud was Wrong*, p. 111.

evidence to show that Bertha's symptoms were probably physical stuff like epilepsy, tuberculosis, or meningitis, and not coming from Freud's made-up idea that trauma is held in the body at all! Or that she had Hysteria, whatever that is. That must have been terrifying for her. She wasn't imagining it or making it up. *They* were!"

"I can't believe what I'm reading in this book!" exclaimed Helen the next time she saw Deborah. "How did Freud get to be so famous with this nonsense?"

"Ahh, well, that's the million-dollar question." Deborah put down her coffee. "Freud, my dear, was brilliant...at marketing. He invented a problem, branded it, and then he sold himself as the only solution. He could give today's online marketers a lesson or two on how to sell an idea. Marketing schools should look at how Freud sold an idea to the world without an ounce of scientific proof whatsoever!"

Helen laughed in disbelief. "Webster goes into a lot of detail about how Bertha's symptoms were actually complex neurological seizures. If Freud was a nerve doctor, how come he didn't see that?"

"As I think Webster points out in Freud's defense, he didn't have the diagnostic tools we have today like MRIs and PET scans, but you are right. Why was he so keen to attribute her symptoms to his theory of the subconscious instead of the physical thing that was staring him in the face? Well, that's why I wanted you to read the book. I suggest you get curious about what is behind the things people are going to tell you on your hotline. The explanations they have been given by doctors, therapists, and family often have a basis in his ideas which had no scientific proof."

Helen was beginning to see what Deborah was pointing at. Her energy and enthusiasm for the subject matter they were discussing was amplifying. "What I find particularly despicable is that they medicalize their erroneous conclusion to make it sound scientific. Like describing Bertha pushing away a drink as *hydrophobia*. In the original case notes, it's a minor event, but when it's written up in their *Studies on Hysteria* it's turned into a medical illness," continued Helen.

"Exactly. Well, you are going to find a lot of that with things like menopause and menstrual issues. Like Dr. Alice said, instead of seeing it as a natural process, women are told they are malfunctioning and broken. Which, in turn, causes more stress, and then they need to be medicated for that too. Call me cynical, because I am, but pathologizing normal is a way to sell drugs. Can you see why I wanted you to read this? Therapists and doctors may not think they are Freudian, but his ideas have seeped into every aspect of how medical professionals, psychologists, and the public are trained to see our minds and bodies as broken machines that need fixing instead of the innate health that is always there."

It had been a few days since the Community Night, and Helen was curious why Patti had been so quiet on the way home. She called her friend and asked if she wanted to meet for coffee. As they sat drinking their cappuccinos in a quiet Brentwood coffee shop, Patti opened up.

Very Well

"So...well, Brian, you see, is not my first husband."

"I didn't know you were married before. You must have been very young."

"Yep, young and vulnerable. I was first married when I was 19. It was a teenage romance that was on and off all the time, and we thought that getting married would hold it together. It was clear that it wasn't going to work so we started the divorce proceedings after just six months. Then we got back together *again*, and I got pregnant. We tried to make a go of it for the baby, but it wasn't working, and we started the divorce proceedings again. At 21 weeks, the baby's health was in question, which now that I know about the effects of stress probably isn't surprising."

She took a deep and painful breath. "After a whole lot of tests and different doctors, I had a miscarriage at 34 weeks."

Helen reached out and grabbed Patti's hand. "Oh, honey, I'm so sorry."

"Thank you ... It was really hard. I was grieving the loss of the baby, my body was a mess, and I still had to go through the divorce. I was on a rollercoaster of hormones and emotions, and I was so young. I remember a few days after it happened, I went for a walk on Ventura Beach near my parents' house. I was feeling fine, and then some stranger said a casual hello to me, and I just started bawling. I rushed back home feeling like I was going to break into pieces. This continued for several months. One minute I'd be fine, and the next, I would be crying my eyes out. I felt like a crazy person; the extreme emotions were unreal. Like, I could feel every emotion all in one day from the highest to the lowest. It was just awful."

Helen was so moved by her friend's story. She had been wondering how thought played into an experience like this and asked Patti if she minded talking about it a little more. "Do you remember what you were thinking?"

Patti paused for a moment. "It's been almost thirty years, but everything is still quite vivid. I used to think the same things over and over. Is this it? Is this my life now? Is life just one miserable, painful experience after another? How am I going to get through it, or when is it going to end? Even when my body calmed down, I still had to deal with divorce lawyers.

"There were stages, like sometimes I could comfort myself and just be okay with the crying, reminding myself that I had lost a baby and that it was normal to grieve. And then other times I would get angry with myself and make myself stop it and beat myself up for being so weak. I think…I think I was scared that if I went too deep into the pain of it, I would get swallowed up and wouldn't be able to get out. Like a black hole, and once I fell too far in, there would be no return."

Patti took a sip of her coffee and looked away into the distance for a minute. Helen was touched by her suffering and her courage; it confirmed she had to keep going with the work she was starting.

"Thank you," offered Helen.

"What for?"

"For your honesty, your vulnerability. For being so

Very Well

brave." Helen gave her a warm hug.

"The inner conversations were the worst. In the morning I would wake up anxious and start wondering how I was going to get through the day, and then at night, I was so terrified of not getting to sleep I would lie awake until 3 am!"

"I'm guessing Brian knows about this?"

"Yeah, he was amazing. I met him about two years later. I was very scared at first about getting pregnant again but he was so supportive, and thank God we have our two boys." She put down her coffee cup, shuddering as a thought passed through her mind. "Helen, imagine if I'd demanded a doctor remove my uterus in the middle of that breakdown. I wouldn't have my boys today."

Helen remembered what Dr. Alice had said about women begging her for hysterectomies, innocently driving themselves to such desperation from misunderstanding how their minds and bodies worked.

"But the loss of the baby, it's still with me. She would have been 28 years old now. I sometimes think about what she would be doing, who she would have married, and what kind of person she would be."

"Of course. I'm so sorry you had to go through that and so glad Brian found you."

After a few coaching sessions with Deborah about dos and don'ts when answering a hotline, Helen felt surprisingly ready. She had thought it would take her ages to get up the courage, but everything she needed was right there under all the busy thinking. Deborah had warned her about not giving out personal information and setting boundaries, not making promises she couldn't keep, and not taking the things distressed people say personally. Also, if there was talk of suicide or harming others she had to let the caller know that they need to inform the proper authorities. Helen knew that even a few months ago, she would not have been able to handle the thought of someone saying they wanted to harm their baby or themselves, but after all she had been through with her own daughters, she felt ready.

Lily was feeling a little better, but there were still good days and bad days.

"Did you know that 1 in 7 moms suffer postpartum and 1 in 10 dads do also?" asked Carl as he handed Helen a coffee.

"*What?* Where on earth did you get that men suffer postpartum depression? Don't tell me, off the internet?"

"Yeah, well, I started researching to see if there is anything I can do to help…I want to be supportive, but it gets hard sometimes."

"Sure, but Carl, you're doing a great job and Lily really appreciates it, we all do. But please don't go scaring yourself or her with this stuff. Think about it for a minute; postpartum depression is due to a huge drop in hormones, right? Well, your male hormones didn't go anywhere, did they, so what's causing your depression?"

"Uh, my…my feelings, I guess?"

"Exactly. For sure you are feeling your thoughts about

Very Well

having a baby, but the funny thing is, the same is true for Lily, even though her hormones did change. I don't pretend to understand it all yet, but you are both feeling your thinking, and right now you have a lot going on. Just love her and remember that both of you, and Flora, have wellbeing, and we are here to help you."

"What's going on?" asked Lily as she came to join them. "Is he freaking out again about his man-baby blues? Don't worry, my darling husband; I heard you and I love you for it. Mom, here are some flyers I made for your hotline. I hope they help."

Helen was very grateful for the flyers. She gave some to Kara to share at work and then drove around on her next day off putting them up in community centers, schools, and pharmacies–places where women in need of support would be. As Helen passed through and around various neighborhoods on the Westside of L.A., she felt a mixture of excitement and apprehension. The thoughts came and went many times over, but she realized she wasn't afraid of them. She remembered the banner that was always behind Deborah on the Community Nights and recognized that Syd Banks's quote about not being frightened of our own experience had changed her world too.

Then, it happened...the first phone call.

8
February

It was 10 am on her day off. Helen stared at the new hotline phone for what seemed like ages, listening to the factory ringtone. She started thinking about how she must change it to something more pleasing and then realized she was up in her head and had better answer. But what was she going to say? She had thought so much about the possible stories and situations but hadn't thought about what to say as a greeting. She felt her blood pressure suddenly rise up in her chest as the insecure thoughts rushed around her head.

"Hi, Hormone Hotline. How can I help you?" *Ugh, that's so lame*, she thought to herself as the caller started shouting at her.

"You need to get here right now! This woman is crazy off her head, and I really don't know what I'm supposed to do with her! We are going in front of the judge in 20

Very Well

minutes, and she is about to run. If she runs, she will be arrested, so you better do something fast!"

Helen gasped. She wasn't expecting this and didn't know what to say.

"Hello, hello? Is anyone there?!" screamed the lawyer.

"Yes, I'm here, but I think you might have got the wrong number or the wrong idea?"

"My client gave me this number and said you could help calm her down, so do your job and *calm her down now*!" The irate lawyer went on to explain that his client had run a red light and was blaming it on her PMDD. "Here, you talk to her, 'cause I can't get any sense out of her. One minute she is normal and the next she is a crazy woman!"

"I can try, but I can't make any promises."

Helen did her best to calm the woman down. She suggested she stay and let the lawyer do his job, and that she call back later so they could talk without the pressure of the lawyer screaming at them both. By the time she hung up, Helen's heart was racing; she was exhausted. She had expected tears and some anger but not that. The PMDD lady didn't call back, but Helen worried about her for the rest of the day. She couldn't help feeling responsible for her, even though she knew it wasn't her fault.

Two days passed before it rang again. Helen had decided that she would turn the phone on in the evenings between 8 and 10 pm and on her days off, and she would see how it went. People could leave messages when it was off, and she would return those calls as soon as she could. This time it was late, about 9:50 pm, and she was about to get ready for bed. Helen answered the phone but there was silence.

"Hello?"

There was more silence, but she could hear very quiet sobs on the other end.

"My name is Helen, and I am so proud of you for calling. I know it's not easy. Do you want to tell me what is upsetting you?"

The sobbing turned into crying, and so Helen just calmly reassured her. "I know that when my hormones got the better of me it felt like *everything* was wrong and nobody understood, but I do. I have two daughters and between the three of us we have been through so many ups and downs you can't imagine."

A soft, quiet voice spoke up, "Every month it's like this. I just can't stop crying." She sobbed a little more.

"I know. It was like that for my daughter. You aren't crazy, and you are very brave for calling. Is anyone with you?"

"No." replied the caller through heaving breaths. "I live on my own." And then she started crying some more.

Helen waited until she had calmed down a little and asked her if she was okay with living on her own at other times of the month. The caller said yes, that she loved it; she loved the freedom to do what she wanted, when she wanted.

"That's exactly what happened to me. Most of the month, I was quite okay with whatever was happening, but for that week before, it was like a magnifying glass was put on my life, and everything seemed impossible."

"Yes, it's like it gets all out of proportion and

Very Well

impossible." The young woman on the other end of the phone perked up a little, realizing she was not alone.

"So if nothing has changed in your circumstances, and it's just your hormones that have gone up and down, then you know that you are okay?"

"*No, I'm not! I hate my life!*" The hormone roller coaster was in full swing.

"I know it seems like it right now, but it's not the truth. Remember how you just told me how much you love living on your own and the freedom you have? I bet you get to make a mess and no one complains, or if you just want cornflakes for dinner, then you can?"

The caller laughed a little through her sobs. "I had cornflakes for dinner last night. I was exhausted; I just couldn't be bothered to cook."

"But that's so cool. You were taking care of yourself," replied Helen. "Are they your favorite breakfast?"

The caller spoke slowly, "Favorite cereal...but my favorite breakfast...would be an onion bagel...with smoked salmon and cream cheese."

"Now you're talking!" Helen was relieved she had stopped crying. "What about getting one tomorrow for breakfast?"

"I guess I could. That would be really nice, actually." They talked a little more about the best places on the Westside for bagels and what she liked to do on her days off.

"There. Do you feel a little better now?"

"A little, but it's not going to last, and if I keep eating like that every time I feel low, then I will look like a house!"

"No, I'm not suggesting you do. But see how you didn't even get the bagel yet, you just thought about getting one, and you felt better? You can have cornflakes or a boiled egg tomorrow morning, but right now, a fresh, new thought made you feel a little better, can you see that?"

"I guess."

"You see, we are always feeling our thinking, even when things are going great. But when the hormones change, it's like everything is awful. It's magnified, and it all feels hopeless. But if you can recognize any sentence that starts with *Everything* or *Always* or *Never,* know that it's just the hormones talking. When you see that these thoughts are unreliable you can let them go, ride the wave, as it were, and wait for it to subside. Just know that it is never *Always* and *Everything*; it just seems that way when you are feeling down."

The next morning Helen woke up thinking about the young woman she had talked to the night before and wondered what she was having for breakfast. Then she wondered about the lady with the traffic ticket. Then she remembered something the young woman had said. She said she loved the freedom of being able to do what she wanted, when she wanted. Helen thought about that for a minute. Then she had an insight, a really powerful one. *Freedom isn't being able to do what you want when you want. Freedom is not getting caught up in your thoughts!*

Very Well

Helen was fascinated by how obsessed Freud was with being famous. "In April 1885, Freud embarked on a curious program of destruction. He gathered together the scientific notes he had made over the last fourteen years, together with his letters, scientific excerpts, and writings, and destroyed them."[18] *Huh?* wondered Helen. The explanation came to light as he himself explained it to his then-fiancée.

"I couldn't have matured or died without worrying about who would get hold of those old papers ... Each one of them (future biographers) will be right in his opinion of the "Development of the Hero."[19]

What?! Wow! What a huge, paranoid ego! thought Helen. *Oh my gosh, he is actually describing himself as a hero?!* As she kept reading, it got worse. In 1885, he hadn't even published anything yet! He didn't even have an idea what he was going to be famous for! Helen didn't know whether to laugh or cry. Freud was so sure that he was going to be famous for discovering *something*, something so earth-shattering, that he was already paranoid about what his imaginary biographers would be saying about him!

This guy was a nut, thought Helen in disbelief.

As she kept reading, she saw words like compulsive, paranoid, mendacious, messianic, and depressed. This was

---

[18] Webster, *Why Freud was Wrong*, p. 45.
[19] Ernst L. Freud (ed.), *Letters of Sigmund Freud* (Hogarth Press, 1873-1939), pp. 152-3.

the account of an intensely neurotic man with a deep and profound fear of being ordinary. Becoming famous, and therefore respected, seemed the only redemption possible.

His first attempt at fame came when he had come across cocaine. "In 1884, he had read an obscure paper about a German doctor who had used cocaine on soldiers suffering from exhaustion. Cocaine, at that time, was a relatively unknown drug whose therapeutic effects had not been documented. Freud immediately sensed the possibility of overnight fame as he began to investigate. Writing to his fiancée:

"We do not need more than one such lucky hit to be able to set up house."[20]

This was what became known as the "cocaine episode" as Freud embarked on achieving his obsession for fame. His friend and colleague Ernst von Fleischel-Marxow had been addicted to morphine. Freud had bought a single gram of cocaine from a pharmacy at great expense and "immediately took a twentieth of a gram of the cocaine himself and found that his depressed spirits were replaced by a sense of exhilaration. He proposed to Fleischl-Marxow that he should free himself from his addiction by substituting cocaine, which was enthusiastically adopted."[21]

Oh my gosh, thought Helen. *He used his friend as a*

---

[20] Webster, *Why Freud was Wrong*, p. 45.
[21] Ibid.

Very Well

guinea pig, took cocaine himself, and all in a state of depression?! Did he not have any idea about the human condition?!

"Like the classic cocaine convert, Freud now became an evangelist for the drug. As well as concluding that he had succeeded in the case of Fleischl-Marxow ... He felt he had discovered a miracle drug ... Seized by the prospect of imminent glory, Freud now engaged in a quite extraordinary rush to publication."[22]

Freud had called it a magical substance and wrote emphatically that it was not addictive. But it was clear that Freud had been writing under the influence of cocaine, as he had admitted he took it regularly. *The fact that the paper had been written and published at such incredible speed kind of proves it,* thought Helen sarcastically.

Two months after the publication another doctor did get recognized for his paper on the anesthetic effect of cocaine which Freud had missed completely! *That must have bummed him out big time*, thought Helen to herself. He had missed his chance at fame and someone else had gotten it instead. But what was even worse was that Fleischl-Marxow had now become severely addicted to cocaine. Freud had become the target of much criticism for his paper, and in an attempt to defend himself, he blamed this new addiction on his friend for being an addict! He had also blamed addiction to cocaine on the fact that people were injecting the drug, conveniently forgetting that he himself

---

[22] Ibid., p. 46.

had recommended this method for its rapid uptake. In fact, he had gone so far as to publicly blame his friend in his paper *The Interpretation of Dreams* by writing, "who had poisoned *himself with cocaine*!"[23] Helen couldn't believe it. What a lying, sniveling coward!

Helen had to put the book down. She was disgusted that such a deceitful and dishonest man had become so famous and respected. And for what? His claims weren't even true!

"Hey, Mom, guess what I learned in school today?"

Helen was getting some dinner ready as Kara came in from class. "What's that, honey?"

"Get this. The Samaritans, a UK hotline, was founded by a Reverend Chad Varah. He started it after he went to an autopsy in London in 1953 of a girl who killed herself because she thought her first period meant she had a disease! He didn't want anyone to feel so alone again that they contemplated suicide."

"Oh, the poor girl..."

"And I found some other juicy statistics for you when I was in the library. 84 percent of crimes of violence committed by women were during the time just before their period; 19 out of 22 Hindu women who set themselves alight were menstruating; five billion dollars is lost a year due to menstrual absenteeism; 45 percent of 276 acute psychiatric patients were admitted during their period." Kara turned the page of her notes. "Of 91 children brought

---

[23] Sigmund Freud, *The Interpretation of Dreams* (1899).

Very Well

into the ER with minor coughs or colds, 53 percent of the mothers were just about to start their period! There is more, but you get the picture. Oh, and Rosemary Kennedy, President Kennedy's sister, was given a lobotomy at age 23 for being 'erratic' and having mood swings! She was left unable to walk or talk and was hidden away in a psychiatric facility until she died at age 85!"

Helen listened to her daughter relaying all these facts expecting to feel some sort of shock, but she honestly didn't. After having read about Freud and listened to Deborah and Dr. Alice, she was beginning to see how women were so often written off due to ignorance and fear. Instead, it simply increased her resolve to help and support as many women as she could.

It was a quiet day at work. There were no movie stars to spy on, just the usual privileged housewives, entertainment types, and the people who enjoyed the superior feeling of looking at all the expensive and exclusive designs but who never actually bought anything. Just before lunch Helen had to take some personnel paperwork up to the executive office. On her way back she popped into the restrooms next to Women's Designer Wear. As she was washing her hands she could hear crying coming from one of the stalls. She stopped and wondered if she should say anything.

"Are you okay?" asked Helen gently.

The crying stopped.

"I'm a member of staff. Do you need help?"

There was silence.

"It's okay. You don't have to tell me anything. I just want to make sure you are okay."

There was a pause. The door unlocked. Another pause, and then it opened, very slowly.

9
March

Nicole was a beautiful woman in her mid-30s. She was dressed impeccably, from her perfectly highlighted hair to her manicured toes, except for the mascara that was running down her face. She stepped very cautiously out of the bathroom stall. She was stunning.

"I'm so sorry. I never do this. I mean...I seem to be crying all the time these days, but I have never sat in a public bathroom and cried before."

"That's okay. No one else is here, and hey, you picked Neiman Marcus to have a cry in, so you have great taste." Helen handed her a tissue as Nicole looked in the mirror to tidy herself up.

"I don't even know why I'm crying! I have an amazing life and..." Another tear ran down her face as she wiped away the mascara.

"Don't worry. I get it. Sometimes it just all seems too much."

"Yes, but it's every month. I mean, everything is going great. I just got an amazing new job and I feel great, and then like clockwork, boom. Everything is a disaster."

"Because your body works like clockwork. It's a phenomenally intelligent machine, and every month it kind of lets us know it."

"But why does it have to malfunction like this every month? Why can't it just do its thing quietly?"

"You could ask why about a lot of things. But I'm pretty sure that our reactions to what it's doing makes it worse. Listen, I have to get back to work, but I want to tell you that I just started a women's hotline for, well, for women like you who are finding hormones too overwhelming." Helen grabbed a napkin, wrote down the hotline number and gave it to Nicole. "Next time you feel overwhelmed, like it's all going wrong, or even if you just want to chat and learn about how to cope better, call me."

Nicole stared at the napkin and then at Helen.

"Oh, it's okay. I'm not a restroom stalker! I work in the shoe department downstairs. You can walk down with me if you like. My name is Helen, and this is genuine help. Both my daughters and I have gone through it and come out the other side, and I want to help other women so they don't have to suffer as we did. You're not crazy."

Nicole took a deep breath, gave her a hug, and they walked out the door together.

"Thank you!"

Very Well

The next few callers had a familiar story about how they were okay most of the month, but then the week before their period, everything seemed so incredibly difficult. The crying and negative thinking, even destructive behaviors, like picking fights with family and drinking to take the edge off were all familiar. It seemed that for some women, having someone to just listen was enough. They felt validated and cared for, and were able to get back to some kind of peace with what they were dealing with. But others were like Kara, where one cycle was barely over and the next was starting with no rest from the onslaught of emotions.

Something that kept coming into Helen's mind, though, was Nicole's comment that her body was malfunctioning every month. Every caller she had had so far believed there was something wrong with them, that they were defective in some way. She kept thinking about the things Dr. Alice had said. It was fascinating, but she had so many questions. Helen decided it was time to consult the expert.

"Hi, Dr. Alice. Is it okay if I call you that?" Helen had been a little nervous to call. She didn't want to be a nuisance and guessed the good doctor must be so busy with her practice and her Three Principles work.

"Sure, it's so good to hear from you. Deborah told me you wanted to be in touch. I think your hotline idea is fantastic. So many women are suffering in silence, and the anonymity makes it nice and safe."

"Thank you. I loved your talk in L.A. It was so helpful, but I have some more questions, if that's okay?" Dr. Alice was more than happy to offer any support and advice she could, so Helen jumped right in.

"First of all, how much is hormonal, and how much is it the anxious thinking on top of the hormones, would you say?"

"Well, there is no direct answer to that as every woman is different, but remember, there isn't any experience that isn't made of Thought. Most women, even women with PMDD, have a normal hormone pattern, but even when hormones are rising or dropping dramatically, like after pregnancy, all of our experience is created by our thinking."

"Okay..." Helen was still trying to get her head around this idea. "A lot of the ladies with PMDD have told me that as they get into their late 20s and 30s, the space between their periods when they used to feel okay has gotten shorter and shorter. What would you say about that?"

Dr. Alice paused for a moment. "As I said, each woman is different and I would encourage them to get checked by a specialist, but I would suggest that as they continued to misunderstand what was happening to them, they have built up a habit of low-mood thinking. Meaning, as they anticipated their period coming, they remembered how bad it was last time and this fear lowers their mood. They get more anxious and more miserable thinking about it all, and so when the estrogen and progesterone start to naturally fluctuate, they are already in an anxious state. And then,

Very Well

after this has taken such a toll physically and emotionally, it takes longer and longer to recover. So it's already next month and they are back into the whole misunderstanding nightmare again."

"Okay, so you are saying that even though there is a physical element here, it's made worse by their thoughts about it?"

"Yes. Now, most of them aren't going to want to hear that. They are in a low mood and want to blame it on something going wrong, that they have a disease, for example. But there is plenty of science to prove that our tolerance of pain and discomfort in a state of mental distress goes down tremendously, so you will feel pain and physical reactions at levels that people who are not stressed do not feel."[24]

Helen was starting to see the connection between thought, emotions, and physical stuff much more clearly. Deborah and Dr. Alice had pointed her in the right direction, but now she was *seeing* it for herself!

The next time Helen switched on the hotline, she felt better prepared than ever when the first call of the evening came in.

"Hello?" mumbled a voice through some quiet sobs.
"Hi, this is the Hormone Hotline."
"Is that Helen?"
"Yes, who is this?"

---

[24] Dr. Bill Pettit, in personal correspondence with the author.

"It's Nicole. We met in the restroom at Neiman's last month."

"Oh...oh, yes of course, how are you?" Helen was excited and relieved that Nicole was calling. She had been unsure if she had done the right thing, offering her number to a stranger.

"Well, it's a month later, and I'm crying again."

"I'm so glad you called. I have been thinking about you."

"Thank you. I wasn't sure, you know, a strange lady gives you her number in a public bathroom, it's a bit weird."

"Yes, you're right, it was a bit weird, but I'm only slightly strange."

Nicole laughed a little. "I came into the store a few days ago and saw you working so I guessed you must be legit, and right now, I hate everyone, so I'm past caring." Nicole started crying again. "I don't know how I'm going to get through work tomorrow. I have a big...thing coming up and...and it just seems impossible."

"I know it seems like that now, but how did you feel in the days after we spoke last month?"

Nicole hesitated as she cleared her throat. "Well, it got better and I did okay, but it always comes back. *Every month!*"

"So did anything change in your circumstances?"

"No..."

"Okay, so it was just some crazy thinking that came and went?"

"I guess, but it's so overwhelming. The voices in my

Very Well

head get really loud, and they don't let up. It feels like they are attacking me!"

"That's what my daughter used to say, but that doesn't really happen to her anymore. Can I share with you what helped her?"

"Sure."

"Well, she saw that she was actually feeling her thinking. During the week before her period, her thinking was completely unreliable and therefore she had no business listening to it. When we listen to anxious thinking, we are living in the feeling of the anxiety. We scare ourselves and things get more and more out of control." Helen paused to give Nicole time to take it in. "When we react to that scary thinking, it makes our nervous systems all revved up, and everything starts to escalate. Could you see that?"

Nicole was quiet for a moment. "But how can I ignore all of my thinking for a week? I have a very demanding job. I can't just switch off; I have to show up. I'm dreading next month!"

"Ah, but we don't have to ignore thoughts; that takes effort. I'm holding my phone in my hand right now and to ignore that fact, I would have to concentrate on something else. The funny thing is, now that I'm trying not to think about the phone, I can feel its weight and shape in my hand. Before I thought of that example, I didn't even notice it. I had nothing on it. What if you just had nothing on that crazy thinking? I bet there are people that you just naturally tune out. When my kids were little, I used to tune out a lot of what they babbled about."

"I tune out my boss a lot of the time."

"Me too! You see, when we are in a low mood, most of what we are thinking is unreliable and so...well, when you lose interest in that crazy thinking, it will die of neglect. Like a stray cat, if you don't feed it, it will go away. It's kind of like turning the volume down on the thoughts and, well, my daughter's and mine, our thoughts just got quieter once we started to understand this. It's very peaceful here now, most of the time."

"That sounds too easy." Nicole was clearly skeptical.

"Maybe mark it on your calendar—*Don't listen to anything I think all this week!*—and see how it goes?"

"I guess I don't have anything to lose."

"There you go. Doesn't that sound better? And call me anytime. You don't have to go through this alone."

Helen and Kara had been checking in on Lily regularly. She seemed okay and then would get really overwhelmed again. Grateful for all the times her older sister had tolerated her teenage outbursts, Kara did her best to listen and be there for her as much as she could. Concerned, Helen asked to come play with her granddaughter and to check that things were okay.

"I have anxiety all the time, and yes, Mom, I know it's just thinking! But I am having other symptoms that aren't anxiety, but they are giving me anxiety because I really feel like something is wrong with me." She was talking fast, and so Helen took her hand and soothed her back to help her slow down. "Like maybe I have some horrible disease or

Very Well

something. Mom, I am so tired. Flora isn't sleeping. My brain is all foggy, like I can't think clearly, but I can't turn my brain off. I'm forgetful and can't remember things. I feel dizzy; I can't focus. And I get all lightheaded, and my heart starts to pound. Does anyone else get this? Am I going to die or is this sleep deprivation or anxiety or...?"

"You are not going to die. You are just overtired, and it feels like your thinking is attacking you. Just look how adorable Flora is, and how well she is doing. Honey, you are not going to die."

Helen reflected on what Lily was going through. She knew there was something more to this that she was not quite seeing yet. She gave Lily and Flora a big hug and a kiss. It would unfold. She didn't know how or from where, but Helen was calmly confident she would see more.

10
San Diego Morning

"Hi, Helen, how are you?"

Dr. Alice was on the phone. Helen automatically felt a surge of excitement and nervousness all at the same time. She was excited that Dr. Alice was calling *her*, but what if she had done something wrong? What could she have done wrong? Helen was amazed at how quickly the insecure thoughts came sometimes, and how freeing it was to recognize it for what it was—that she was just being human. She laughed to herself as she answered.

"Hi, Dr. Alice, how nice to hear from you! I'm doing great, how are you?"

"Oh, me too, thank you! Now here's something interesting. I just heard about a health conference in San Diego, and one of the most prominent research psychologists in women's menstrual health will be

Very Well

presenting her latest work. It's called '*From Menarche to Menopause: The Role of Stress and Hormone Sensitivity*,' so it should be exactly what we need. I'm flying in, would you like to join me there? I think it's just a two-hour drive from L.A., right?"

"Oh, wow, that sounds amazing! I...I would be honored!" Helen couldn't believe it. What an amazing opportunity.

"Wonderful. I'll email you all the details, as you will have to register. This will be such a great chance for us to hear what the scientists are saying, and we'll get to catch up. You can tell me all about how your hotline is going."

Helen was stunned. She used to be a housewife; she sold shoes in a department store. How did she get to be invited to hear a Ph.D. scientist present research at a medical conference?! *Life is funny*, thought Helen to herself. *You have no idea what is going to happen next if you just keep showing up.*

Julie was happy to swap her day off in order to help Helen out with her adventure. The drive down to San Diego was simple; she had driven it many times to take the girls to see their grandparents in La Jolla. She found the downtown conference center and picked up her badge at the registration table. Helen started to feel very self-conscious. She wasn't a doctor or doing research. What was she thinking? All the other participants seemed to be medically trained or academics or something important. Her insecure thoughts started to speed up. What if she couldn't understand the science, or what if someone asked her why she was there?

I'm not supposed to be here; this is for smart people!

It was like an insecure radio station was going on in the background of her mind. Like an internal monologue from your worst critic who knows all the right buttons to press. Helen intuitively knew not to listen to the unreliable babble. Knowing that the uncomfortable thoughts would pass and didn't mean anything, she looked for her new friend. Dr. Alice was sitting on a big, comfy sofa nearby, reading the conference brochure. She was as elegant as ever and jumped up gracefully as soon as she saw Helen.

"Hello! I'm so excited you could come! These medical conferences can be pretty dry, but I thought you and I could discuss what she says, and that will make it so much more enjoyable. We might even learn something."

Helen was thrilled that Dr. Alice was so happy to share this with her. She still couldn't get over the fact that the good doctor valued her opinion so much, but was very happy to be there with her.

"Me too, but I have to tell you, I think most of this is going to be beyond me. What if I don't understand all the science?"

Dr. Alice responded kindly, taking her arm, "Oh, don't worry about that. If there is something technical you don't understand, let it go and just stay in the moment. Academics love to show off, use four long words when two short ones would do." She laughed at herself. "I know it can be a bit daunting, but I'm sure this one is going to be very

Very Well

interesting. You can always ask me later, and besides, no one else here is going to get it all anyway."

They went into the main conference room for the presentation and found their seats. Helen felt a little better, but as she looked around at the other attendees, they all looked way too comfortable to be feeling as stupid as she was.

"So do you know the doctor who is speaking?" asked Helen as she watched those thoughts go by.

"No, but she is from the Women's Mood Disorder Clinic at UNC.[25] I have read some of her research papers. I'm so curious as to what is being offered medically as an explanation for these so-called disorders."

The lights flickered to get everyone's attention as one of the organizers came to the podium to introduce the speaker. Dr. Susan Girdler, an elegant, middle-aged woman in a red and black dress, came to the podium to deliver her presentation.[26]

"It is absolutely an honor to be here. I am so delighted. I was thinking on the plane ride here, when I was doing my Ph.D. dissertation I actually wanted to study something

---

[25] University of North Carolina.

[26] The following are notes I made from a lecture given by Dr. Susan Girdler, professor of psychiatry and psychology, vice chair for faculty development, and director of the Stress & Health Research Program at the University of North Carolina, given at the 2016 NAPMDD Conference. The only changes made are for ease of understanding. This lecture can be found in full at:
https://www.youtube.com/watch?v=_eZAhOG2l0I&t=902s

else, but my supervisor suggested I look at PMDD, and to be honest, at the time I wasn't even sure if I believed PMDD was real. But as I started working in this area of reproductive mood disorders, I began to see it for myself.

"In research laboratories, women with PMDD do amazingly well on stress tests during their follicular phase,[27] but given the same tests during the luteal phase,[28] they might break down in tears to the point where we had to stop the testing. There was one participant who was so stressed that she had documented her panic attacks and was so agoraphobic that she never left her house on her own. She needed her husband to bring her into the lab to do the testing. Still I was skeptical, until I analyzed the data, the biological data, and saw that it mapped onto their cycles."

Helen settled into her seat, her mind slowing as she took in the information.

"Women are twice at risk for depression than men, and this becomes evident when we reach puberty and remains so during reproductive years. This leads us to believe there is a relationship with sex hormones, and can be seen clearly at times of large fluctuations such as post-birth and

---

[27] The follicular phase starts on the first day of menstruation and ends with ovulation. Prompted by the hypothalamus, the pituitary gland releases follicle stimulating hormone (FSH).

[28] The luteal phase begins after ovulation. It lasts about 14 days (unless fertilization occurs) and ends just before a menstrual period. During most of the luteal phase, the estrogen level is high. Estrogen also stimulates the endometrium to thicken.

Very Well

perimenopause. But what I really want to share with you is the clinical phenomenon of reproductive mood disorders such as PMDD, PPD, and perimenopause depression. I want to spend time today giving you evidence that women with these disorders are actually vulnerable to *normal* hormonal change, which defines the hormonal sensitive phenotype."[29]

Helen wondered what a phenotype was and got a little scared again that this was going to be too technical for her to understand. She needed to make some notes, so she looked in her purse to find some paper, but all she could find was a Pizza Shop coupon and a report from work about changes in pensions and benefits. She started to take notes on the back of the report. There was so much great information; she didn't want to forget anything.

"I would like to share with you evidence about stress, the relationship with stress, and how that plays into the pathology of how reproductive mood disorders work. So, as you know, the HPA axis[30] and cortisol play major roles in the sympathetic nervous system that releases adrenaline. This has been implicated in mood disorders for a long time now, but in stress, they work together to drive heart rate, and in response to stress, they act in a positive role for the

---

[29] A phenotype is an individual's observable traits, such as height, eye color, and blood type.
[30] The hypothalamic-pituitary-adrenal (HPA) axis is a mechanism that mediates the effects of stressors by regulating numerous physiological processes, such as metabolism, immune responses, and the autonomic nervous system (ANS).

sole purpose of mobilizing energy stores and to get oxygen to working muscles."

Helen didn't quite get all that, but she knew from Deborah that prolonged stress was not good for the body.

"And that system was exquisitely designed for dealing with short-term physical stressors that require a physical response, but today, our stressors are not physical or short-term, and so the problem arises when the stress response continues in excess of what the body needs, and when that is maintained for a long time, it sets the stage for disease development and mental illness."

Helen was following so far. Basically, she was saying that our bodies weren't designed for such long periods of stress, and this leads to physical problems, just like Deborah had taught them about chronic pain. She started to relax as her thoughts settled down again.

"Okay, let's start with puberty," continued Dr. Girdler. "Events that happen in puberty have an effect on the body; it's a time of high stress. And that stress impacts the still-developing adolescent brain. Girls report more stress than boys, particularly in interpersonal, family, and peer domains. Adolescent girls report greater depressive symptoms under stress than boys. Another interesting fact from research shows the significance of pubertal timing, that is, the age at which the changes related to puberty start."

Dr. Girdler took her reading glasses off the top of her head and looked at her notes. "One piece of research showed that girls who matured earlier showed greater depressive symptoms from seventh to twelfth grade. So why might

Very Well

early development be linked to stress?"

Good question, thought Helen.

"Think back to when your body was changing. Did you feel uncomfortable at all?"

The crowd murmured in recognition of her question.

"Imagine, if you develop early you will stand out, and this adds a whole other layer of challenge for adolescent girls in social interactions and where they fit in with their peers. Another more sobering statistic is that child sexual abuse is associated with early menarche.[31]

"In a large-scale study of over 67,000 children in the U.S., the amount who reported sexual abuse at the age of 12 was the same as those who didn't. That is an astronomical figure! So what might be a behavioral model that could explain this development of depression or anxiety in adolescent girls? We know that child abuse has a long-term impact on the cortisol stress axis—it sensitizes it. It creates a 'pathway' that leads to depression and anxiety."

Helen's heart sank at the thought of the weight of all the pain caused by so much trauma and misunderstanding.

"Women's menstrual cycles have been of interest for centuries. We women have been burned at the stake, locked up, and undergone forced surgeries. But it wasn't until 1931 when a New York psychiatrist, Dr. Robert Frank, first systematically documented in 15 of his patients the cyclical occurrence of a variety of complaints. He termed this *Premenstrual Tension* in recognition of the tension and

---

[31] Meaning the stress of abuse can bring on early menstruation.

anxiety that tended to eclipse other symptoms."

Dr. Girdler clicked her pointer at a large screen behind her and showed a photograph of Dr. Frank's original 1931 report. The document, torn and brown with age, was typed with a manual typewriter, but you could clearly see his observations.

```
Severest tension
Suicidal
Incapacitated
Impossible to live with
All most crazy
Unbearable shrew
```

Everyone laughed at the "shrew" comment.

"But it was clear that all these symptoms went away with the onset of menstruation. He was the first to hypothesize about the cause, that it was an excess of hormones, and so his remedy was either a dose of X-rays to the ovaries or eliminating them altogether, and this treatment was, of course, effective. It has been five decades from this report to the diagnosis of PMDD becoming official."

Dr. Girdler then put up some slides showing graphs of women's cycles to show how the rate of physical and emotional response goes up drastically before menstruation and drops after. "As you can see, the emotional symptoms eclipse the physical symptoms, *but* very importantly, for there to be a diagnosis of PMDD, there is a complete

Very Well

remission of these symptoms shortly after the onset of menses. But as research shows, many women become symptomatic at ovulation, and it escalates until the onset of menses. So these women spend half their reproductive lives suffering from this disorder.

"Now, we know that estrogen and progesterone are very potent modulators of mood, and a lot of research shows that they have a beneficial effect, buffering the physiological response to stress and countering the inflammatory processes in depression. But when we look at how estrogen and progesterone are elevated, at their highest, this is when women diagnosed with this disorder are experiencing the worst symptoms of anxiety and depression. And when estrogen and progesterone are at their lowest, they are symptom-free. So just the opposite of what you would expect is happening if estrogen and progesterone are anti-anxiety and antidepressant agents." Dr. Girdler scanned the audience to see their reaction. Helen was a bit confused. It sounded like the body was behaving backwards for women with PMDD. "Let's go back to puberty to try and understand this a little bit better."

Dr. Girdler then went into some very uncomfortable descriptions of mouse experiments that Helen found quite hard to hear, but it seemed to prove something very interesting. It appeared that if the mouse was stressed during puberty, the anti-anxiety and antidepressant qualities of estrogen and progesterone disappeared!

"So the experience during puberty has lasting effects on the responses to estrogen and progesterone in later life. It appears to reverse or eliminate the anti-anxiety and antidepressant qualities of estrogen and progesterone. Therefore, PMDD is better conceptualized as a stress disorder."

Helen heard that loud and clear. Stress was at the bottom of this, and that was something she could help women with.

Dr. Girdler put on her reading glasses again for the next slide.

"*Clinically distinct subgroups of women for whom historical factors provide a context of vulnerability for stress response dysregulation and perhaps for the development of the disorder.*"

Helen had to read this a few times very slowly to get what it meant.

"*Clinically distinct subgroups of women...for whom historical factors...provide a context of vulnerability...for stress response dysregulation...and perhaps for the development of the disorder.*"

Helen paused to think about this as Dr. Girdler went on with some more science. *Historical factors, like say, early development, abuse, or trauma...made some women vulnerable...which can lead to them having a bad reaction to their cycle?*

"So under the leadership of Dr. Eisenlohr-Moul, we started to look at what exactly predicts the hormone-sensitive phenotype of half the women with PMDD, and after the break, I will tell you more about what we found."

Very Well

"What's a phenotype?" asked Helen excitedly as they got up for the coffee break.

"Well, it's a combination of things, really. Traits, I guess you could say," answered Dr. Alice as they walked out to the lobby. "Things such as height, eye color, and blood type. If I remember correctly, some traits are largely determined by the genes, while other traits are largely determined by...environmental factors."

"Environmental factors? You mean like...stress?"

"Yes," answered Dr. Alice with an impressed smile. "So what do you think so far?"

"It's fascinating! I mean, I doubt I got all the science, but it sounds like she is saying first of all that PMS and PMDD are not a result of too many hormones or something going wrong with the levels or...or quality of hormones?"

"Exactly!"

"But that's huge! I always thought it was because our hormones were messed up or malfunctioning or something! I think most women do. We say things like 'oh, my hormone levels are all off this month' or 'it's just my hormones gone crazy!' In fact, in that first piece of research she put up, the first guy in New York in the 1930s who said the woman was an unbearable shrew, he said it was an excess of hormones! But she is saying that PMS isn't something wrong with the level of hormones at all!"

"Yes, and that's what I was saying when I came to speak in L.A."

"I realize that now, but it hadn't sunk in. Sorry, I'm a bit slow."

Dr. Alice shook her head in disagreement.

"But why, when the research shows that this isn't true, don't the scientists or our high school biology teachers tell us the truth?"

"I suspect it's either ignorance or a money thing; it usually is. All those hormone repair kits, mindfulness programs, and hormone-balancing diets, not to mention the billions in pharmaceuticals. It's like the whole chemical imbalance theory not being true."[32]

"Yeah, Deborah told us about that, but no one believes me when I tell them that the people at the NIMH who invented that theory now admit it was made up!"[33]

The two ladies got themselves iced cappuccinos from a coffee cart in the lobby and found a table away from the other participants to sit down. The conference center was buzzing with speakers, delegates, and visitors so it was nice to find some quiet.

"Thank God for air conditioning." Dr. Alice was fanning herself with her program. "I'm remembering why I like Colorado right now."

Helen grinned. "Yes, we're only a few miles from

---

[32] "There are no objective tests in psychiatry–no X-ray, laboratory, or exam finding that says definitively that someone does or does not have a mental disorder." Allen Frances, MD, Professor Emeritus and former Chair, Department of Psychiatry, Duke University. He was Chair of the DSM-IV Task Force. Check out the latest research article showing there is no scientific proof for the chemical imbalance theory: https://go.nature.com/3vkZMZP

[33] Look out for my next book, *A Tale of Two Boys!*

Very Well

Mexico. It gets very hot here. Okay, I have so many questions."

Helen wasn't sure where to start, but Dr. Alice jumped straight in. "So what did you think about all the talk about puberty?"

"Well, I developed early," replied Helen, "and I can remember how uncomfortable I felt. My body was changing fast and...I knew it was normal, but my friends weren't showing yet, so, yes, I kind of stuck out, literally! I suddenly had these big boobs, and I didn't know what to do with them."

Dr. Alice laughed. "As you can see, I never have, but I remember my first boyfriend had a twin sister and she had huge boobs. She would...*maneuver* them to make sure I knew it, as if to say, this is what real women look like! So whether we feel self-conscious because we develop early like you, or late like me, it's the self-conscious thinking that is creating the experience. If we had known that it was our thought-created experience that was making us feel the way we did and not our bodies, then maybe we wouldn't have developed a strong stress reaction? I think what she was saying is that when you have an early life stress experience[34] that creates a...what did she call it? A pathway?"

"Yes," agreed Helen, looking at her notes. "She said a 'pathway that leads to anxiety and depression.' But that's what we would call a low mood, right?"

---

[34] This can be abuse or trauma, but also prolonged anxiety and stress about our bodies, family, or the future can all be factors.

"Yes. So much of what she described this morning is a low mood. And in a low mood, we are more sensitive to insults or rejection or...or anything uncomfortable, including the severe fluctuations of our hormones as well. If you develop a strong startle response early on, then it makes sense you are going to be jumpy at, well, anything, including a natural rise or fall in your hormone levels."

"And remember she said PMDD is better described or...conceptualized as a stress disorder? See, this is what I don't understand. When I took my daughter Kara to the psychiatrist back when she was in her teens, suffering terribly, he called it PMDD. Yes, her symptoms were really bad as her cycle started and would go away after her period, but as the years went on, the days when she was distressed got longer. Her distress started well before her period, and as it got worse, it would take her longer and longer to get over it. So she would start worrying about next month to the point where there were only a couple of days in the middle when she felt vaguely okay. By the time she went away to college, she was never off the roller coaster!"

"Oh, the poor thing. So yes, a diagnosis of PMDD does require that it's cyclical, that it's directly connected to the menstrual cycle, as opposed to bipolar or borderline personality disorder or PTSD, for example," offered Dr. Alice. "Which is what makes it a different diagnosis according to the DSM.[35] Those other diagnoses are either all

---

[35] Diagnostic and Statistical Manual of Mental Disorders, 5th Edition (DSM-V).

the time or at random times. Women with PMDD can predict pretty much when their stress symptoms are going to come and go by looking at the calendar."

"But that's my point, and that's why I was confused. Her psychiatrist said it was PMDD, but by the end, she was a mess all the time. So was it really PMDD or...bipolar or PTSD or, as I see now, she was suffering from the misunderstanding of what was really creating her experience?"

Dr. Alice raised her eyebrows in agreement.

"The truth was, her father had died tragically and our life went up in smoke. No wonder she was reacting so much. I just had a thought. If a woman's personality changes so dramatically at certain times of the month, why is it not multiple personality disorder?! One day Kara would be the sweetest kid, and the next, she was a demon from hell...until the demon ate her up completely. At times, there was no respite and I thought I'd lost her completely. It seems to me that all these diagnoses are pointing at the same things, they all have the same symptoms–anxiety, depression, mood swings, etc. I know I'm not a doctor, but...well, what difference does it make what you call it? It really is just a misunderstanding of how experience is created, isn't it?"

When they came back into the conference room, the audience had grown with the addition of some late arrivals. Helen was feeling a bit more at home and not so insecure about being there. Understanding where her feelings were coming from was a huge comfort.

"Welcome back, everyone. So I want to pick up where we left off. We are now going to look at what exactly predicts the hormone-sensitive phenotype of half the women with PMDD. Dr. Eisenlohr-Moul recently published this data." Dr. Girdler put up a slide that looked to Helen like two crazy scribble pictures her daughters would have done at age two or three. They were actually graphs with anxiety levels on the vertical, and days of the monthly cycle on the horizontal. One was for estrogen and one for progesterone.

"My kids did pictures like that when they were little," whispered Helen.

The slides were a mess of lines going in all directions, but through the middle of each graph was a red line which Dr. Girdler said was the average. "When you look at the average, there really isn't a difference between changing hormone levels and symptom severity. But the other lines are individual women, 66 in all, with tremendous differences in their personal experiences. And, for some, it really does look like changing hormone levels is related to their symptom severity. So what is going on here? What predicts this hormone sensitivity?

"Well, a few years ago we started to ask questions about histories of abuse." Dr. Girdler went on to describe how data was collected to report levels of sexual, physical, and emotional trauma. "And when we looked at this data, we saw that women with PMDD had a substantially greater history of abuse. Then we went back and reanalyzed the data, and we saw that the women with PMDD had greater

Very Well

symptom sensitivity to their *normal* fluctuation of hormones."

She then showed other data showing things like higher thyroid response in women with PMDD. "Which, incidentally, is consistent with soldiers with PTSD, so it's as if the thyroid axis is responding to a life-threatening stressor. For the vast majority of women in our studies, well," she hesitated for a second, "well, it's been decades since their last abuse experience. Most of these traumatic experiences were in their childhoods, teens…in puberty, and so their physiological responses to stress may represent an adaptation gone awry."

Helen and Dr. Alice looked at each other with surprised excitement.

"When the body continues to prepare the individual for a severe stressor *that no longer exists*, this somehow remains encoded in the brain."

She then showed the audience results from a study that showed women with histories of eating disorders, anxiety and mood disorders, PTSD, substance abuse, nicotine dependence, etc., and the highest indicator by far for who was likely to develop PMDD was 'any qualifying trauma.'

Helen glanced at Dr. Alice again. Dr. Alice gave her a knowing smile back.

"It's time to take a break now for lunch, and after we reconvene, we will take a look at postpartum depression and menopause. Thank you so much for your attention this morning."

There was applause as everyone started to make their

way out to get something to eat. Helen and Dr. Alice settled down to their lunches but had plenty more to digest.

11
San Diego Afternoon

"I need to tell you about Marilyn Bowman's book,"[36] said Dr. Alice as they tucked into their lunches. "It's not a Three Principles book; it's a textbook, really. Marilyn is a research psychologist, and her book is a fascinating collection of reports of trauma from all over the world that points to the fact that we all have different responses to traumatic experiences."

"Because we all live in different realities," agreed Helen as she enjoyed her roasted salmon pad thai.

"Exactly. In the traditional model, psychologists and social workers believe that certain things are inherently stressful...like moving house, for example. It was third on the list of 'known stressors' when I was in med school, after

---

[36] Marilyn Bowman, *Individual Differences in Posttraumatic Response* (Routledge Press, 1997).

divorce and the death of a parent. But how can we generalize? Moving house is certainly a lot of work and very disruptive, but what if you are going to retire in Hawaii, or start a new job or new family? It might be the best thing that ever happened to you; it's what you make of it. So, yes, we are all living in our own thought-created reality, but something is only stressful if you *think* it is. And in this book, Marilyn shows that not everyone reacts the same way to the same events. Some women survive a violent rape, for example, and are able to go on and have very productive lives, and others might hear about a family member being attacked and are incapacitated."

"It depends on state of mind," observed Helen. Dr. Alice nodded in agreement as she finished off her salad. "So that would explain why not all the women in her research groups reported abuse but still had PMDD?"

"Yes! Remember she mentioned PTSD and soldiers? She said something really interesting, really important, in fact. She said, 'It's been decades since their last abuse or traumatic experience.' She was saying that when people who suffer trauma don't understand what is happening, they suffer things like repetitive intrusive thoughts, flashbacks, and panic attacks, and their–"

"And their physical responses to stress is...what did she call it?" Helen looked excitedly at her notes again. "'An adaptation gone awry.'"

"I'd say!" exclaimed Dr. Alice. "Many of the women I see in my office are frantic, even suicidal! They are feeling their stressed out *thinking* about the traumatic event now,

Very Well

not the event that happened in the past."

"Yes, Deborah explained this to us when she talked about her own experience of trauma.[37] So what is really happening is the misunderstanding of how Thought is creating their experience and has made them over-reactive to anything and everything. So they are jumpy, easily startled *and the natural change in hormones is just another thing to set off that overreaction*."

Both women sat quietly for a few moments as they reflected on the evidence, the science that was confirming what Sydney Banks had seen 30 years before. Thought is *The Missing Link*.[38]

After lunch, the audience gathered again in the conference room and waited for Dr. Girdler to restart the fascinating presentation.

"Okay, so now I want to talk about postpartum depression, and like PMDD, it is predicted by severe life stress, including histories of trauma."

That's a pretty strong statement, thought Helen. It never occurred to her that Lily had experienced any trauma, but like Kara, her father had died suddenly and tragically when she was just a teen.

Dr. Girdler pointed to a chart showing that the more incidents of trauma, the more likely the possibility of depression. Dr. Alice nudged Helen.

---

[37] Chana Studley, *The Myth of Low Self-Esteem* (Amazon.com, 2019).
[38] Sydney Banks, *The Missing Link* (Lone Pine Publishing, 1998).

Chana Studley

"What?"

"Maybe I should give her a copy of Marilyn Bowman's book?" whispered Dr. Alice with a grin.

"Women who were tested in pregnancy and showed a higher cortisol response to stress were more likely to develop PPD. Now, I have been lucky enough to receive an education from my colleagues in this area, and as you know, we call it postpartum depression, but the reality is that women with PPD really have pure anxiety."

There was a pause as the audience took this in, and Helen and Dr. Alice looked at each other again as if to say, *she does get it?*

She continued, "So it's really more of an anxiety disorder." Dr. Girdler then went into some basics about pregnancy hormones, describing in detail the tremendous plummet of both progesterone and estrogen after birth.

"What is the evidence that women with PPD have a hormone-sensitive phenotype? Research shows[39] that women with a history of PPD react adversely to their increase and decrease of hormones much more than women without that history. So either the addition of hormones or the withdrawal of hormones increases the dysphoria,[40] ill temper, and panic, and reduces wellbeing effects not seen in

---

[39] Dr. Crystal Schiller, UNC, 2016.
https://www.ncbi.nlm.nih.gov/pmc/articles/PMC4811338
[40] Dysphoria is a state of generalized unhappiness, restlessness, dissatisfaction, or frustration, and it can be a symptom of several mental health conditions. (Or is it another way of describing a low mood?)

Very Well

women without a history of PPD. So this is just more evidence that reproductive mood disorders may be characterized by a vulnerability to normal reproductive hormone changes."

Someone in the audience insisted on asking a question, but Helen couldn't quite hear it. Dr. Girdler's answer, though, was very interesting. "The exposure to the huge plummet in hormone levels in vulnerable women may *sensitize* them."

Vulnerable? thought Helen. She guessed that the doctor was referring to their history of trauma, but it was becoming so obvious that anyone who misunderstands where their experience is really coming from is suffering innocently.

"Okay," continued Dr. Girdler, "so we made it through adolescence, we've experienced about 500 menstrual cycles, and have given birth on average to two children. Now the menopause transition. *Bring it on!*" She gave a big grin as some murmurs and knowing laughs came from amongst the older women in the room, including Helen.

"All joking aside, this is also a time of vulnerability for depression. Major depression rates can increase two to fourfold, and this is true even if you have never had depression in the past. So about a third of women suffer depression during this time."

Helen thought about her own experience. She had never thought of herself as having depression. She didn't have time for it. She had been stressed. Her husband had died, her life had been turned upside down and she had to completely reinvent herself. Not to mention bringing up two daughters with all their problems and struggles. Helen realized she didn't need a diagnosis. She had struggled with many, many long, dark nights of depression, she just hadn't seen it that way before.

Dr. Girdler put her glasses on again to read some more graphs that illustrated that women with a history of depression, anxiety, and stress were more sensitive to hormone fluctuation in menopause. "*Again, this suggests that it's the sensitivity to hormone levels, not the hormones themselves.* Midlife for women is associated with a lot of psychosocial changes. Changes in relationships, work, and professional status. HRT is not the answer for everything, as this drawing suggests." She put up a slide of a hand-drawn *New Yorker* style cartoon depicting two women sitting in a restaurant.

I was on hormone replacement for two years until I realized I needed a Steve replacement!

There were some more murmurs of laughter. Another graph was put up on the screen. "As we approach our final menstrual period, we see there is a slow but erratic decline in estradiol[41] levels and a slow but erratic increase in FSH.[42] By

---

[41] Estradiol is an estrogen steroid hormone and the major female sex hormone. It is involved in the regulation of menstrual female reproductive cycles.

[42] Follicle-stimulating hormone is a gonadotropin hormone. FSH is synthesized and secreted by the anterior pituitary gland and regulates the development, growth, and reproductive processes of the body.

Very Well

the time you get to about two years outside or after your last menstrual period, your estrogen levels are nice and low and stable, and your FSH levels are nice and high and stable."

She took a big sigh as she continued. "But...in that transition, right in here, there is *no* hormone stability. In this next graph, you can see that the fluctuation in estradiol, progesterone, and FSH levels is extreme. In fact, estrogen levels can be higher than they were before a woman was ever peri-menopausal and then plummet down! So what is the trigger for these symptoms in certain women if this pattern is common to all women in this age group?"

Dr. Girdler went on to describe some research she had just completed where they tested the estrogen levels of perimenopausal women in relation to stress levels and discovered that in the 14 months that she tested, it was only the women with high life stress and high variability who developed clinical depressive symptoms.

"So to try and understand what mechanism there might be for that, we bring them into the laboratory and expose them to the Trier Social Stress Test,[43] and they have to do it in front of these people."

She put up a slide of a very mean and serious man and woman in white lab coats with clipboards looking very sternly right at the audience. Everyone gave a nervous giggle.

"While you are being recorded, these terrible Testers are

---

[43] The Trier Social Stress Test (TSST) is a laboratory procedure used to reliably induce stress in human research participants. It is a combination of procedures and was created in 1993 at the University of Trier by Clemens Kirschbaum and colleagues.

trained to make the situation unpredictable and uncontrollable. This has a huge effect on stress levels. By month eight, we saw that women with high estradiol variability were also showing more negative emotional responses, especially in terms of being hostile and angry, and reporting high levels of sensitivity to rejection."

On the graph she was showing, the labels Anxiety, Fear, Anger/Anxiety, and Rejection were all clearly marked as separate subjects in their testing and scores. Helen was curious how the tests or questions differed for these supposedly different things. Surely they were subjective; surely they were all coming from low-mood, insecure thoughts?

"And, this high sensitivity to rejection predicted the development of depressive symptoms in women with high baseline stressful events.

"So to wrap this up and tie this all together in some way, early life adversity is a risk factor for all reproductive mood disorders, but I want to underscore that it does not mean that every woman who has had an adverse life event will go on to develop a reproductive mood disorder. But, if you have that history, we know that this history can sensitize the response to stress and can have long-term effects. And that may be one pathway to reproductive mood disorders.

"Now, if you are vulnerable, you are more likely to develop reproductive mood disorders. So we now know that it's not just physiologic stress responses that were found in relation to hormone fluctuation but *emotional responses*.

"So, I've been a bit of a Debbie Downer by talking about

all the moods and stress, but things are looking up when we transition out of menopause. We have a lot to look forward to! Thank you."

There was some nervous laughter from the women in the audience as she opened up for questions, and everyone applauded her impressive presentation.

"In my practice, I ask a lot about personal histories but more about relationships, marital status, etc. Should I be asking about abuse?"

Dr. Girdler raised her eyebrows. "I'm not an interventionist. I just bring them into the lab and stress them out; you are the clinician. So let me ask you. Why do you want to know? I mean, would it affect your treatment of your patient? You know this more than I do, that this may be the first time they have told anyone so if you do, you will need to help them process this."

Helen's heart sank a little as she imagined these poor women who had already been through hell being sent off to well-meaning psychologists who would drag them back into the past for some low-mood therapy which inevitably would make them feel worse and prolong their hormonal distress.

"Can PMDD be transmitted or inherited?"

Dr. Girdler removed her glasses to answer. "Anecdotally, many women report that their mothers had PMDD. Can it be genetically transferred? Well, we don't know the source of that sensitivity yet. There needs to be more research."

Yes, we do! thought Helen to herself. *They are terrified by their thoughts and feelings. Grow up in a home with a stressed out or hyperreactive mother who blames it on her body, and of course the daughters are going to pick that up.*

"What percentage of women with PMDD have a history of abuse?"

"About 50%. That's of the population who are willing to be part of our research and not the general population, but that is astronomically high."

I bet the other half were stressed out for long periods too, they just didn't recognize it like I didn't, thought Helen.

"If someone has a diagnosis of PMDD *and* a history of abuse and they get treatment for the abuse, will that eliminate their PMDD?"

Dr. Girdler smiled widely. "Great question! We don't know, but I think it is worth trying. But to the extent that an effective behavioral intervention could help with dealing with an exaggerated stress response, greater sensitivity to rejection, interpersonal problems that are mapping onto physiology, mapping onto symptoms, so my guess would be, yes."

YES! screamed Helen in her head. *Of course it would! Ask me and my daughters!*

"Does it help to adjust hormone levels?"

The doctor shook her head. "There is no empirical evidence that adjusting hormones will help. In fact, there is no such thing as estrogen dominance–that's the construct of some *American quack*! You see, two women can have the same levels of estrogen and progesterone and respond to

Very Well

them in very different ways.

"I think that's all the time we have for questions. It's been my absolute pleasure, and thank you for your attention."

The presentation ended, and everyone applauded as they stood to leave.

"That was amazing! Thank you so much for inviting me. I'm quite fired up with all this info." Helen was buzzing as they gathered up their belongings. "Are you flying back tonight?"

"Yes, I have to get back to work."

"Can I drive you to the airport?"

"Oh thank you, that would be wonderful. We can chat more on the way. Maybe get a coffee at the airport, if you have time?"

"Definitely! I have so many more questions!"

As Helen drove them towards the airport she thanked Dr. Alice again for inviting her, and she had so much she wanted to talk about. "So she was basically saying that life stressors and trauma are a predictor of reproductive mood disorders. But from an understanding of the Principles, that's only half the story. If these women were shown how trauma and stress are created when they were younger, they wouldn't have had to suffer their whole lives. I mean, if you knew you were okay no matter what happened to you, that you had innate health and wellbeing, you wouldn't get as messed up by life's experiences. You would know that it's going to pass."

"Exactly. Your natural resilience and wisdom would guide you back to common sense to get help where needed. Which is why your hotline is so important. Tell me some more about the calls you are getting."

Helen described some of the women, the variety of stressful thoughts they were having, and how they all seemed to be in a reaction loop.

Dr. Alice checked in for her flight. The airport was bustling with all kinds of passengers. Some were rushing, distracted with hectic schedules, others were tired, waiting, and wondering when they could move on to their next adventure or maybe home to sleep. The two women bought coffees and sat in one of the coffee shops, content to reflect on their day.

"It was interesting that she said 'any qualifying trauma,'" reflected Helen. "I mean, I wonder if she sees it as anything that can make you *feel* traumatized. I had one lady who was crying on the phone to me that she is single and all alone, and the next call is from a woman who wants to get away from her annoying family for some peace and quiet! They both were innocently thinking their circumstances were what was causing their stress, and if that just changed, then they would be okay."

"Maybe you should have connected them so that they could swap houses for half the month!" laughed Dr. Alice. "No, but it's the misunderstanding that they are...doomed to feel that way because of their circumstances that has 'sensitized' them and their nervous systems."

"Something else I found fascinating," observed Helen.

Very Well

"She says trauma and a history of abuse can be a predicting factor for these disorders, but don't they say that about obesity and alcoholism and...well, every other disorder?"

"Yes! I think that's why she is saying PMDD symptoms are at their worst when we are stressed, experience an acute trauma, or are living with chronic trauma conditions like CPTSD,[44] but when we look further upstream, we see that it's listening to negative thinking and misunderstanding that is the real primary cause. And that's what makes us 'vulnerable,' as she puts it."

Helen looked in her notes again. "Here she actually says that really, postpartum and I'm guessing all the other reproductive mood disorders are 'pure anxiety!' So it's like she is agreeing that it's all coming from the same cause?"

"Yes, but wellbeing can't be reduced. I mean, it can be covered up with all the negative thinking and old ideas, but it can never diminish or disappear. It's innate; it's resilient."

Their reflections on the day were interrupted as Dr. Alice realized she had to get to her gate for boarding.

"So when she referred to finding out what the 'mechanism' is for all this, it's understanding the Three Principles, right?" asked Helen.

"For sure it is! Talk to Deborah about this, I think she will have some input from her work as a trauma coach and the chronic pain studies she has done, but you are on the right track and are going to help so many women!" Dr. Alice hugged her goodbye, Helen waving as she disappeared

---

[44] CPTSD - Complex Post-Traumatic Disorder (i.e., continued abuse).

amongst the passengers. It had been a fascinating day. So much information and yet so simple once it was seen as thoughts and moods that are always moving through. So much innocent suffering. So much more work to do.

Helen jumped into her car for the ride home, the lights of the freeway passing in the night as she listened to some of her favorite music. As she passed La Jolla, San Clemente and the sign for Capistrano Beach, she wondered if the swallows had returned from their winter in Argentina. Every year these elegant birds return from the heat of South America for a cooler Californian summer. *That's wisdom*, thought Helen.

12
April

Kara was excited to hear about Helen's trip to San Diego. She was so impressed with her mom for taking this project seriously. Other people's moms were sometimes cool or fun, but Kara was actually amazed by hers. As a teen she had taken her mother for granted, but now as she was getting older, she could see the depth of who her mother really was, even if Helen couldn't.

"I'm so jealous of you! Tell me all about it!"

Helen grabbed her notes. "Well, Dr. Girdler, the presenter, was very nice and a little intimidating at first, but then I realized that was just my insecure thinking. I know, I know, but it was really intimidating, full of Ph.D.'s and super smart types. She said that she had been skeptical that PMDD was even a real thing! Which was kind of good to hear as it showed she was curious and open to new ideas. She explained a lot of the physiology of PMS, PMDD, postpartum, and menopause, which she called reproductive mood disorders. Most of which went over my head, to be honest, but she confirmed what Deborah always says about prolonged stress. It really is what's at the root of the problem. But this is what really blew my mind. She said that it was not the number of hormones or that our hormones are dysfunctional in some way that is causing the problem, but rather our reaction to it!"

"Yes, that's what Dr. Alice said when she came."

"I realize that now, but I just couldn't hear it before. Maybe I'm too old and stupid for all this science stuff? I mean it goes against everything I have ever known about periods and moods. I guess I had to go to San Diego to really hear it."

"Don't beat yourself up, Mom, Deborah says that most of us need to hear new ideas several times before they sink in and we really *see* it, as Syd would say. Give yourself some credit. Most people wouldn't have even had the nerve to go, let alone try to understand. So, what was her explanation of what is causing it?"

"Thanks, sweetheart. Well, this was the fascinating thing. She basically said it was a history of trauma, you know, abuse and such things. But I think from what I have learned from you and Deborah and Syd's books is that trauma is relative. I mean, I don't want to...well, dismiss anyone's suffering, but it really depends on how you process it, right?"

"Sure," agreed Kara. "Two people can go through the

Very Well

same thing and have completely different experiences of it. I mean, Lily and I both lost our father as teenagers, and yet, we handled it very differently. I have met women at the clinic where I'm working right now who have lost their husbands, and they are in pieces, whereas you picked yourself up and made a life for yourself."

"Well, I had to. I had you girls. I couldn't just give up. I didn't really have a choice."

"But that's my point, Mom. Life is what you think. Some women in exactly the same situation–losing a partner and with kids–do give up. They fall apart and need social workers to come in and help them. Some never come out of it, believing they are damaged and lost for the rest of their lives. I'm seeing it and reading about it all the time. Remember what Deborah said? We are all doing the best we can with the thinking we have in that moment. And that thinking might be pretty low. So she is saying that the habit of overreacting to life stuff has 'trained' our nervous systems into overreacting to even hormone fluctuations?"

"Yes! It's as if the very fluctuation itself is just another thing, another frustration, that our nervous system can't cope with." Helen looked back in her notes. "It's as if the fluctuation itself is a kind of trauma. It's hypervigilance gone crazy. But here's something I found odd. She picked...a sensitivity to rejection at that time of the month as a significant or specific thing, which I found odd. I mean, why rejection, specifically? If everything is made of thought, why pick on one certain bad feeling? Why not anxiety or anger?"

Kara smiled an insightful grin. "I know why. When I was in the depths of that darkness, rejection was a very big part of it. Yes, it's insecure thinking, but at the time, all I knew was that I hated everybody, and I knew that everyone hated me! I knew I was out of control, and so I was terrified that you or my school friends would just get fed up and leave me, and I'd be in this hell all on my own, so I would lash out at you first. It was all an innocent misunderstanding but so very painful."

"So understanding that it is all made of Thought really is the answer."

It was an interesting new experience for Helen to go from family stuff to work to research, and in and out of the lives of the women who called the hotline. When she was at work, she would think about them and how they were doing. Maybe they were doing a little better today? Maybe they felt just a little better knowing someone understood? What if they — her musings were interrupted as William from Men's Shoes and Katrina from Women's Designer Wear came and sat with her for their coffee break.

"Darling, you were miles away," laughed William as he sat down next to her in the break room.

Helen laughed, too, as she told them what she was thinking about.

"You do what now?" William was confused. "My mother is a nightmare. She's going through her, you know, 'Change.' Why on earth would you want to bring all that crazy into your lovely life?"

Very Well

Katrina, a woman in her mid-40s, reached across the table and gave him a friendly slap on the shoulder. "You are so mean. It's probably you who's driving her crazy! I think it's an amazing idea, Helen. There are plenty of women in their 50s who come into my department who are plain nasty, and I just hope, for their husbands' sakes, it's their hormones or else that's the way they always are!"

Helen and William laughed as they sipped their coffees.

"So what is it you do for them?" asked Katrina, she seemed genuinely interested.

"Well, listen mostly. I share some very amazing ideas that I got from a doctor in Colorado and a coach here in L.A. that really helped my daughter with PMDD. My other daughter is going through postpartum depression, and my own journey has given me a lot of experience to share."

"That's amazing!" replied Katrina.

"So I'm going to give your number to my mom then; she is sooo nasty at times. But she is my momma and I do love her."

"Please do!" Helen handed each of them a flyer from her purse.

William finished his coffee, got up, and wished Helen good luck as he left to go back upstairs.

"Okay, so now that idiot has gone, tell me more. I have been getting hot flashes, and I'm only 43! I'm not pregnant, and it's got me so worried. Maybe I have a tumor or something?"

Helen reached out and patted her arm. "I know, it can be quite uncomfortable, but it can be lessened if you understand what's happening. I doubt you have a tumor; it sounds more like perimenopause, but please get checked by your doctor, as we don't want to miss something that could be causing it. But no matter what is causing it, your reaction to it is going to create your experience."

Katrina looked confused. "Well, of course, but I can't change that?"

"Oh, but it's not about changing thoughts. It's more about...observing them, you could say. What if you knew that all thoughts are neutral until you react to them? What if you didn't react and just watched them go by?" Helen felt clumsy as she tried to give over her understanding of the Principles, but knew she had to try.

"Well, that's easier said than done. I was up all last night terrified there is something wrong with me, and I found all these reports online that say I might have a tumor or some disease or something!"

"But can you see that you were just scaring yourself? Please go to the doctor and get it checked out, and whatever the results, please let's talk some more."

Katrina agreed as they both finished their coffees and went back to work.

That night she had a couple of callers who were just checking it out and needed someone to listen, and then she got her first drunk.

"You don't know what I'm going...through. You...have...no...idea!"

"Are you on your own right now?"

Very Well

"OF COURSE I'M ON MY OWN! THE HUSBAND LEFT, THE KIDS DON'T WANT TO KNOW, AND IT'S JUST ME AND THE VODKA RIGHT NOW!" The caller started crying.

Deborah had warned Helen that this might happen and so she told the caller to be safe and call back when she was sober.

"Okay, so when hell freezes over then... Ugh...oh, get lost." The caller hung up, and Helen stared at the phone for a minute, feeling very grateful for her life and family. When her husband had died and her life was turned upside down, there were times when she wanted to drown in a bucket of booze, too, but she knew it wasn't the answer. The bills and the girls would still be there in the morning, so why suffer the hangover? Then the phone rang again. Maybe it was the drunk calling back?

"Helen?"

"Yes, who is this?"

"It's Katrina from work. I made the doctor's appointment, but I'm so scared. What if it is something bad?"

"Oh, hi! Well, I doubt it, but can you see that you are scaring yourself again?"

Helen had barely finished speaking, and Katrina was off telling her the story of her mom's breast cancer scare and something she had heard on the TV and...

"Katrina, slow down. This is what the problem is. You are going so fast that your brain doesn't have a chance to slow down and let you sleep."

"Sleep? It's only 10 pm, I have so much to do before I go to bed."

"What, like worrying and stressing yourself out for a few more hours?"

Katrina took a breath. "Well, when you put it like that, I suppose I could ... But if my mom had breast cancer, then don't I have, like, a seventy-five percent chance of getting it too?"

"I thought you just said it was a scare?"

"Yes, it was. They thought it was cancer, but it turned out to be benign."

"So if it wasn't cancer, then you are not in that category either, are you?"

"But if she almost got it, I could almost get it!"

"Katrina! Slow down and take a breath. Breathe with me." Helen did some loud slow breaths and got Katrina to slow down a little. "Now, promise me you won't google anything more tonight, and if the urge comes, then just watch it roll by. Watch those thoughts roll through your mind like the ticker tape you see on CNN."

"Okay...I know you're right. I just get myself so worked up each month."

"Well, there's your clue!" said Helen, vindicated. "If this happens every month then you definitely don't want to listen as it's never true. Watch it go by, and we will talk soon. Good night."

As she was getting off the phone, something occurred to her. *I wonder if the same women will call at the same time each month?*

Very Well

Something had shifted for Lily. She seemed to be getting a bit better every week. Her mind was slowing down, and she seemed to have got the hang of observing her thoughts rather than reacting to them. It was still tough going at times, but whenever she heard anything slightly destructive she learned to ask for help, and either Helen or Kara would go to keep her company, take care of the baby and help her ride the wave. It became clear she had not handled her father's sudden death as well as Helen had thought, and the fear of something suddenly happening to the baby or herself or Carl had been constantly on her mind.

Lily had never seemed stressed when she was a teen, but maybe it had been eclipsed by the passion of Kara's emotional tornado. It seems Lily had kept it to herself and toughed it out, not wanting to burden anyone with her very private sadness. Lily was beginning to see that all her understandable worries about the baby were a story, a scary story that she could watch pass by, and that her wellbeing was always there to support her.

Katrina called almost every night for a week, scared about what the doctor might say, what would she do if they found something, or how was she going to tell her husband if they did. Helen kept reminding her nothing had been decided yet and that she was torturing herself with her own thinking, but it wasn't sinking in. It was like every time she called, she had forgotten everything Helen had told her the night before, and they had to start all over again.

Kara suggested she stop taking so many of her calls, but

Helen knew she would only get it at work if she didn't, so she kept looking for where Katrina was beginning to understand, ignoring the innocent confusion. She knew that Katrina, like Lily, was okay under all the noise, but couldn't help wondering how on earth Katrina's husband put up with it.

Deborah was calling on Helen's regular phone. "Hey, I just had an idea!"

Helen was intrigued.

"Remember Dr. Alice told us about Bertha Pappenheim, you know, Freud's client, Anna O.?"

Helen murmured a yes, unsure of where this was going.

"Well, I think she and Freud were pretty much the same age, and they were around at the same time. Why not compare their lives, what they got up to and when? It would be fascinating to see what happened to them after that first meeting, don't you think?"

"Okay. But...why? Why me?"

"I think you will find it interesting. It was kind of the beginning of women being heard and having a say in their own lives."

"I thought Anna or...Bertha...or whatever her name was, didn't have any say? I thought that was part of the problem."

"She didn't as a young woman, but then she started talking. A lot. Why not find out what happened next?"

"Do you have any books on Bertha? Are there any books on Bertha?"

Very Well

"I don't have anything, but you could probably find something online."

Helen was just finishing her morning coffee break when Katrina spotted her in the staff break room.

"Come with me up to my floor! Come on, it will only take a second. I want you to see something!"

"But I have almost finished my break. I have to get back to my floor. My manager is in a foul mood today."

"It won't take a second. Come on!"

Helen succumbed to Katrina's pushiness and reluctantly followed her up the escalator, past the ground floor where her own department was, and then up again to Ladies' Wear. Katrina walked quickly to her area in Designer Wear and stood in the middle, pointing up.

"Ta da!"

Helen looked up. All around the top edge of the displays just below the ceiling was an electronic notice board with the names of new designers going round and round.

"It's that ticker tape of thought you keep talking about! I had no idea what you have been on about all this time, but last night I had a good sleep, and then this morning I came in and saw this. The names just keep on scrolling round and round. Sometimes I notice them, and sometimes I don't, but it doesn't stop. It doesn't care if I read it or not; it just keeps going! Then a customer who I know has been in here 1,000 times just spotted it, and I thought, how did she not see it before? It's just like you said. Thoughts are constantly moving, and I don't have to scare myself by reading or listening to them all the time!"

Helen started to laugh. She loved it. "Yes! That's exactly it! You would go nuts reading that all day long."

"Oh, believe me, I have, and it gave me such a headache."

Helen had to stifle her laughter as customers turned to look at her. "I have to get back, but this is brilliant, Katrina!" Helen was so excited that she was seeing something new. "Keep looking in that direction. Well, not that one up there, but in the direction of seeing that thought is always moving and that you don't have to listen to it!"

Helen waved goodbye as she went back down the escalator. She felt so good that she had hung in there. Knowing that Katrina had wellbeing, even though Katrina couldn't see it, had made all the difference. It was right there, right when she needed it.

13
May

Helen's theory that the same ladies would call at the same time every month was turning out to be true. Nicole and two new callers, Georgia and Sharona, all called around the same dates the next month. They had different worries, but the same escalation of anxiety and stress happened. They felt awful, would get really down about it, and then stress themselves out until they were an anxious mess. Then they would need to deal with the aftermath of exhaustion that would take them right into dealing badly with the next month.

Helen suggested they mark on their calendar: "Don't listen to my thoughts this week." Some of them said it would be a waste of time, but that they would try. There were other calls, too. Some ladies were going through perimenopause, another had endometriosis and one had postpartum depression.

"I was in a parent teacher thing last night. I really didn't want to go, I'm exhausted and find everything too much right now. I had to take my baby with me which just made it even more overwhelming. In fact it was a nightmare. My baby was pretty quiet most of the time while the principal was speaking, and so when she got a bit fussy, I took her outside. Then this *witch* follows me out and says that the baby is bothering everybody, and I had no business bringing her! I mean, I was already feeling rotten, and it had taken everything I had just to get there to meet my big kid's teachers and she says that to me! I couldn't believe it!

"I screamed at her. I told her she was an inconsiderate, nosey b-word, and then I was beside myself for talking like that and had such horrible shame I wished the ground would swallow me up. I hadn't been able to shower in days, so getting ready and making myself get out the door was like climbing a mountain. I actually felt violent. I wanted to punch her, the stupid cow, but then I just crumbled. I was terrified I was going to drop the baby! I cannot believe I could even think these things. It's so violent and frightening."

"Oh, you poor thing."

"She wasn't so bad. She actually took the baby for me so I could go back inside and meet the teacher I needed to see. But the next day I called one of my friends who was there and asked if the baby really was a nuisance, and she said no!"

Helen smiled. "I'm so sorry you had to go through that. You see, when we get into a low mood, it feels like

Very Well

everything's wrong. You and that lady were both in a low mood. Who knows what her reason was. Maybe her teenager was failing all her grades and she was struggling in a bad mood herself."

"I don't care! She had no right to tell me off. I'm dealing with a newborn and severe postpartum!"

"Maybe her kid is sick and is missing out on too much school?"

"But I'm sick! I have a newborn and severe depression!"

"Maybe she's a single mom and struggling to bring up four kids?"

"But..."

"Maybe she lost her baby and the sound of a crying baby was too much for her?"

"Okay, okay, I get it. So we were both losing it."

"When we are in a low mood, everything looks bad. When she said it was bothering everyone, she really meant it was bothering her. She could have no idea what anyone else was feeling, but her discomfort made it feel so bad for her that she imagined everyone must be feeling that way, too. Is your partner there to help tonight?"

"Yes, he's amazing. Oh my gosh, I can't imagine what it would be like to do this alone."

The next morning Kara asked Helen how she was doing with the hotline. She was becoming concerned her mother was maybe taking on too much.

"It's fine. I only turn it on for a couple of hours in the evening and part of my days off. There are messages to return, but it's so rewarding. Don't worry, honey, I switch it off if I'm too tired, and I'm meeting Deborah today so I am taking care of myself, too."

"Hi...uh...I'm not sure if this is allowed?" A man with a strong New York accent was calling on the hotline, and he seemed very nervous. "My name is Clarke and my wife is...well she's...suffering."

"Hi, Clarke. Yes, of course it's allowed. I wasn't expecting it, but I'm so glad you called." He sounded older so Helen guessed his wife was going through menopause. "What's happening?"

"Well, my wife, she is such a brave, sweet girl. She's always been my angel. We have been together for 35 years, since high school, you know, and we have always got on well. Brought up three lovely boys and always been the best of friends, but since she, you know, started 'The Change,' she has been...*a real bitch!* I don't know her most of the time! She screams at me no matter what I do. She is mean to the grandkids and cries all the time. She has to have the air conditioning on full blast all night, even though I'm freezing, and she is always...sweaty. She is just so mean and nasty!"

Helen tried not to laugh. "Oh no, that sounds awful."

"I know she can't help it, and when she realizes what she's done, she hates herself and feels even worse, but it's been a few years now, and I can't take it much more. When is it going to end?"

"I'm so sorry you are having to deal with this. It can't be

Very Well

easy for either of you. Do you think she would talk to me?"

Clarke immediately shot down the idea. "Oh, you don't want to talk to her, sweetheart. She will just shout at you and call you names! You don't want that."

"Okay, but maybe I could help. What is her first name?"

"Geraldine."

"Lovely. Will you tell her that I have been through it, and that I really do understand."

"I can try."

Deborah and Helen met for coffee later that day. It was one of those glorious Los Angeles late afternoons with pure, blue sky. There was a faint smell of sea air as they walked along the boardwalk on Venice Beach. The usual variety of tourists and local characters wandered by with their ice creams and designer sunglasses. Skateboarders and an excited dog off his leash weaved in and out of the crowd. They each got an iced coffee and went down to the water to watch the waves.

"Oh, that feels good," said Helen as she stretched out her feet in the sand.

"So how's it going with the hotline? Are they driving you mad yet?" asked Deborah curiously.

"No, actually. I thought they would, but I have noticed a few things already. I have a theory that the same ladies with PMS will call at the same time each month, surprised that they are sad and anxious again, but I think they are catching on. Most of them are making themselves more miserable by their reactions to their symptoms, like I learned in San

Diego, and they have often been given really bad info or advice by doctors. I mean I'm no expert, but already I know that surgery to have your ovaries removed should be the last option, not the first?! Oh, yeah, and I have a colleague at work who is in perimenopause, and she just had an amazing insight about Thought." Helen told Deborah about the designer names "running" around Neiman Marcus.

"That is so L.A.!" laughed Deborah. She still had her very English way of seeing things, even though she had been in California for over a decade. "I'll have to send some of Joe's movie star clients there to have a look. It might help them to have an insight, too!"

"And then send them down to shoes and ask for me! I'll be happy to help them spend some of their insightful money!"

Deborah giggled. "That's great. Have you had any difficult calls?"

"I had one drunk. She was pretty harmless, and a guy who said his wife was nasty. The others are all pretty much just needing someone to listen to them."

Deborah paused for a moment. "I used to think I was a great listener until I found the Principles. As my mind quieted down, I realized that I was a terrible listener. I was basically biting my tongue waiting for them to shut up so I could tell them what to do!" Deborah covered her face in embarrassment. "Listening with a quiet mind is such a different experience. Listening to connect, to get close, is real listening. Without that quiet, well, the information I think they need is shallow and empty."

Very Well

"I do find myself wanting to fix them, to help them out of their misery. If they could just see that their suffering is coming from their *thoughts* about their bodies or their partners, or whatever, they would be so much calmer."

"Sure, it's natural to want to help people. You are a natural helper. Have you heard of the term empath?"

"Yes, but I thought you hated labels and all that psychobabble stuff?"

Deborah laughed again. "I do, but it's good to know why it doesn't make sense. I hated the word 'triggered' for a long time, but couldn't put my finger on why until I saw it was a very Outside-In way of blaming others for how we feel. *She triggers me. That movie triggered me.* Nothing on the 'outside' can ever make us feel anything. It's always our thinking about it."

"The word empath has taken on a whole new meaning for me recently, too," continued Deborah. "Empathy is a noun; being empathetic is an adjective. But in psychobabble language, being an empath has become a thing, a person. We love to thingify stuff! I was talking with one of my clients[45] and her insight about this really helped me see the misunderstanding." Deborah showed Helen a text on her phone.

> - I do not feel other people's pain, I feel my thoughts about other people's pain.
> - I feel my thoughts that I feel other people's pain.

---

[45] Marlene Fuchs, in a personal communication with the author.

- I feel the thought that I am taking on other people's pain.
- I feel the thought that I could make other people's pain bearable by taking it over.
- I feel the thought that people in pain feel better because I take over their pain.

"Wow!" replied Helen. "That turns the whole empath thing upside down!"

"Yes, or it will just annoy them. But anyway, can you see how much we make up? It's amazing to care and to show that we care, but see how it can easily become twisted into a self-serving thing when we misunderstand thought?"

"I do. You know how you taught us that the whole chemical imbalance thing is untrue? I was thinking. It's the same with this whole hormone imbalance thing, too. It was a theory put forward by a doctor back in 1931 and has stuck around ever since, and yet science doesn't back it up. But I see now that wanting to change hormone levels which are normal for most women is an 'outside-in' misunderstanding too. Hormones are 'outside,' aren't they?"

"Yeah, it's a little weird to get your head around, but hormones, pain, even thoughts are 'outside.' They are experienced with the gift of Thought, but in that moment, they have taken the 'form' of hot flashes or cramps. And form is an outside-in illusion."

"So what is inside?"

"I think it's what Syd called Formless. As you know, Thought, the Principle of Thought is a creative energy, and before it comes into our minds, before it comes across our

Very Well

screen of consciousness, as it were, it's...a formless energy. I have no idea what I'm saying right now, but it's mystical, a spiritual energy. But then as it moves, it morphs into thoughts and images and sensations, and it becomes Form – it has taken a form. But then as it passes out, it becomes formless again...I think."

"So that's how we can't get damaged?!" exclaimed Helen. Deborah looked at her quizzically. "You are always quoting your mentor, Dr. Bill Pettit, that we are never broken and can't be damaged, right? Well, that's because we, in our pure sense, are formless, and, well, you can't break a...a formless thing, can you?! It has no form to break; it's spiritual! It is our essence, our very nature, and we are all connected to that same unbreakable source." Helen was overcome with her own insight. She paused. She felt a gentle sensation of gliding, lightness, of weightlessness.

Deborah smiled. "Yep, that sounds about right." She pulled a piece of paper out of her purse and quoted Syd Banks.

"This inner world is a spiritual world. It's a spiritual reality and it actually exists. As a matter of fact, it is the only thing that exists."[46]

Staring out at the glimmering Pacific Ocean under the late afternoon sun, they both relaxed. The sound of the waves and a few children playing was all there was in that

---

[46] S. Banks, "Bellevue" (lecture).

moment.

After a while, Deborah turned and asked, "How are you doing with Bertha and Siggy Freud?"

Helen fell over into the warm sand with laughter. "Oh my gosh, I don't know whether to laugh or cry! When I read about Freud, it drives me crazy! I know, I know, nothing can make me crazy; it's just my thoughts about him, but really? The man was a paranoid junkie, and Bertha...well, she was so brave! She had suffered so much but went on to help so many people and yet we have never heard of her."

When Helen got home, more calls came in.

"After my last baby was born I went to a psychiatrist. I hate psychiatrists." The caller spoke very nervously. "He told me that maybe I was fighting against my femininity and that is why I have postpartum depression. Does that make any sense?"

"Uh, well, that sounds very...ridiculous, actually." Helen knew better than to believe everything someone says when they are upset. The psychiatrist sounded like a friend of Freud, but really? In this day and age?

"How are you doing now?"

"Well, he put me on medication and that didn't work, and...then he upped the dose and that just made my blood pressure go up so they gave me a med for that, and now, I'm on six meds a day, and I feel worse than when I started. Now they say I have PMDD as well."

The caller sounded very lost. Her story was dramatic, but there was no passion in her voice, no feeling that came

Very Well

with it. Helen guessed it was the meds that were dampening down her personality, but couldn't help wondering why she continued with a doctor who was insulting and not listening to her. The caller told Helen that her name was Lori and continued to tell her a terrible story of medications, side effects, hospitals, and miscarriages. It was painful to listen, leaving Helen feeling quite inadequate. If only Lori had been directed to an insightful therapist at the beginning, instead of being put straight onto addictive drugs in what was probably an inadequate ten-minute chat with the doctor, things could be so different now. Helen listened patiently and suggested she stay in touch.

"What about a community night for these people who call you?" asked Patti on the phone later that night. "They could meet and support each other and that would take some of the workload off of you?"

Helen thought for a moment. "Maybe, but I really do enjoy it. My girls are all grown up and doing their own thing now, so I feel really useful for the first time in ages."

"Okay. It's just an idea, but I think it would be great."

"Let me think about it."

"You can have it here, at my place, if you like. Do you think anyone would show up?" Patti was clearly excited to help.

"Are you sure? Some of these women are out of their minds."

"Helen, I feel like I let you down after the fundraiser disaster. I didn't pull my weight like I should have, I was just interested in the glory and excitement of it. I'm really sorry for not standing by you, and I'd like to help with this. Real help, like having your meetings here. And hey, I get to listen, too, right?"

Helen was touched by Patti's thoughtfulness. She wasn't sure what Patti had seen as far as understanding the Principles, but she did seem a much nicer, more aware person these days.

"Please think about it. We could try one and see how it goes?"

Smiling, Helen promised Patti she would think about it. She wondered if things were moving too fast. She had just gotten the hang of the hotline and now another project? Helen felt her thinking speed up and then, just like Deborah had promised, she caught it. The sudden sense of urgency woke her up to the fact this wasn't the best time to think about it. She was tired and instinctively trusted she would make the right decision another time. The uncomfortable feelings left, and Helen went back to watch her TV show.

Helen's search for books about Bertha was not so easy. There was nothing currently in print, so she started looking in secondhand book stores until, eventually, she found one. As she was reading, she thought about Patti's idea. She guessed they could try it. For the next month, Helen asked the women who were making the most sense if they would like a support group. There was a mixed response, as some were too nervous to meet new people or go to new places. Others loved the idea of getting support from women who

Very Well

understood, and some were just afraid to commit as they had no idea how they would feel on the day. Helen was beginning to feel a deep sense of trust. Things were unfolding. They could try it a couple of times and see what happened.

14
June

Sharona and Georgia called again the next month with all kinds of stories, but the same stress and anxieties, and Helen reminded them to look at their calendars.

"Did you write 'Don't listen to my thoughts this week' on your calendar?"

"Yes!"

"Did you look at it?"

Georgia said she forgot, and Sharona said she did, but it just made her angry. Then Helen realized why Deborah kept saying that techniques don't work. They are great when you're in a good mood, but that's when you don't need them, and when you are in a low mood, you just can't make yourself do them! It made perfect sense to Helen to suggest it, as she was in a good mood at the time. Her common sense had said, *Don't listen to anxious thinking*, but now that

Very Well

Georgia and Sharona were in a low place, it was just a stupid waste of time.

What was she thinking by suggesting such a silly thing?

Helen started to doubt herself and then realized that was not a helpful thought either. Not listening to lousy thinking the week before their period was a great idea; she just needed to point them inward, so they could have their own insight with it. Having them rely on hers wasn't going to work. They needed their own. Maybe a community night was a good idea.

The next call was different. She described herself as a healer and started telling Helen what to do to help her callers. She insisted that hormone problems were coming from toxins in foods and laundry detergents.

"Did you know that sixty percent of the chemicals from your makeup end up in your bloodstream?"

Helen thanked her for sharing, but that she wouldn't be recommending her line of hypoallergenic cosmetics. That night, she finalized with Patti what their community night would look like. They decided to call it "The Women's Club." Helen would lead a discussion on a certain topic, and Patti would be the hostess with the mostess.

They would keep it simple and general, with a focus on pointing everyone to the Principles. It wouldn't be about supplements or nutrition, but if they wanted to share that with each other, that was fine, too. Deborah couldn't join in as she was traveling with Joe, but she was so happy to share with Helen her experience of leading groups of pain clients.

She wished them all the best, and Kara was thrilled to be included. Helen invited the women she thought would most benefit, who would actually show up. By the time the night came, she had gathered a group of about fifteen ladies.

"Hello, hello! My name is Patti, please come in."

Georgia came in, followed by Sharona and a woman called Noreen. Clarke's wife, Geraldine, came and a couple of newer ladies, Alex and Carina. Julie and Katrina came from work, but Michelle declined. Kara helped with teas and coffees, and Patti handed around some very nice dainty cakes from the Brentwood Patisserie.

"Ooh, I shouldn't but I will, just don't tell my husband!" giggled Geraldine.

She didn't seem to be the witch Clarke had described, but then most people are on their best behavior with strangers, thought Helen.

The ladies came from all over the Westside of Los Angeles and ranged from Sasha in her mid-20s to Geraldine, a grandmother. Sadly, Nicole couldn't make it. She had called to say something big had come up at work, but she was very grateful for everything she had learned so far. Geraldine turned out to be a hoot. Helen was curious. She couldn't see why Clarke had described her as nasty.

"I'd go on that hormone replacement therapy stuff, but there are plenty of other things that need replacing first!" laughed Geraldine as they all introduced themselves.

Helen gave a general introduction and told them about herself and her story of her own nightmare with menopause

Very Well

and bringing up her daughters after her husband died. She pointed out that within the group, there were ladies with PMDD, miscarriage, PPD, perimenopause and menopause, and a few other situations like endometriosis and polycystic ovaries where hormones seem to get the better of them. Everyone was welcome and what she was sharing would be true and helpful for all these experiences. Kara then talked about her journey with hormones, how she found the Three Principles, and how it had made an amazing change in her experience.

"As you know, I'm not a doctor, and I don't pretend to be any kind of expert," added Helen. "I'm also not here to promote any kind of treatment or supplements or any other kind of, you know, natural remedies. I think we have all tried many different things. Some work for some people, and some work for others. We don't want anyone to be in any discomfort, so if you want to share with each other what worked for you, please feel free to do so privately, and that way, we can stay focused on seeing something new here in the group."

Everyone agreed, and so Helen continued. "So what I think made the most difference for me was to understand that *I am always feeling my thinking*. When Kara first said that to me, it kind of made sense, but as I understood it more deeply, it gave a whole new meaning to the hot flashes I was experiencing. When I would get a night sweat, for example, and I would wake up in a burning heat..."

"Oh, me too. It feels like my inner child is playing with matches!" giggled Geraldine.

"I know," laughed Julie. "I have to have the AC on all night; my husband is freezing and I'm in an oven!"

"Yes, exactly," agreed Helen, trying to keep them focused. "Well, when it was happening to me, my reaction was always, *Ughhh*. I would then start thinking about how unfair it is, when is this going to end, and how terrible my life was, and before I knew it, I was in a very ugly and frightening dungeon of self-pity. I would then dread the next hot flash and the next one, to the point where I had only just gotten over one and the next one was already starting. It was unbearable."

Noreen put her hand up to say something. "But that's biology. That's not thinking."

"Yes, there's definitely biology, but how do you know that you are sweating?"

"I can feel it, see it, even?"

"Yes, and this is what I find fascinating. Did you know that your brain has one job? Its sole purpose is to keep you alive and safe, and it can't do that without your five senses. I mean, your brain doesn't speak English, and it's stuck in this box called the skull."

Helen pointed at her head, and they all laughed. "My brain has to rely on the information it is getting from my five senses to stay alive. In fact, I read this story of a lady who had a stroke and lost her eyesight. But her eyes worked just fine. It was the visual processing part of the brain that was damaged, and so she couldn't see, even though there was nothing physically wrong with the structure of her eyes. Your five senses are only as good as the thoughts they

Very Well

produce. That lady's experience proves that sight happens in the brain, and our brain activity is only as good as the thoughts it produces. Otherwise, how would we know anything?"

Noreen didn't take a moment to reflect. "Okay, I get that, but you can't say a hot flash is thinking." She was quite insistent. "I had one while you were talking, and I wasn't thinking anything. I was listening to you!"

Helen hesitated and searched for a better way to explain it. "Right, and that's because our experience can show up in many different forms–from images and music to dizziness and sweating. Thinking is just one of the ways the creative power of Thought can show up. Sweating, seeing, and anxiety are other ways. Thought is an amazing, creative power, and it constantly creates our experience. And this insight helped me see that I didn't actually have to react badly to night sweats! There is no rule that says you must get annoyed and miserable because you are sweating! This was the ticket to freedom for me. Now I barely get them, and if I do, so what? No big deal!"

"Are you really saying that by...by not overreacting to the hot flashes, they went away?" Sasha's tone held an air of disbelief.

"Pretty much. I mean, the body needs to do what it needs to do as we go through these changes each month, or after a baby, or as we reach menopause. But if I react badly to it, my brain is going to get the message that there is something terribly wrong and puts me into fight or flight, which then adds a whole bunch of adrenaline, cortisol, and glucose into the bloodstream. This makes us feel even worse and more scared, and then we react to that. It just gets worse and worse until we are a sweaty, miserable mess."

Helen moved on to explain that it wasn't that their hormones were messed up or that they had too much or not enough. But rather it was a history, a lifetime, for some of them, of overreacting to life, keeping the stress response revved up and on hyper-alert, that was causing the discomforts and anxieties they were all feeling. Some of them got it, but some were very skeptical, wedded to their belief there must be something physically wrong with them. They had believed and been told for so long that it was their bodies that were broken and malfunctioning, or that their brains were lacking something, that the idea that this could be solved by something as simple as a shift in thinking didn't make any sense.

"My PMDD went undiagnosed for years," said Jen, a woman in her early 40s, "until I had a hormone saliva test every third day or so over a month. I collected my own saliva first thing in the morning and then sent it off to the lab. My doctor said it showed such low dips in my estrogen and progesterone between ovulation that it was like my body thought it had had or lost a baby each month! So I get that some of you have ups and downs because of your...*thinking*, but mine really is bad hormones!"

Helen didn't want to argue. "For sure some of us do have biological abnormalities, so I'm glad you got yours checked. But here's what I'm thinking. Back, way back before any of my hormone problems started, I was already

Very Well

very much 'up in my head.'" She pointed up and patted herself on the head. "I see now that I was a perfectionist, wanting everything to be perfect and the best. Not wanting to make a mistake or look bad. I had to have the right school bag in junior high or the right hair in high school. In college, I was desperate to fit in and stressed about so many things, and that was all before I got married and started a family. That kind of mind is going to overreact to anything and everything that isn't 'right,' even natural biological changes. Yes, some of us have biological conditions that need medical attention, but how we think and feel about it is what is creating our experience. In fact, it may be that we have innocently created that hormonal deficit ourselves without realizing it. But the good news is that if we created it, it can probably be fixed."

There was a pause, and then Kara shared what made sense to her. "You see, even back before my PMS became PMDD, before I even had periods, back when I was a little kid, I was anxious. I didn't know it was anxiety. I was little so I didn't have a word for it. But I can remember telling Mom that I couldn't go to school because I didn't feel well. She would ask me what was wrong and I would say I felt...'neck sick.'"

Helen went back in her memory to when the girls were little. She couldn't remember Kara being anxious, but she remembered this strange illness Kara would talk about. "I remember that. I'm so sorry, honey. I never understood what you meant."

"I don't think I did either, but now that I'm thinking

about it, I think it was anxiety. The muscles in my neck were so tense that it made me feel nauseous. And I don't think there was anything horrible going on. I was just nervous about school and friends and...well, life."

"I'm so sorry, my love, I had no idea." Helen felt uneasy that she had totally missed that her baby girl was suffering.

"It's okay, Mom. If I didn't know, how would anyone else?"

"And there was no abuse or anything?" asked Sharona nervously.

"No. I think I was just up in my head trying to cope with confusing feelings, like Mom just described. I just wanted to understand. So when my periods started and my body was changing, it was just another confusing thing to try and understand. I had already developed a habit of being jumpy and hyperreactive about everything. And by the time my father died, I was already a mess and unable to cope with the slightest thing."

"I think I get what you are saying," offered Patti as she thought aloud. "If we are constantly scared of either our surroundings or depressed about the past or worrying about the future, that constant anxiety is...well, it's training us to be super sensitive. Our nervous systems are now overreacting to everything, *even* our hormones going up and down."

Before Kara or Helen could agree, Noreen spoke up fast. "I'm sorry you were a...a messed up kid, but I wasn't. I wasn't all anxious and nervous. So it isn't that for me. Mine is definitely an imbalance or something wrong inside! I

Very Well

know there is something wrong with my endocrine system, like Jen, or whatever it is. Otherwise, why would I be in such a state at the same time every month?"

Helen could feel Noreen's overreaction from the other side of the room. Maybe she felt threatened, as if what they were suggesting meant she was weak or to blame in some way? Deborah had discussed with Helen that sometimes people will lash out at you when deep down they know it's true. It was ironic. Noreen's lashing out was an overreaction, the very thing she said she didn't have.

"Honey, you are going to be just fine." comforted Geraldine with the gentle love of a grandmother. "We are all going to be just fine."

"I didn't think I was anxious either," admitted Helen. "But as I get a better understanding of these ideas, the more I see that I really was. I don't think I saw it back then, because it had become normal. It was normal for me to always be worrying. I worried about the kids when they were little; I worried about how I was going to keep a roof over our heads when my husband died. But I also worried about what shoes to wear with what outfit to go to a PTA meeting, and what if there was nowhere to park, and if you would like me or not. It was constant. And now, well, I've just lost interest in so much of my thinking, as my friend Deborah says."

"So..." Jen was reflecting out loud. "So even though my hormones are doing a dance, I could handle it better? Is that what you are saying?"

"Yes. I mean, you seem to be handling it really well, but

the more you understand the nature of Thought, the easier it will be. As I said, there is no rule that says that because something is uncomfortable, we *have* to be annoyed. I used to get annoyed with customers who wasted my time, you know, the kind that wants to try on every style of shoe and then doesn't even buy anything. But I have noticed it just doesn't bother me anymore. Sure, I'd like the commission, but I have lost that indignant, judgy reflex. It's just faded away. The same thing happened with my hot flashes. I still get one occasionally, but...so what?"

"I could see that." Jen gave a smile and shrugged.

When Helen and Kara got home, they kicked off their shoes and slouched onto the sofa. They were tired, but it was a good tired.

"Well done, Mom. You did an amazing job."

"Thanks, honey. You were a big help. We make a good team. I'm just so sorry I didn't notice your anxiety when you were a kid. I..."

"It's really okay, Mom. You are the best mom I could wish for. It was my stuff, and like I said, I didn't even know myself."

Helen grabbed Kara's hand and kissed it.

"Shame Lori didn't make it."

"Who's Lori?"

"She's the one on six different meds. I hope she's okay."

Kara switched on the TV as the Channel 7 news came on. She picked up the remote and started to flick through the channels to see if there was anything on.

Very Well

"Hold on, turn back a minute!"
"What? It's just the local news, Mom."
"No, that's...that's Nicole!"

15
July

Nicole had been waiting for this big break for a while. She had started as a production assistant and worked her way up to senior production manager at Channel 7 News. But like most of the aspiring young people who had come to Los Angeles over the last 100 years, her dream was always to be in front of the camera. On the day of the first Women's Club, the regular news reporter had taken ill, and Nicole was in the right place at just the right time.

Before she knew it, she was on her way to The Griffith Park Observatory up in the Hollywood Hills with a news crew to interview an astrologer about a passing comet. Location for such movies as *Rebel Without a Cause* and *Terminator,* Griffith Observatory was Los Angeles and Hollywood history. She stood nervously in front of the iconic building overlooking L.A. glittering under the night sky below.

"I was terrified!" admitted Nicole as she told Helen all about it a couple of days later. "I thought my heart was going to pound out of my chest! Are you sure you couldn't see me shaking?"

"No, you were amazing! You were so professional, as if you had been doing it for years."

"Oh thank you. Well, I'm no Katie Couric, but I have big dreams. I just hope my crazy hormones don't let me down. I do so want to become a TV journalist; it's what I studied in college."

Next, Helen called Lori to see if she was okay. She replied that she was overwhelmed. The doctors had put her on an antipsychotic to make her sleep, only it made her blood pressure soar again. Helen suggested she talk to Dr. Alice, at least to get another medical professional to check all these medications she was being given. The awful thing was that Lori was more anxious and depressed than she had been before she'd started to take all those drugs. They weren't even helping her, and now she had all these side effects to deal with.

In fact, thought Helen, *nearly everyone she had ever met who was on antidepressants...was depressed!*

Deborah's idea about comparing Freud's life with Bertha's intrigued Helen, so she decided to turn it into a project. She stopped at the huge stationery supply store on Lincoln

Boulevard on her way home from work and got some highlighters, paper, and pens.

Siggy and Bertha

She got a folder and wrote their names on the front cover. It felt like she was embarking on a kind of spy mission. The first thing she discovered was that Freud was only three years older than Bertha. She folded a sheet of paper in half down the middle to write significant dates in order to start her timeline.

Bertha Pappenheim 1859–1936–Sigmund Freud 1856–1939

1880–Bertha, the daughter of a wealthy Jewish family in Vienna, was obligated to nurse her dying father. She became distraught and very ill.
1881–Freud, the son of a Jewish merchant, graduated medical school / Bertha's father dies, but she is too ill to travel to Pressburg for the funeral.
1882–Breuer abruptly ends Bertha's treatment after two years. Bertha is suicidal and sent to a sanitarium.

Helen paused; Bertha's father had just died, a relationship that was so difficult she was violently ill over it, and then her doctor suddenly abandoned her? Of course she was struggling! *What is the matter with these people?* wondered Helen. She remembered a phrase she had heard in

Very Well

college, "some people are caretakers and some are caregivers." It seemed like they were trying to take care of Bertha, but had anyone actually given her care?

1883 – Breuer writes, "I have seen the little Pappenheim today. She is totally healthy, without pains or anything else." Bertha is released and described as cured.
1884 – Freud begins studying the psychological effects of cocaine.
1885 – Freud goes to Paris to study Hysteria with Charcot at the Salpetriere Hospital / Bertha is still ill and spends four months in the Inzersdorf Sanitarium for "Hysteria" and "somatic disorders." Freud's fiancée, Martha Bernays, visits Bertha and writes that she still has hallucinations at night but is released.
1886 – Freud marries Martha Bernays / Bertha is one of their first visitors.
1887 – Bertha is readmitted for "Hysteria" and "somatic symptoms" for a third time. She remained in the sanitarium for 18 days and was then released, never to be hospitalized again.
1888 – Bertha's first book is published, *Kleine Geschichten für Kinder* (Little Stories for Children).
1890 – Bertha's second book is published, *In der Trödelbude* (In the Junk Shop).

Helen looked over this information. What was the life of a nineteen-year-old girl in Victorian Vienna like? she wondered. What was the connection between the Freud and

Pappenheim families, and how was Bertha publishing books a year after being released from a mental hospital? It's not as if they had self-publishing on Amazon! She would have needed a publisher. How on earth did she manage it?

Helen's next new caller was heartbreaking. Chrissy seemed quite cheerful on the phone, but as her story unfolded, Helen could hardly believe her ears.

"Oh, it's hell. Not only do I have perimenopause, but I got severe PMDD all at the same time!"

"How old were you when it started?"

"50! I am 56 now. All the treatments make me suicidal. I was locked up for the first time in my life at 51, two weeks after they put me on the Mirena coil.[47] It drove me insane and pushed up my blood pressure sky-high. I had preeclampsia three times with my pregnancies and the blood pressure tablets do the same thing as synthetic birth control. It is very scary. My blood pressure is 220/120, and I cannot take any more tablets. I am under Dr. Michaels at Cedar Sinai Hospital and Professor Statler."

Helen didn't know any of these names but they seemed impressive.

"He is a cardiologist specializing in hormones who works with Dr. Michaels. They can't fix me, I am 56 and still having periods. The GnRH[48] did not work, pushed up my

---

[47] Birth control device.
[48] A hormone made by a part of the brain called the hypothalamus. GnRH causes the pituitary gland in the brain to make and secrete the

Very Well

blood pressure, and made me insanely suicidal."

Helen couldn't believe what she was hearing, but it got worse.

"I jumped off of Santa Monica Pier into high tide at 2 am, just after the GnRH injections. Miracle I survived![49] A dog walker saw me and pulled me out. I woke up in Cedars ICU, and my period had started. I was on day 11, but had been given blood pressure tablets again. I don't know how I am still here."

Helen couldn't understand what she was hearing. "Oh my gosh, you poor thing!"

"One thing the psychs and gynae agreed on was not to give me a hysterectomy, as they said they knew from research that I would get deep depression and want to kill myself, and as I was 51 when it happened, I would be through the menopause soon. No such luck."

"How could they know for sure you would go into a deep depression?" asked Helen. "I mean, no two people react the same way to anything."

"I don't know, but that is what they said. My FSH levels are 11, which is that of a 34-year-old. Dr. Michaels said I am Benjamin Button; I'm going backwards! I have been tested like crazy by the mental health team. If I can't get them to understand, then nobody can."

Helen couldn't help thinking that she needed a new

---

hormones luteinizing hormone (LH) and follicle-stimulating hormone (FSH).

[49] Based on a true report!

kind of help.

"I was in the hospital for my own safety last week and was literally forced to take a blood pressure tablet. It sent me insane again and did not bring down my blood pressure." Chrissy was talking fast. "One thing that has been a life changer, though, is that Dr. Michaels has put me on an antihistamine made from grass pollen with no side effects. Who would have thought histamine is the main cause?"

"Histamines?" queried Helen. All Hellen knew about histamines was that they had something to do with allergies. How would an antihistamine help?

"Yeah! My diet consisted of totally high histamine foods, which I thought were healthy. Avocados, bananas, spinach, strawberries, you name it. I am a different person now. I am so glad I didn't die when I jumped. My youngest is at Stanford University studying engineering, and I can't believe he got there with me being in and out of the hospital for the last five years. I'm sure I have PTSD from all that."

"That sounds like hell," replied Helen when Chrissy took a breath. "What were you like before? Did you have any history of stress?"

"Not before all this. I did insist that I get my tubes tied when in the middle of my last C-section. The surgeon was from Denmark and she said that they did not tie tubes in Denmark, as it was known to cause severe depression. That was 20 years ago. I thought that she meant I would get depressed about not being able to have another baby. I insisted. I was high on morphine and whatever. I wish I had listened to her. My reaction to the tubal ligation is why they

Very Well

won't give me a hysterectomy. What is done cannot be undone!" Helen listened very carefully. *Maybe Chrissy just wasn't aware of the levels of stress in her life? Maybe there was more to the story?* "Oh, sorry, I'm on day two, not four; my mind is really foggy. The blood pressure tablet is coming out of my system, too. It is incredible that hormones and meds can do this to me."

Helen was having a hard time following the story.

"Five years, I did the nasal spray and was locked up in the mental ward after three sniffs of the GnRH. Nothing worked. But this antihistamine does. Dr. Michaels had known about this for twenty years and only told me in February! I was a journalist for years for women's magazines. We did not write about this in those days. I need to write, but my brain does not work anymore. It's just mush."

Chrissy said she was tired and needed to go but thanked Helen. Helen was exhausted just listening and trying to make sense of it all.

Chrissy called back a couple of days later. "The suicidal thoughts before my period and the high untreatable blood pressure are my biggest problems. It's still relentless."

"But I thought you said the antihistamine was helping?"

"Oh, it is, but this PMDD has destroyed my life, my children, my family. I'm okay today, but I know next week it will all come back again. I've been having periods every two weeks since starting the GnRH in 2018. I'm on continuous bio HRT which should be suppressing my ovaries, but it's not. They are all baffled."

"I'm not surprised," said Helen, trying hard again to follow.

"I was told by the psychiatrist that it's in my head!"

"Well–" Helen hesitated. She knew that Chrissy was experiencing her thought-created world just like everyone else, but she also knew that it would not be helpful or kind to tell Chrissy that it was her thinking. "What do you think is your main problem now?"

"If I think about your question, I will spiral down. I wish I could wipe away these last five years. I can't deal with the flashbacks and the fact that it happened to me!"

"Chrissy, I have some ideas that I think would really help you. It sounds like we have a couple of days right now while your mind and body are fairly calm. Would you be willing to meet with me so I can share with you what has worked for me and my daughters? I want to see if we can help you have a better time of it next month."

"Okay, I guess. It can't get much worse, can it?"

Helen met Chrissy at a cafe in Santa Monica the following evening after work. They talked about thoughts and low moods and how Thought is always flowing. The next day Chrissy came into the department store to meet Katrina and see the digital ticker tape in Women's Designer Wear before meeting Helen in her lunch break. They met again that night.

"I was finally offered a bed last night in the psych ward. I don't need it now. The blood pressure tablet is wearing off, and I am on day three. It is incredible how the mood lifts. I

Very Well

can't face going near the hospital, so I just didn't turn up. I will call them in a while, but it will go against me, I know it will, as I have refused help. I was waiting seven days for a bed but I got through it! I don't think I will get through the next time, though."

"Wow, slow down," said Helen. "Come back and join me in Wednesday evening. You are doing great. See how your mood lifted?"

"Sure, but that's the hormones shifting. Every month, up and down, up and down. It will happen again, and it will be terrible."

"Yes, hormones fluctuate, but that is normal and natural, it's why we call it a Cycle. But what if your thinking is calm? What if you felt safe and taken care of? Your experience of it could be quite different. Now that you know what's happening, you know what to expect and that takes away a lot of the fear."

"I always dread it coming. I can feel it creeping up, and I get so scared."

"And that scary reaction is what is sending your nervous system into panic and making it ten times worse. Could you see that?"

"I guess. There was one time when I was really bad and I called the Samaritans and they hung up on me! I was laughing at that so much that I could see how ridiculous everything was!"

Chana Studley

"Oh my gosh, that's like my colleague Michael.[50] He has a story about calling them and they were busy! But that's exactly it. When you saw how ridiculous it was, you laughed. That changed your mood slightly, and you got through it. That is your innate resilience; it's there all the time. I'm going to be with you every step of the way this month, holding your hand as much as I can. We will see it coming. It won't be a surprise, so you don't have to panic. Chrissy, you have all the courage, resilience, and wisdom you need to manage this."

Helen didn't know what was going to happen, but she knew it could be so much better than it had been. They kept talking and stayed in close touch.

"On day 11 now, so I'm teetering on the edge. Just trying to get motivated to do things today. Scott came back from college yesterday, and I had Jonny, my eldest, home with his girlfriend. I did not sleep very well so I need to go have a cold shower and get moving. My mood is up and down but doable. The video clip you sent is excellent.[51] I think my perception has changed a little."

"I'm glad you liked it. It's my friend Deborah's. She works a lot with people in chronic pain, but the ideas are the same with hormones. Watch those scary thoughts go by.

---

[50] Michael Neill, "Why Aren't We Awesomer?" TED Talk, June 24, 2014.
[51] Chana Studley, "Understanding Chronic Pain."
https://www.youtube.com/watch?v=5MUHrCiD3Do

Very Well

Remember they are like clouds always moving, and you don't have to listen to them."

As the days went by, Helen became a little nervous. Chrissy had been in a locked mental ward last month; how would it be this time? Giving this a try was far better than what Chrissy had been going through before. Either Chrissy would cope with her next period...or she wouldn't.

The phone rang just as Helen was about to turn it off; she was tired and ready for bed. Afraid it was Chrissy she picked up, hoping she wasn't calling from the hospital or a police station.

"Is this the Hormone hotline?!" cried a new caller, clearly distressed.

"Yes, my name is Helen, try to breathe slowly and tell me, how can I help you?"

"*They lied*!! Those soulless, heartless, so-called doctors lied to me!"

Helen was relieved it wasn't Chrissy calling from the emergency room, but what was this about? "I'm so sorry, what happened to you?"[52]

"Back when I first went to my doctor and told him about the awful symptoms I get every month, he said there was nothing physically wrong with me even though it felt like my guts were digesting acid! I told him I had piercing headaches and my emotions were all over the place so he sent

---

[52] The following story is a true account reprinted with permission by Dr. James Davies from his book *Cracked* (Icon Books, 2013).

me to the gynecologist. She agreed there was nothing wrong with me physically and decided I had some psychological disorder called PMDD. She put me on this "*special*" medication just for women specifically with menstrual problems. She gave me a drug called Sarafem."

"So what was the lie?" asked Helen curiously.

"Well, it wasn't created for PMDD, was it? It was goddamn Prozac under a different name! The liars just changed the name and put it in a pink box!! *I've just found out that I was taking Prozac for years and didn't know!*"

16
August

"What?!" exclaimed Kara the next morning as her mother spilled the story from the night before. "Is that even legal? I mean that's...that's got to be against the Hippocratic oath or trading standards or something?!" Kara was as outraged as the caller and went to school to see what she could find out.

"It really is." Helen had sent a meme to Chrissy that said, "Freedom is not taking everything personally." "I am working on this. My cycle is normally 14 days! Last month was 26, and it was hell. Not sure what is happening this time, but it feels like a 14-day cycle. I am cramping already."

Helen couldn't keep track of Chrissy's days and wasn't sure if Chrissy could either.

"I'm batting the thoughts away like you said. I have the dentist at 10:30 am. My tooth snapped in half a few weeks ago. Just another thing to remind me that I'm falling apart. Happy I have got both my boys at home, though. Just need to get myself into gear and keep busy. I have loads to do."

"Sorry to hear about your tooth!" Helen reflected on how she could help Chrissy see that she didn't have to do anything with her thoughts. In fact, the more she reacted to them the more it would rev up her nervous system again. "So what if instead of batting away the thoughts...can you see that they will leave on their own? Like clouds, all thoughts move on. Their nature is to move, no help needed. In fact, the less attention you give them, the easier they can leave and be replaced by fresh, new ones."

In that moment, it was so clear to Helen that batting thoughts away, reframing, or any technique was just more anxious thinking. It was like Chrissy was innocently putting more garbage in the trash to get rid of the garbage!

She invited Chrissy to join them for the next Women's Club, hoping desperately she wouldn't be in the psych ward again.

That evening Kara came home with information about Sarafem. "Okay, so Eli Lilly made Sarafem and promoted it as a wonder cure exclusively for the very female condition of PMDD. They spent $30 million on advertising this '*unique*' wonder cure and made $2.6 billion in one year![53] And your

---

[53] Shankar Vedantam. "Renamed Prozac Fuels Women's Health Debate." Washington Post, April 29, 2001.

Very Well

caller is absolutely right, chemically Sarafem and Prozac are exactly the same! The only difference was they changed the packaging and the names, oh, *and* they charged more for it!" Kara's disgust was palpable. "It's so sneaky! The patent for Prozac was about to run out so this way they were able to squeeze more money out of it. Which means thousands of women were deceived into taking Prozac and didn't know it!"

"Oh my gosh! That's terrible!" Helen sat down. She was stunned. "You say 'were?' Did it stop?"

"Yes, but not until 2020. And the only reason I have found so far for why it was stopped was for 'business reasons.' Ha!" Kara drew in a sharp, disgusted breath before she continued. "But do you see what it means, Mom? Eli Lilly was experimenting on these innocent women without them knowing!"

"Well, we don't know that. I mean, slow down a minute."

"But they were being given an antidepressant when they didn't have a diagnosis of depression. You can't diagnose something and then medicate for something else! It's like something out of a George Orwell novel! Antidepressants have all kinds of side effects, sometimes nasty ones, and terrible withdrawals. You can't put people on a drug without their full consent and that means knowing all the facts ... Mom, don't you see...*that could have been me.*"

Kara went to call one of her friends to rage some more while Helen went back to her books. She needed the distraction.

Chana Studley

The life of a young woman in Vienna in the late 1880s wasn't so great, even in a wealthy family. Bertha had been given a genteel and limited education and was now living the life of "waiting to be married off" with no life of her own inside or outside the home. She was basically the property of her father until she married, when she would become the property of her husband. Her world had been small and chaperoned; her only outlet had been her imagination, of which Bertha had seemed to have a lot. She'd created numerous stories to amuse herself, fantasies about fairies and imaginary places to escape to.

Joseph Breuer, the family doctor, had been brought in to attend to Bertha's cough. Nursing her father's tuberculosis had taken a toll on her health; she was anemic and weak from starving herself. Helen made a note; *Anorexia maybe?* If she had been anorexic, that meant she was already struggling with some pretty heavy thinking. Tied to the house, isolated and overprotected, watching her younger brother pursue higher education and go wherever he chose must have been torture for an obviously intelligent young woman who had been restricted to being a nursemaid. By all accounts, Wilhelm Pappenheim had been a bully and tormented Bertha on top of everything else. Helen couldn't imagine it. Bertha had developed anxiety, fatigue, missing moments of consciousness that she'd called "absences," and then she had started to have strange physical issues.

Breuer had been fascinated by her array of symptoms and spent a year and a half seeing her almost daily. At the

Very Well

time, he was 38 and married; she was 21, beautiful and charismatic. Bertha would describe what she had called her "private theater" of fantasies to Breuer in long discussions as he attempted to study her case. Her symptoms had grown, including headaches over her left eye. She had felt like the walls were collapsing in on her and her right arm cramped in an extended position. Her right leg was twisted, and she couldn't turn her head.

Yeesh! thought Helen. This poor girl!

Breuer's diagnosis, based on those symptoms, had been Hysteria. Helen remembered Dr. Alice mentioning something about the womb wandering. She googled Hysteria.

Hysteria is a pejorative term used colloquially to mean ungovernable emotional excess and can refer to a temporary state of mind or emotion. In the 19th century, hysteria was considered a diagnosable physical illness in women.
https://en.wikipedia.org > wiki > Hysteria

Huh, thought Helen as she was interrupted by a new caller, Candace.

"I get off balance, a kind of drunk feeling, not alcohol but a dizzy feeling during the week before I bleed. Have you ever heard of anyone else having that?"

"Actually, I used to get that when I was going through perimenopause. I would get really dizzy just before each hot flash. You poor thing, I know how horrible it is."

"Oh! No, I'm not that old! *Are you saying I'm going through menopause?!*"

"No, no, not at all. What I meant was it's part of hormone fluctuations." Helen hesitated. Or was it the result of her history of overreaction to her hormones fluctuating? The caller's overreaction was surging into the phone. "What does your doctor say?"

"My doctor says it's vertigo and gave me meclizine[54] to take as needed."

"Okay, do you want to take it?"

"Not really, I read it has side effects."

"I don't know, I'm not a doctor, but I know that when my thinking slowed down, the dizziness went away."

Candace was curious, and so Helen invited her to the next Women's Club. She then wondered about Lori and sent her a text. Lori eventually replied, but it just said,

Sad

As the women arrived at Patti's beautiful home for the next Women's Club, Helen kept a lookout for Lori. Georgia and Sharona had hit it off, becoming good, supportive friends, and Geraldine was on form. Katrina and Julie came from work, and Sasha brought a friend. Noreen didn't make it this time, but Nicole did, and just as Helen was about to

---

[54] Meclizine is used to treat or prevent nausea, vomiting, and dizziness caused by motion sickness. Dizziness is a common symptom associated with both acute and chronic anxiety.

Very Well

start the discussion, the doorbell rang again. It was Lori.

Lori was petite, dressed in jeans and an old t-shirt. Her dark, unwashed hair was pulled back in a messy ponytail. She looked frail and scared, as if she might change her mind and run away into the night at any moment. She hesitated.

"Come in, please, come in," welcomed Patti warmly. She showed Lori into the living room to join the others. They all introduced themselves as Lori sat down on the sofa with Alex and Carina.

"I thought we could talk about moods tonight," offered Helen kindly. "We talked a lot about Thought and thinking last time, and I know we have all had experience with moods."

"My husband calls me a moody cow," snorted Carina.

"I won't tell you what my boyfriend calls me!" laughed Alex.

"My husband says to me, 'Gerri, you have a tongue, bite it!'" cried Geraldine, and they all giggled in disbelief.

"Yes, well, we all have moods, including men, I might add. I know my husband could get into a real grumpy mood when things weren't going his way," continued Helen. "So let's talk about regular moods for a moment. Everyone goes up and down during the day; it's normal and natural. Deborah, my mentor, uses the analogy of an elevator in a department store to illustrate this, and as I work in a department store, it makes total sense to me. As most of you know, I work in Women's Shoes and it's on the ground floor at Neiman's. There are beautiful chandeliers; it's bright and open. We are mostly in an okay mood, even if we are faking it a bit sometimes, right, Julie?"

Julie laughed. She knew it was true.

"Now, when you go down to the lower level, you come to Housewares. There are gorgeous designer vases and table linens from France, top of the range, super sharp German knives, and exquisite china from England. But the products are more compacted together, the ceilings are lower, and Giovani who works there is, well, he's not the most positive person. If you ask him how he's doing, he will tell you all the things that are going wrong. How his orders were late and that his customers are so demanding, that he never gets a chance to breathe, and the other staff are so lazy."

Julie nodded in agreement.

"Now, down in the basement is Mr. Grumpy Guts. He is the most miserable man you could possibly meet. He is a cantankerous old fart. He complains all the time; he thinks everyone else has it easier than him, even though a lot of the day he sits on his backside. The basement is dirty and dark. It smells, and no one wants to hang out with him down there, so he is all alone."

"Sounds terrible," said Patti.

"Sounds like my husband," laughed Geraldine.

"So let's take the elevator and go back up. Up past Housewares, past Cosmetics to Women's Wear. And here we have…"

"Me!" interrupted Katrina.

"Ha ha, yes, Katrina, who is doing so well!"

Helen and Katrina shared with the other ladies the insight about the designer names going round and round.

Very Well

They all said they would come in to visit her and have a look.

"Katrina is doing really well. She has ups and downs, like the rest of us, but she can see when she is getting caught up in her thinking and pops out of it now, don't you?"

Katrina made a fake bow and grinned.

"Now, if we go up again, we come to the Men's department where we have...Felipe. Felipe is really happy. He is genuinely happy. He loves his job, grateful to be working in such a cool place with beautiful products to sell. He gets to serve Brad Pitt and Justin Beiber with their Rolex needs. They ask his opinion on style and the latest fashions. He can look out the windows at the beautiful view, the Pacific Ocean, and the snow on the mountains in the spring. Because he is present and authentic, his customers love his natural charm. They sense his genuine interest and come back for more, so his boss loves him, too. He'll probably be promoted soon."

"Who's Felipe?" challenged Katrina in disbelief. "I don't know anyone named Felipe who works at the store! I need to ask him a few questions!"

"I made him up," replied Helen as they all giggled. Katrina put on a big pretend sulk. "So what has this all to do with moods? Well, our moods go up and down, like the elevator at the store. Can you see that?"

Everyone nodded, so she continued.

"Now, see how the different characters on the different floors have certain moods. Mr. Grumpy Guts in the basement and fabulous Felipe on the top floor are in very different moods. *They are feeling their thinking*. It's an analogy, of course, but the analogy is pointing at a reliable system. We are all those characters in one person. We can all be up and down at different times. When we are thinking low, miserable, insecure thoughts, we cannot be in a good mood, right? And when we are thinking happy, joyful, abundant thoughts, we cannot be in a low mood. Everyone with me?" Helen looked over to Lori to see how she was doing. Her eyes were glazed and she didn't quite seem present. It was like she was there but somewhere else at the same time. "Moods, therefore, are a reflection of the quality of our thinking."

"I think I get what you are saying, but it's my hormones that are making my moods go up and down," said Alex despondently.

"I know it seems that way, and certainly there is a fluctuation happening in your body, but there is no rule that says we have to feel terrible because of it, and how would you know you feel anxious or that your temperature changed unless you had some kind of thought about it?"

Alex shrugged her shoulders.

"You see, there are no exceptions. There isn't any experience that isn't made of the gift of Thought, and our moods reflect our thinking."

"As Alex said, maybe regular moods, but hormone mood changes are physical," added Nicole.

"I know this is a little hard to get, but...well, whatever our bodies are doing, be it hungry, itchy, or sweating, we would only know because they produce an experience that shows up in our consciousness, and our reaction is what

Very Well

governs what happens next. If we panic or freak out, that sends danger messages to the brain that sets off the stress response which uses stress hormones to get things moving in the body. This kind of constant reaction affects the amygdala and hypothalamus and makes the pituitary gland over-sensitive, which makes the brain more susceptible to hormones released by the endocrine system."

The ladies sat in silence for a moment to soak this in.

"Mom, did you swallow a medical textbook when I wasn't looking?" asked Kara in disbelief.

"No...I just did some reading..."

"Can you say that again, but in English this time?" asked Carina. The other ladies agreed; they were all a bit confused.

"Sure. The stress response, sometimes called the Fight or Flight response, is designed to go into action when we are in shock or crisis. Adrenaline and glucose are pushed into the body to give us energy to survive. This all happens with the help of a hormone called cortisol. Cortisol is manufactured with the help of progesterone. We know about progesterone because that's one of the culprits that fluctuate in our monthly cycle."

"So me getting all stressed and anxious about my period coming was actually what was causing my next period to be even more stressful?" cried Carina.

"As you know, I'm not a doctor, but yes! It seems that way from what I can put together."

"So how is this related to the department store?" asked Katrina, still confused.

"Oh, yes. Well, imagine Felipe up there in his lovely

mood. He is serving Liam Neeson or helping Vanessa Williams choose a gift for her nephew, and something happens."

"Oh, like the shoplifter who fell down all the floors and nearly broke his neck!" interrupted Julie.

"What?!" cried Kara.

"Ah, yes. Or let's say someone returns $2,000 worth of goods, and Felipe loses that commission. But because he is in a good state of mind, he will be like, 'Oh well, I guess that commission wasn't mine after all,' or 'Probably best they don't waste their money.' He naturally rides the wave of disappointment. He doesn't get all twisted up and overreact to it. His natural resilience keeps him afloat.

"Mr. Grumpy Guts, on the other hand, who is always in a bad mood down in the basement, can't see anything good in anything. If you listen to his language, it's very extreme; *Always* and *Never*. 'No one appreciates me, I can never get a break, and I always work harder than anyone else.' Even when something good happens, he'll say, 'Well that's not going to last.' You see, these different characteristics can only live in these different moods."

"But that's a horrible job to be down in the basement all the time," responded Alex.

"Actually, he has a nice clean office. He often pulls his chair out into the warm sunshine when he is waiting for a delivery and sits there most of the day with his cat and a coffee."

"That sounds really nice!" laughed Candace.

"Exactly. It all comes down to perception, and

Very Well

perception is made of our thinking. He perceives his job to be terrible, so he is living in the dark feeling of his thinking, even though he is actually sitting in the sun."

"Huh? Sorry, but I'm not following you," said Carina.

Helen smiled and thought for a different analogy, "Well...okay, how about this. Not far from here, south near the Mexican border, there are deserts, really hot deserts where not much grows. It's barren and desolate. And in northern California, we have amazing snow-capped mountains. A cactus probably can't grow up at Lake Tahoe, and a pine tree cannot grow down in the Mojave Desert. They are two very different environments and so have very different plants. And like a cactus cannot grow in the snowy mountains, we can't overreact and scare ourselves when we are in a good mood."

Carina looked even more confused. Kara asked if she could add something. "You know how when you drive up to Big Bear Lake, as you go up from the desert to the mountains, the trees change? The palm trees change to pine trees. In fact, as you go higher and higher, there are no trees above a certain height. It's called the treeline. Trees don't grow above the treeline. I mean, there are no trees on Everest, right? It's not about trying harder or finding the right technique; it's just not possible. Trees need a certain amount of oxygen, and they just can't live at that high altitude. It's an analogy. Insecurity and anxiety can't live in a good mood; they need a low mood–"

"And you can't feel good when you are in a low mood down in the 'basement!'" interrupted Katrina excitedly. "I get it! Now I get what you mean by always feeling our thinking! It's impossible to feel bad when you are in a good mood, and yucky thinking needs a dark, miserable basement to thrive and grow!"

"Yes! It's not the actual basement that is causing Mr. Grumpy Guts' mood. It's his thinking about the basement. The same way hanging out with Brad Pitt is not causing Felipe's good mood either."

"It would for me!" laughed Geraldine.

"Sure, wouldn't that be nice, but it would be our thoughts about Brad. You know he's almost 60 now? So to a young woman he's an old man, and she would probably not be so excited. Could you see that? It's your thoughts about him that are creating the excitement. So let's bring this back to our physical situations. What I'm saying is that when we get a hot flash, a drop in hormones after birth, or our monthly cycle comes around, and we are stressed, anxious, and in a low mood, it's going to be a much much worse experience than if we are in a better mood, no matter what is happening physically."

The ladies were quiet for a minute.

"I think I get it," said Nicole. "When I'm in a low mood, my monthly cycle is going to be a much tougher experience. And as I hate it more, the more stressed I get, the worse it gets. If I'm in a better mood, then whatever is happening with me physically will be much easier to handle and less reaction means less escalation. Is that it?"

"Yes! Go to the top of the class!" cheered Helen and Kara. "The intensity, heaviness, and urgency that you feel at

Very Well

that time of the month are letting you know you are in a low mood and, well, there is no good information in a low mood, so stop. No need to follow that thinking."

"The low mood *is* the information," added Kara.

"Yes."

They all talked about it some more, how they all had certain characteristics or "stories" that would show up in their low moods, like this is never going to change, no one understands, it's not fair, my life is awful, and what's the point. These stories were a big fat signal to stop listening and look the other way. They started to see that freedom was not getting sucked in and being able to rise above the noise.

"Lori, would you like to say anything?" asked Helen gently.

Lori looked up slightly. She smiled slowly and said, "I think you are all so brave. I don't know if I can do this much longer."

Everyone paused and looked at her, glimpsing the pain and dark place she was in.

"We are so glad you are here, and the fact that you came out to be with a bunch of strangers is huge. I think you are much braver than you think."

Helen wrapped up the evening and encouraged them to come back next month. Kara gave Lori a hug and chatted with her after the others left.

"I'm worried about her, Mom," said Kara on the way home. "She seems so lost and confused."

"I know. All we can do is love her and show her the way through."

17

September

"Helen!" It was Nicole on the phone and she sounded out of breath. "Okay, are you ready for this?"

"What? Are you okay? What's going on?"

"They have offered me a personal interest spot in the news report, you know, I can pick something and report on it!"

"That's wonderful! Amazing, well done! What do you have in mind?"

"You! I mean the work you do with the hotline! It's social news, it's drama, it's amazing, it's...it's *HOT*!"

Helen laughed. "You're not serious."

"I am. I presented the idea to my producer and he liked it. He said it was...edgy."

"Well, that's one way to put it, I guess? I mean, I have had to talk a few ladies back off the edge a couple of times.

Very Well

But...but I promise people anonymity. I'm not sure there will be much you can report. And I'm not going in front of the camera."

"We don't have to use names, and we can use stock footage, but yes, you! Why not you?"

Helen was taken aback by Nicole's suggestion. "Because that's not me. I don't want to be known as the Hormone Lady or the...the *Hotline Hostess*."

"Okay, well, do you mind if I ask any of the ladies from the group?"

"I guess not. I mean, as long as you make it clear that we respect people's anonymity, that...that I'm not a doctor and it's all voluntary."

"Perfect. Would you be willing to talk off camera?"

"You mean, like a shadow talking behind a screen?"

It was Nicole's turn to laugh, "No! We don't want to make you seem like a criminal; this isn't about backstreet abortions! No, we would do it very elegantly with you talking over film of women enjoying their lives or something."

"I...don't think so."

"Okay, but you'll think about it."

Helen laughed again. "I can see why you are good at your job, but NO!"

Kara was so excited when Helen announced it to her that night. They were at Lily's visiting her and the baby, and even Lily couldn't help smiling.

"Granny's going to be famous," said Kara as she picked

Flora up and gave her a cuddle.

"No, I'm definitely not. I made that very clear; it's not about me. The hotline and the good information we offer, alternatives to all the toxic meds and surgeries and...and crackpot remedies are what need the attention, not me. I know you are going to say it's my insecure thinking, but..." Helen hesitated. She knew that when people say, "I know it's my thinking, but..." they really hadn't seen the truth about the nature of thought at that moment. She paused as Kara grinned at her.

"Why don't *you* do it, sweetheart?" replied Helen.

Kara wasn't expecting that. She stopped and took Flora to play in the garden.

"It's okay, Mom, you don't have to. Not everyone has to be in front of the camera," offered Lily kindly.

"I know," agreed Helen with a confident smile. "I'm actually totally okay with saying no. It's not insecurity; I just don't feel like it's the right fit for me. Anyway, darling, how are you doing? You seem a little better."

Lily sighed. "Well, Carl noticed...well, he said that I don't really engage with Flora so much. I mean, I take care of her and everything, diapers, feeding, but he noticed I don't really smile at her, enjoy her. I'm taking care of her, really I am. He wasn't being mean; he was trying to help me see that maybe I was too caught up in doing it all perfectly that I had forgotten to enjoy being with her."

Helen came and sat on the sofa with her daughter.

"I know what he means. As soon as he said it, it made sense. Mom, I'm scared that I don't feel connected to her.

Very Well

All that effort to be perfect, and I don't even have the one thing a mother should have. *Kara loves her more than I do!*" Lily started to sob as Helen put her arms around her eldest daughter.

"Oh, honey, it's okay, it's okay. I know that you love her and so does Carl. You're just feeling the really yucky thinking that is passing through right now. And it will pass. And there may be other yucky thoughts, but it's not who you are and you don't have to listen to it. Can I tell you what I discovered? Your child will bring you up maybe more than you bring up your child. It's wisdom all the way. And also how little is on us. Love and being present means way more than all the other myriad things we think and scare ourselves with."

Gin Li had called the hotline a couple of times already. She was experiencing PMDD *and* perimenopause. Like Chrissy, she was considering going on antidepressants but was nervous after hearing about the side effects. Helen had introduced her to the Principles, and she was already doing so much better.

"So...I am now on day 60 of no period. According to my period tracker, I should have started yesterday. I noticed, as did my husband, that I was a little edgy today. I had a mild hot flash this evening as well, but no depression this time! I will keep you updated, but I'm hoping for no more periods. I go to the specialist on the tenth."

Helen was so excited; this is what she had hoped for. "My periods were regularly irregular at the end. I got three a year for the last three years of my cycle. They would come at Easter, July 4th, and Halloween every year! It was hilarious. I called them my '*holiday guests.*' And then they stopped altogether." Helen shared with her about how the Principles had helped her so much, and that life was very smooth these days.

"That's awesome! I definitely believe my reaction to my thoughts has been controlling my behavior quite a bit. I know what you've shared with me has helped so much already. I'm looking forward to watching the last video you sent."

Helen went back to her books and continued reading about Hysteria. The information she found was either presented as "fact" or feminist–sometimes very angry feminist. She read it all with a pinch of salt, wondering about these Victorian women who had been poked and prodded in the name of science, misunderstood, and often locked up. Women like Bertha who had been at the mercy of their circumstances, innocently ignorant of what was actually happening to their bodies. It was clear that belief in the superiority of the male body went all the way back to ancient history. Aristotle described the female body as a male body "*turn'd outside in.*" Women's bodies were therefore faulty, defective, and deficient. But because women possessed that most invaluable of organs–the womb–they were defined and limited by that purpose with no other redeeming qualities. To be a woman was to be ruled by her biology, and because for centuries no one knew

Very Well

what the inside of a body looked like, the most weird and incredible explanations of a woman's cycle were told as fact by men who were even more in the dark themselves.

Helen had found a website called "*The Wandering Womb.*" It seemed to be that the prevailing idea for centuries was that the womb could move out of place and wander around the body, suffocating women as it made its way to the head. This, they believed, explained *all* women's physical problems, diseases, and derangements, because, after all, a woman's worth was only in her ability to produce offspring.

Because men "knew" that the female body was inferior, women could not be trusted to give an accurate account of how they felt about their own bodies. Men's opinions, on the other hand, were all based on their own suppositions, superstitions, and fears. This attitude continued down through the ages as men witnessed what they didn't understand, confused by women's excessive emotions, and scared by unpredictable moods. This idea that women exaggerate, are weaker and attention-seeking, has survived until the present day.

Helen was fascinated by the names of books that were published about women's health by men, some of whom, like priests and monks, had never even talked to a woman, let alone examined them. Shrouded in propriety, they pontificated about their speculations.

1640–*The Sick Woman's Private Looking-glasse*–John Sadler (who claimed to have cured all the "evil qualities" of the uterus).

Chana Studley

1683–*A Brief Discourse of a Disease Called the Suffocation of the Mother*–Edward Jorden (who believed that if the womb was not secured it would suffocate the woman).

Next came witch burning. 45,000 people were executed for witchcraft in the 1500s and 1600s. Most were women, and most were over 40 years old. Helen knew why. It was menopause! If a woman was overcome by "paroxysms of frenzy and mental aberrations, as if under the dominion of spells," and was no longer able to produce children, then she must be evil, right?

I know I felt pretty evil at times, thought Helen to herself when she remembered how dreadful she used to feel.

She continued to make notes. The word "hysteria" came from the Ancient Greek word for the uterus, *hystera*. A description of the theory of a "wandering womb" came from Aretaeus, a physician from Cappadocia in the 2nd century A.D. He wrote that the uterus could move out of place and float within the body.

In the middle of the flanks of women lies the womb, a female viscus, closely resembling an animal; for it is moved of itself hither and thither in the flanks, also upwards in a direct line to below the cartilage of the thorax, and also obliquely to the right or to the left, either to the liver or the spleen, and it likewise is subject to prolapsus downwards, and in a word, it is altogether erratic. It delights also in fragrant smells, and advances towards them, and it has an aversion to fetid

Very Well

smells, and flees from them; and, on the whole, the womb is like an animal within an animal.[55]

Hold on a minute, thought Helen, *that sounds suspiciously like Freud's idea of the subconscious!* An animal within an animal? Erratic, floating nervous energy? She knew that Freud had a formal education and would have been educated in the Classics. Helen went back to the Freud book to see how he had described it: "*...associations and impulses that are not accessible to consciousness. An autonomous region...with its own wishful impulses...a turbulent and beleaguered force that needed to be tied down.*"[56]

Hmm, so now we can add plagiarism, not to mention unoriginal, to his list of fine qualities, scoffed Helen to herself.

Chrissy called the next time Helen was on the hotline. "Well. I started spotting yesterday, day 12. I got through it. This morning I went back to the dentist, as I got the day wrong before. My head is such mush. Got the right day this time, and my big fear that my tooth that I broke two weeks ago was not going to be able to be saved was put to rest."

"Oh, that's good."

"I seem to have stopped spotting, but I'm cramping

---

[55] https://en.wikipedia.org/wiki/Aretaeus_of_Cappadocia
[56] Sigmund Freud, *Introductory Lectures* (1916), describing what he later called the id.

really badly now. This happened last time. I barely spotted for two days, and then wham, but this time, my mood lifted instantly. I was weepy this morning. You know, I could feel it coming but I never really know when, and listening to you talk about how thoughts pass and I don't have to listen to them has really worked."

Helen was so pleased.

"Yesterday was hilarious. Normally if I had been at that stage and I'd turned up at the dentist on the wrong day, I would have had a serious meltdown. That would have triggered the end! But no. I went and got waxed, nails and eyebrows done. What the hell was going through my head before? It was like I was the normal me again. I have not treated myself to a wax for years. I have my son Scotty home from Stanford for another week before he goes back to school for the fall semester. He is so lovely. Jonny and his girlfriend have stayed with me since the hospital last week, so I am in heaven. I even cooked dinner from scratch last night. On day one I'm usually lying around and eating crap. I've fallen in love with the cats again. Like, really in love. I feel like me for the first time in five years!"

"Oh, that's amazing. I'm so happy for you!"

"Yes, I have that serene feeling that I had when I was pregnant and breastfeeding. It can't be a coincidence. But I'm scared I'm just too happy."

"That's understandable, after all that you've been through, but that's just a thought, too. Watch it pass by and don't pay it any attention. You can be as happy as you want to be."

Very Well

While she was on the phone with Chrissy, Gin Li left a message: "Well... 'Aunt Flo' paid me a visit this morning. Guess it's not over 'til it's over. The good news is that I had very few symptoms this time! The last time was the worst, as far as mental and emotional symptoms go. I was depressed, lethargic, and in a state of hopelessness for many days, but you know what's odd? My husband has kind of followed the Three Principles his whole life without even knowing about them. He has actually said similar things to me for years, and I just thought he was unusually strong and that I wasn't. Weird, huh? Speak soon, bye."

It was mid-morning in the department store. Helen was thinking about what she would share at the Women's Club that evening when she spotted Barry Manilow sampling some Joe Malone scent for men over in the Perfume department. It occurred to her that last month's meeting had been a bit heavy with all the biology stuff so maybe best to go back to the Principles and talk about what "Outside-In" means. As she looked across the store, she saw Rod Stewart step onto the up escalator. She giggled to herself. She couldn't help noticing how remarkably similar their hair was. *Maybe they had the same hairdresser?*

All the lovely ladies showed up as usual. It had become a really nice group, everyone appreciating the support and encouragement. It was the end of summer vacation and kids were going back to school, so there was talk of the craziness of carpooling and school supplies.

"You may have heard me mention the idea of things being Outside-In? I wanted to talk more about this tonight, as it's an insight that I think you will find very helpful. When I was trying to fix my problems, I was convinced that things and people needed to change for me to be okay. If only my husband hadn't died, when I get a better job, why isn't my body behaving, etc. If they can heal heart disease and all those other things, why can't they fix my hormones?"

"If they can put a man on the moon, why can't they make him stay there?" laughed Geraldine. Everyone was getting used to her funny comments, and Helen was kind of grateful as it kept the room light and in a good feeling.

"Ah, so that is my point. I was convinced that if only things and people would change or go away, then I would feel better. This is what we call an Outside-In understanding of life, meaning, I thought things on the outside of me were governing how I felt and creating my moods. This logically makes sense, but then that means I am a victim of everything and everyone. For as long as I held everyone else responsible for how I felt, I had a hard time controlling, avoiding, and managing you all!"

The ladies gave a little laugh as they all knew how much effort they had put into trying to control their surroundings and relationships so that they would feel okay.

"It's such hard work! As soon as you have one thing under control, something or someone else misbehaves. It's a nightmare! Now that I know that how I am feeling isn't coming from my circumstances or other people, I don't

Very Well

have to get all exhausted or frustrated trying to control everything anymore. My feelings are always coming from my thoughts about those outside things. This is what we call an Inside-Out understanding and as Syd Banks says, it's psycho-logical."

Brandi, a new member, spoke up. "Yes, and that's why we need to look to our divine healer within for our strength."

Helen wasn't quite sure what to make of her comment. It sounded good but she was suspicious it was leading to a technique, so she smiled and continued. "Yes, knowing that we all have Innate Health means we don't have to get stuck in needing the outside things to change. This is powerful, especially when our physical bodies feel out of our control, too."

"Yes, I dance in my living room because it's the most Feng Shui place in my apartment," added Brandi. "It brings my inner goddess into the room. I find sacred breath work to be very helpful, too."

Kara looked at her mother as Helen tried to stay focused. "I'm so happy you have found something that works for you...but we are...well, we are looking a bit further upstream in this group. We are looking past the techniques and the rituals to how the mind works."

"Oh absolutely," agreed Brandi.

"You see, even our physical bodies are 'Outside.' If my mood goes up or down because of my weight or bloating or even my reaction to my hormone levels, then that is also Outside-In. So anything that we think is causing our discomfort, or our wellbeing for that matter, is Outside-In. Could you see that?" asked Helen.

"What do you mean by causing our wellbeing?" asked Carina curiously.

"Well, I know I used to think if I could just get down to the beach, then I would feel better. Or if they would just behave or...or if I took a hot bath, then I would feel better."

"But a hot bath does make me feel better."

"Oh, me too," agreed Helen. "I love long, hot baths, a walk on the beach, or a hike up in Topanga Canyon, but it's not the bath or the beach or the canyon that is giving me my wellbeing. It's my thinking about the hot bath or nature that has made me feel better. Our wellbeing is with us all the time. I hate steam rooms and saunas, for example, I feel like I'm going to suffocate, but the physiology is probably almost the same as a hot bath. Could you see that I'm just experiencing it differently with my thinking?"

Carina thought for a moment, and then Alex spoke up. "You mean both are making your body warm, but your thoughts about them are creating different experiences?"

Helen nodded in agreement, but before she could continue, Brandi got in first. "Releasing your emotions and expressing your divine goddess will help you with your fear of the steam room."

"Thank you, Brandi, but I don't need to," replied Helen with a big smile, the clarity of what she knew to be true filling her with confidence. "You see, fear is made of Thought, and all those thoughts I had about saunas have already left years ago, so there is actually nothing to release."

Very Well

She kept talking to keep the meeting focused on the topic. "And here is something that blew my mind. *Thinking is also Outside-In.*"

"*Huh?*" replied a few of the ladies in unison, including Brandi.

"Let's go back to what we have seen so far about Thought, the creative energy of Thought. It flows; it's always moving and never stays still. Like fire is always hot, water is always wet, Thought always moves. Another way to say it is, fire can never be wet and Thought can never get stuck. Before Thought comes into my consciousness, it is formless. It's some kind of spiritual energy that is, I don't know, flowing around over here."

She pointed to her right and moved her arm around as if she was stirring up something. "As Thought moves through my 'screen of consciousness,' as it were, it takes a form–could be a thought or it could be cramps and bloating or it could be an image."

She drew a box in the air around her face like a TV screen. "And then it moves on. It goes back to being...well, formless, over there somewhere. I don't know where spiritual stuff goes, but it's moved on. So when it's in our consciousness and it's taken a form of some kind, it's become kind of Outside-In. It's outside of the spiritual me, in that it took on a form."

There was silence again for a few moments.

"Wow, you have gone too far upstream for me this time!" remarked Geraldine.

"I get it!" cried Sharona. "You mean, when Thought is

in my mind and I'm reacting to it, I'm reacting to its *formed* form, i.e., I'm reacting to the illusion of the form it's taken? Am I on the right track?"

Helen smiled as Kara jumped in, excited to continue. "Yes! And that's why it doesn't feel good to fight it, because it's not real. It's still energy, but just an illusion that the problem is real. I spent so much time fighting it, but it was never real."

"But you still need to release those emotions. They cause all kinds of harm when they aren't dealt with." It was clear that Brandi was wedded to her ideas and could not see where Helen was pointing to.

"Harm?" asked Kara. "How do you mean they can cause harm? I mean, how could they if they are only made of thinking and have already moved on?" Kara didn't wait for an answer. "Brandi, don't you see? We can't ever be harmed or damaged because Thought is formless. You just can't break something that has no form, and when it takes on a form, it's an illusion, so that can't be broken or damaged either."

Helen quickly read Brandi's expression, recognizing that they had been correcting her ideas a fair bit that evening. She didn't want her to feel ganged up on, so she wrapped up the evening with a smile and warmly invited them all back next month.

"Wow, Mom! That was amazing. You should definitely be thinking about going back to school. You could write a paper on this. I think you could run circles around my

Very Well

teachers."

Helen gave her a gracious grin.

"And you can't say you are winging it anymore... What?" Kara stopped as she noticed an unusual look come over her mother's face. "Are you okay, Mom?"

"Yes, my love, but...I think I just had an insight. When you said winging it, I...I just got this amazing feeling of...flying?"

Kara smiled at her.

"Like a bird, like my arms were outstretched and I could feel warm, strong air holding me up."

They both paused for a few moments.

"We are not winging it. We are held...we are...gliding."

18
October

Nicole had worked hard preparing her special report. It was a small piece, but it was her first chance to really show what she could do. Even though it was just a local evening news show, it was a local Los Angeles news show, so that was pretty big in many ways. She had already recorded Georgia and Sharona talking about how distressing their symptoms were and how the hotline helped to understand what was happening to them in a new and helpful way. She had even gotten Clarke and Geraldine to talk about how her menopause symptoms were affecting their relationship and how much sweeter it was now. Helen had stuck her designer heels in about not being on camera, and so Kara, with some considerable nudging from Nicole, had bravely agreed to be interviewed live in the studio the following week.

Very Well

Helen had a couple of new callers on the hotline, as well as the regulars.

"Can you relate to this?" asked a new voice. "I can't think straight. I hate everyone. I want to eat chocolate all day and curl up into a ball and just cry. It's Halloween tomorrow night, and I'm dreading all those spoiled brats banging on my door, the little beggars. Actually, I think I'll just switch all the lights off, hide in my room and eat all the candy myself!"

Helen tried not to laugh; she wasn't sure if the caller was being funny or serious.

"I thought that when my periods stopped it would all be over. I'm 53, and still I have to put up with this?!"

"Oh, yes, totally! I was like that and so were my daughters. For me it was menopause, but for them it was PMDD and postpartum. You are not alone, and it doesn't have to be like this."

With each new caller, Helen hoped she was making a difference. Every story carried similarities. Was it any wonder, with the history of being told they were defective by doctors who often didn't have a clue?

Helen continued to be intrigued by her discoveries about Bertha and "Siggy" Freud. Bertha was reported to have been suicidal, threatening to jump from her bedroom window. She remembered there were times when Kara had felt like this, and Helen started to wonder if Bertha would have been diagnosed with PMDD had she been around today. These threats had led Bertha to be transferred to a sanitarium where Breuer had continued to see her. "Breuer lied about this when he later wrote her case history (with Freud) for *Studies on Hysteria*, claiming that she has merely been taken to a country house."[57] Dishonesty was added to the list of Freud's wonderful attributes in Helen's notes.

By this time, Bertha was being drugged with morphine and would go from states of euphoria to dark depression. Electric eels had been placed on her face, and she had been treated with arsenic and electric shock treatments. She was basically tortured and surprise, surprise, it didn't help. Bertha's illness was often referred to in the literature as being the result of her repressed rage. Brandi had also mentioned this idea of repressed and hidden emotions, so Helen decided to ask Deborah what she thought about it.

"Hmm. Okay, so this is what I think about the concept of repressed rage. I mean, I read and heard a lot about it when I was doing my chronic pain research." Deborah took a sip of her glass of wine. Joe was inside working in his office as the two women sat overlooking the Venice Canals from the deck at Deborah's house.

"If something is suppressed or repressed, that means it's been put somewhere or is hiding or underneath something. If it's hidden from view, it must be covered up by something, right? I always ask someone who believes this idea, how exactly is it buried or covered up? Or better still,

---

[57] Melinda Given Guttmann, *The Enigma of Anna O.: A Biography of Bertha Pappenheim* (Moyer Bell, 2001), p. 57.

Very Well

what is it they think is keeping it from being seen? They usually say something like feelings or old ideas or...or memories or trauma. I then ask, so what are those made of? What are trauma and feelings made of? Have you ever asked yourself what memories and suffering are made of?"

Helen grinned inwardly, knowing exactly where Deborah was going with this line of reasoning.

"If I ask them enough questions, the right questions, they will eventually admit that memories, feelings, and trauma are all made of thoughts or thinking in some way. *Ha Ha,* I say, or rather think to myself! So you agree it's all made of Thought! They then disagree, of course, because they think I'm talking about thinky thoughts, or that I'm suggesting they are imagining it or exaggerating, but I don't push it because there is no point going around in circles. However, once you see that Thought is a creative power and it's always moving, then there is no place for it to hide. No possibility or mechanism for it to get suppressed or repressed. Then you see that it can't actually get stuck anywhere, real or otherwise. Thought and thinking is never just *anywhere*; it has no substance. It's energy, always in motion, it's...spiritual."

"So how do the Principles help us understand it differently from all those other therapies?"

"Well, there are a lot of therapies and psychological theories that see experience as coming from thought. But what I think is unique about the Principles understanding is that thought is neutral until we have a reaction to it. Thought in and of itself has no power or life of its own, therefore it can't *do* anything to you. It can't *get* you, or use things to trip you up. It's not a devious entity with its own agenda. As Sydney Banks said, a thought only lasts as long as the time it takes you to think it. The Principles, as far as I know, is the only understanding that says that outside of the normal ups and downs of moods, our minds are completely healthy."

Helen was following so far.

"But what Freud and everyone who came after him are saying," continued Deborah, "is that people act and feel and behave in ways that they don't intend to because it's coming from a level of thought that no one can get to. And because it's hidden or 'repressed,' somehow, it's out of reach, inaccessible, and therefore we need to work hard to find it."

"And he was the only one who knew how to do that!" laughed Helen.

"Exactly! *And,* because he and his followers don't see Thought as a creative energy, it must have some other quality...a nervous, devious life of its own. They see it as unpredictable and unmanageable, frightening even."

Deborah paused before she continued. "So put his two ideas together:

A. You have something devious, even malicious inside of you that is not within your control, or worse, is possibly out of control;

and

B. You can't get to it?

What a terribly scary idea! It's the stuff of nightmares and horror movies! It's like...like *the monster from the black*

Very Well

lagoon! Personally, I can not subscribe to a theory that sets out to scare people into submission, which in and of itself is made of fearful thinking!"

Helen sat back in her chair, the impact of this beginning to sink in. "It's like Freud created a psychological monster that has been terrifying people ever since. So Freud really did get it wrong."

Deborah nodded in agreement. Helen suddenly remembered to tell Deborah about Nicole and the TV project. From a deep place of clarity, she calmly knew she didn't need to be in front of the camera.

"It's just not me. I'm not doing this for fame or fortune. I don't want to be recognized in the market for having been through a difficult menopause. Anyway, Kara has said she will do it, but she is really nervous."

"That's understandable. I don't blame you, and if you like, I can go with her. In fact, Joe knows all about this stuff. He coaches his clients to do TV stuff all the time." Joe was in the kitchen pouring himself a drink so she called to him through the open window. They explained the situation to him and he happily agreed to come along to make sure she was prepared.

The next morning, Lily called. She was okay but just needed some reassurance from her mom.

"Honey, this is such a normal, commonplace thing to go through. You are doing just fine. Lily, take the baby and look at her."

Lily put the phone on speaker and picked Flora up out

of her crib. She sat in the rocking chair in the corner of her room as Helen continued.

"Isn't she cute? See how simple it is. Just give yourself the time to be with your baby. Forget the list running through your head of the millions of things you have to do next; they will wait. When your mind is full of all of the things you need to do, it's hard to spend time with the loving thoughts. When you have thoughts of love, you feel love."

Lily listened carefully to what her mom was saying. She wasn't sure she fully believed it yet, but looking down at Flora's adorable little face, she was sure she felt the start of...something beginning to bubble up to the surface. Maybe she really could do this after all.

Deborah and Joe picked Kara up and drove over to the Channel 7 News studios. A PA gave them a quick tour and showed them into the studio where the interview would happen. Joe had coached Kara on how the cameras worked, what to expect, and how to not trip on the cables or touch anything. It was all very exciting. Nicole was thrilled to see them and went over what they would talk about before introducing her to the producer. He had insisted at the last minute that Channel 7's resident doctor had to be present to give it some legitimacy, even if Nicole only asked him a couple of questions, and so Kara was introduced to Dr. Richard Sanchez. Dr. Sanchez shook her hand casually, leaving immediately to make a phone call.

As the time crept closer and closer to being live on the air, Kara started to feel really nervous. Her stomach was

Very Well

doing bungee jumps and swirling like a whirlpool, but the moment she sat in the chair opposite Nicole, it vanished; she was in the moment and totally focused. As the prerecorded tape finished up, the studio floor manager counted down with his fingers: four, three, two...

"Kara, you suffered terribly when you were younger." Nicole smiled at her encouragingly. "Can you share with us some of your experiences?"

"Yes...it was awful, I mean, every woman has experienced some moodiness in their cycle, but this was off the charts. I would feel so anxious and angry...frustrated, hurt...scared, lost. I would have this simultaneous burning urge to run away from home but also to collapse and sleep for the whole day. My body would feel like it was on fire with this furious rage. I was so afraid of what I might do."

"That sounds awful. You were in high school at the time?" asked Nicole sympathetically.

"Yes, I was at home living with my mom and sister. I don't know how they put up with me. It was really difficult for all of us. It wasn't so much the cramps and physical stuff, it was the emotional rollercoaster that was so hard. Any small conflict that was brewing in my mind–sometimes it was school or friends or my family–and I would come to a raging boil and then I'd feel like, like this is it, I need to run away and disconnect forever."

"So how did you cope?"

"My mom was amazing. She really supported me. She always let me know that I was loved and accepted, no matter what I was feeling. Studying and keeping friends was really hard, and I only just made it through high school. I felt so suffocated and working on the anxiety with all those techniques, like expressive writing and meditation, just made me worse. It was a waste of time."

"So what happened? Did your doctor offer any help?"

"My doctors just offered psychiatric drugs, which scared me even more. I have seen friends and family members have a terrible time with side effects and withdrawals from medication, so I didn't want to do that. I know now that there are some great alternatives, but back then, I just toughed it out until I discovered a new paradigm in psychology. When I understood how the mind works, well, it just helped me to calm right down. It changed my life."

"Wow, interesting...but how does understanding how your mind works calm down your hormones?"

Kara knew Nicole had to lead her in this direction with the interview, and here was her chance to share what really helped. "Well, so I'm not a doctor...but what I can tell you is that, for me, I used to get into a vicious cycle. I would have a terrible time in the week leading up to my period–all anxious, exhausted, and reactive, even suicidal–and then it would calm down. But because I knew next month was coming, I would start to get nervous that I was going to have to go through that *again*. I mean, it's definitely coming, right? It's not like a fight with your sister or your boss that might blow over, this monster is coming right at you and it's going to be horrendous! Look how bad it was last month!"

Kara put her hands up to her face to express how

Very Well

frightening it always was. "So I was already getting all anxious and worked up just thinking about it in the weeks before my period. This, in turn, activated my stress response which then set all kinds of stress hormones and adrenaline running around my body, and hey, presto, I'm having an even worse nightmare. So then it took me way over a week to get over it and calm down. This vicious cycle made my cycle, well, vicious! By the end, it got so bad that there was only about a day or two in the middle of the month where I felt vaguely normal."

Nicole turned to her other guest. "Dr. Sanchez, is this what is called Premenstrual Dysphoric Disorder?"

"Yes, Nicole. PMDD, as we call it, is when the extreme ups and downs of emotions that Kara described are clearly connected to the menstrual cycle and can be predicted monthly, unlike other mental illnesses and disorders that have more random timing. The chemical imbalance is aggravated each month."

Both Kara and Nicole wanted to challenge the doctor's use of chemical imbalance, but there wasn't time, and it wasn't the place.

"Thank you, Dr. Sanchez." She immediately turned back to Kara. "So how did understanding how your mind works help the vicious cycle?"

"Well, before, I would just freak out as I didn't know what was happening, and that always made it worse and last longer. But once I saw that I was feeling my thinking, that I was scaring myself by listening to and believing my crazy thoughts, I stopped. I had this amazing insight that I was torturing myself with my own thinking and that was making my monthly experience much worse. Within a couple of months, my symptoms calmed down, and so I was calmer, and so my cycle was easier. It was like, like I'm now on a gentle cycle."

Nicole smiled, struggling to stay professional. "That's incredible! So simple and yet, well, as you said, life-changing?" Kara nodded and grinned in agreement. Dr. Sanchez just stayed with his TV face of knowing condescension as Nicole continued, "Now, you mentioned your amazing mom. Tell us a little bit about her."

"Yes. Well, she is amazing. She stood by me, even when I was taking it out on her. She got me whatever help I needed, but then later, she had her own difficulties with, you know, uh, going into menopause. So when I came back from college, I shared with her this new understanding of the mind that had helped me so much, and she got it. I mean, she *really got it*, and it totally changed her experience of suffering from hormones, too. And so she set up a hotline for other women to help them with hormonal distress, and is now helping so many women see how they don't have to suffer so much either. She really is amazing!"

"Wow, that is awesome. I know all the women I interviewed were very grateful for what she has done for them." Nicole turned to the camera. "So, if you or someone you know is experiencing this kind of distress, here is the number of the Hormone Hotline." As Nicole wrapped up the segment, Helen's phone number rolled across the screen. "Just to clarify for the audience, your mom is not a doctor

Very Well

or medical professional. This hotline is for support and counseling, and not affiliated with any hospital, treatment, or organization, correct?"

"Right. It's a grassroots project. She is a volunteer. It's all free, and she does an incredible job. I'm so proud of her and the work she is doing."

"Well, thank you for coming in tonight and sharing your story. I know there are many women who need this kind of support. Thank you again." Nicole turned back to the camera. "This is Nicole Perry for Channel 7 News. Join us again after the break for the weather report with Jules Kawolsky, your number one Channel 7 Weatherman!"

The camera's lights turned off, and Nicole took off her microphone. "Oh my gosh, you were amazing!"

Kara buried her face in her hands. "I have never been so terrified. How do you do this every day?"

"But you were great!"

Deborah and Joe came to give Kara a big hug; they were buzzing with excitement too. "You are a natural!" congratulated Joe. "I might have to sign you up to my agency!"

"You know what this means, don't you?" Deborah held Kara by the shoulders, looking her straight in the eyes. "Your mom's phone isn't going to stop ringing."

19
November

As Kara walked through the door of their apartment, she could hear her mother was already on the phone.

"No...no, you are not going crazy." Helen looked up at Kara in amazement. "Yes, I know what it feels like. I have had all those symptoms myself. No, no, your body isn't malfunctioning."

Kara made them both a cup of herbal tea and sat on the sofa with her mother while she finished the call.

"The phone hasn't stopped ringing. I just know there are a ton of messages to return and—" The phone rang again.

"I'll get it," said Kara. "You drink your tea."

"Is this my postpartum making me do this? I mean, is my disease making me do these dangerous things?" asked the caller. "It's urging me to completely break away from my

Very Well

partner and show zero tolerance and zero remorse? How does one navigate this minefield and defend one's emotions, while at the same time not letting the disease cloud one's judgment and sabotage one's life?"

"It's not a disease. You are just feeling that awful thinking," offered Kara.

When she was done with the call, Helen thanked her for helping. "You were amazing on TV. I am so proud of you! I loved the vicious cycle, gentle cycle thing!"

"Oh my gosh, I was terrified! But the funny thing was, as soon as the cameras went on and Nicole asked me the first question, all the fear just vanished. I was so in the zone that I didn't feel it. It was an amazing experience." Kara carried on, talking about the studios and the producer and Dr. Sanchez and seeing some celebrities.

"Are you thinking of changing careers? I'm sure Joe will sign you up, if you want a career in TV. I can see it now, Kara Vargus, social worker to the stars!" laughed Helen.

"No, but I know now what I want to do when I'm done with my master's."

"Yeah? What's that, my dear?" asked Helen as she sipped her tea and relaxed on the sofa before the next call came in.

"I want to work with you."

Helen looked at her daughter.

"Think about it, Mom. This is getting too big for just you already. You are going to need help. More volunteers, and maybe staff? Qualified staff who can really work with these women. Maybe a clinic? You have really started something here, Mom. You are an amazing leader!"

Instantly, the phone rang again, and Helen took it into the kitchen while shaking her head at her daughter.

Luckily the next day was Helen's day off, so she sat at the kitchen table catching up on the messages. There were calls about postpartum depression, menopause, perimenopause, and PMDD; several from boyfriends and husbands; and even a couple of doctors and social workers. She called them all back and left discreet messages when it was a voicemail, as Deborah had trained her to. Kara was right. She would need help if this continued. It would be too much for her alone. It didn't take her long to decide it was a good thing, a strong thing, for her to ask for help. She called Lily, Chrissy, Patti, Georgia, and Sharona and invited them over for a get-together with her and Kara.

"This is so nice," said Sharona, tucking into some veggies and dip that Helen had put out on the coffee table in the living room.

"Yeah, Mom, what's this about?" asked Lily. She held Flora in her lap as the other ladies all smiled adoringly at her gorgeous baby.

"Well, thanks to Nicole and our darling Kara here, the hotline phone hasn't stopped ringing. It's on silent right now, but I know there will be at least ten messages by the time we are done."

"You were sooo good on TV, Kara!" acknowledged Georgia, and the others all agreed. "Watch out, Oprah!"

Very Well

"Yes, you were all amazing. I was so proud," admitted Helen. "But this is getting too much for just me. I need help. I need volunteers to help answer the phone."

The ladies sat in silence for a second as they realized why they were there. "There are seven of us here. We could all take a shift, a turn at answering the phone. That way..."

"Count me in," interrupted Sharona.

"Me too," said Patti and Georgia simultaneously.

Kara sat grinning on the sofa next to Lily. She raised Lily's hand. "We're in."

Helen's heart was bursting. "Thank you."

"Me too, me too!" agreed Chrissy with a big smile.

"Amazing! Thank you so much! Kara already knows what to do, as she has had to listen in on many calls and can help straight away, but I think some training will be a good idea for the rest of you, if you are willing?" They all agreed; even Lily was excited to be part of something new. They had a lot to learn and were very keen to support Helen, so they decided to meet again the following week.

"I can help you now with the messages, if you like." offered Chrissy. "You know, listening to them and writing down the numbers for you to call back. I don't need training for that, right?"

"Oh, that would be amazing. Thank you, Chrissy. So let me know what evenings you all prefer and what nights you really can't do and I'll work out a schedule. And if you can't make it sometimes, don't worry, it's okay; one of us will cover. I don't want this to be a burden to anyone."

After the others had gone, Lily stayed to chat with her

mom for a little while.

"I'm so glad you made it, honey! You seemed really calm today."

"Yeah, I guess. It kinda blew my mind back when you said we don't have to listen to our thoughts. I never knew that. I've been talking to Carl about it, and yeah, I just feel calmer. It's kinda weird."

Helen was so pleased. Seeing how this understanding was helping to heal her family was more than she could have wished for. "You are going to be such a help to the women who call in. Many of them are new moms, and they are just scared and need someone who understands."

"I hope so. I mean, I do love Flora very much. I just felt so disconnected from her before, when I was up in my head all the time. I didn't realize how simple it could be to just spend time loving her."

"You are going to do great."

Helen was grateful for her Bertha and Siggy project. It gave her a distraction from the constant calls of distress. She enjoyed the volunteer work. Some of the calls were even funny or informative, but digging into Vienna in the late 1800s was fascinating. Helen looked back in her notes:

1888–Bertha's first book is published, *Kleine Geschichten für Kinder.*
1890–Bertha's second book, *In der Trödelbude,* was published.

Very Well

She continued to find dates.

1893–Freud begins formulating his Seduction Theory (which he later drops, partly from having no real scientific evidence and partly because of the backlash from colleagues. Freud's implication that incest and rape were rampant in Viennese aristocracy led him to be ostracized, so he dropped that as the basis of his theory of trauma. Helen added "coward" and "spineless" to his list of fine attributes).

1895–Bertha becomes director of an Orphanage / Freud and Breuer published *Studies on Hysteria*. Anna Freud is born.

1896–Freud first uses the term Psychoanalysis *(It was Bertha who came up with the idea of the 'Talking Cure,'* thought Helen, but by now she wasn't surprised by Freud's antics).

1897–Bertha publishes *A Woman's Voice on Women's Suffrage.*

1899–Bertha translates Mary Wollstonecraft's *A Vindication of the Rights of Women* and publishes her first play, *Women's Right.*

1900–Freud publishes *The Interpretation of Dreams.*

Bertha was 38 years old when she became the director of an orphanage in 1895. It was a huge change for her. She had decided to dedicate her life to altruistic work and began to live a much more austere lifestyle, one that she felt could be a role model to the girls she was taking care of. She had left the life of a daughter of a wealthy family and began the career of a social worker and reformer, making real change in the lives of others less well-off than herself.

Bertha had become an ardent feminist, and translating Wollstonecraft's book into German had put her at the forefront of the German feminist movement. Helen could see why the book had appealed to her. Wollstonecraft argued that traditional treatment of girls left them empty-headed, frivolous, and barely competent to raise children. This must have resonated deeply with Bertha who had escaped the life of a so-called "respectable" woman. "How many women waste life away...who might have practiced as a physician, regulated a farm, managed a shop and stood erect, supported by their own industry... How much more respectable is the type of woman who earns her own bread by fulfilling any duty, than the most accomplished beauty!"[58]

Helen paused for a moment and thought about her own life–how she and her girls could have all the higher education they wanted, could just go out and get jobs, rent apartments, or buy cars as equal citizens. Until 1908, women were legally forbidden to assemble, participate in political organizations, or engage in politics in any form at all, and it wasn't until 1974 that women were allowed to apply for their own credit cards!

Helen was fascinated by how Bertha had gone from a sheltered, suffering mental patient to an accomplished

---

[58] Mary Wollstonecraft, *A Vindication of the Rights of Women* (1889).

Very Well

professional woman in her own right in just a few years. The only thing Helen could see was that she wasn't being controlled by her circumstances anymore. Freud, on the other hand, had been dealt all the best cards and just had to show up.

The phone rang constantly for the next week.

"Two nights ago I was hospitalized due to a panic attack or maybe hypoglycemic shock. No one knows what caused it. I get shivers and tremors and insanely fast heartbeats for days, debilitating social anxiety and weakness. In the past, I've self-medicated with pot, but I don't think it's an option right now, not with a baby to take care of."

Another call.

"Nine days out and I can feel the monster settling into my soul again. I'm bloated as hell, cramps, nausea, side pain, back pain, shortness of breath. I'm so uncomfortable I can't walk."

"Is sensory overload a sign of PMDD?" asked another caller. "Noise, talking, chewing gum, and loud people all bother me. It makes me feel violent; I'm really afraid I might hit someone!"[59]

---

[59] "If you google Hyperacusis, misophonia and tinnitus, you will find evidence of a link of these symptoms to the white cell ratios and other blood results that have come to be identified with the presence of (CSI) chronic systemic inflammation ('to be on fire'). CSI is a manifestation of a chronic low-grade activation of the HPA stress response." Personal correspondence from Dr. William Pettit, Jr. with the author.

Chana Studley

"I certainly have had that, and I know my daughter Lily did when she was suffering after her baby was born," offered Helen. "I find that the more stressed I am, the more sensitive I get to noise, and then *everything* annoys me."

"Yes, it just gets worse and worse."

"So what will help is for your mind to slow down. Your thoughts are very speeded up right now, and we need to turn the volume down on them. Have you ever wondered what thoughts are? Have you ever noticed that every negative thought, bad mood, or hurt feeling you ever had always passed? It always does. Thought is always moving, like…like clouds across the sky. There are big white puffy ones and gray stormy ones but they always move on. You are the blue sky." There was silence. "Are you still there?"

The caller hesitated. "Yes…I have no idea what you're talking about, but I feel much calmer. Thank you."

The hotline ladies arrived for their training session the next week. Helen knew what she wanted to tell them, but she had asked Deborah to come and share her experience and support, too.

"This takes me right back to when I trained in London, 20 years ago.[60] Those women trained me, I passed it on to Helen, and now she is passing it on to you. *I love it*!"

Helen and Deborah shared with the volunteers what they had learned, suggestions of how to handle inebriated or

---

[60] Chana Studley, *The Myth of Low Self-Esteem*.

Very Well

angry callers, or anything that seemed dangerous. After the others had left, Helen had a chance to sit down with Deborah for some advice.

"Deborah, my women's group is going really well, but I have a question. New ladies are joining. Should I keep going back to the basics or go further?"

"I would share what comes to you each week. Trust your wisdom, and don't be afraid to change it up sometimes. I just had a thought. How about asking Nicole to get that TV doctor to come one time? You could do a Q&A?"

Dr. Sanchez was a charismatic man; it was obvious why the TV cameras had been attracted to him. He was dressed in an air of authority that complimented his expensive suit, softened only by his charm, as he walked into Patti's living room and sat in the big armchair. He made it clear he was an internist, not an OB-GYN, but he had trained at Yale, Stanford, and UCLA so his credentials were impeccable. Helen thanked him for coming as he informed the Women's Club candidly that he was only there as a favor to Nicole, but that he hoped he could be helpful to their little group. It went downhill from there.

"I've been told I now have PME. What is that exactly?" asked Sasha.

Dr. Sanchez sat back in his chair and put his fingers together like he was about to deliver a seminar in a university library. "Premenstrual Exacerbation refers to the worsening of the symptoms of another disorder, such as major depressive disorder or generalized anxiety disorder, but please get checked by your doctor."

"I'm just curious," interrupted Georgia. "On the TV show you referred to PMDD as a disorder?"

"That's right. It's in the DSM. Do you know what the DSM is?"

"Yes, I do, and I also know that it was written by a bunch of white men who were paid by big pharmaceutical companies, companies that make medications for the normal ups and downs of life they say are illnesses just to sell more drugs, and published by the American Psychiatric Association, which is not a government department but a private business!"

"My dear, I am delighted you are taking such an interest in this topic, but please do not confuse your google search with my six years of medical school," condescended Dr. Sanchez.

"And please don't confuse your one hour lecture in medical school on PMDD with my living with it for ten years!" fired back Georgia.

"My dear," continued Dr. Sanchez firmly. "Everyone who comes into my office and the offices of my colleagues is experiencing some kind of stress-related illness these days—asthma, heart disease, obesity, eczema, migraine. These are real medical problems."

"Please don't *my dear* me! Can't you see it's all coming from misunderstanding and greed? Medicalizing normal behavior isn't helping us!"

"Yes!" agreed Sharona. "You said on TV that we have a

chemical imbalance. Don't you know that's a whole made up story just to sell more drugs?!"

"Okay, okay, let's not do this. We all have a valid reason for being here, and our experience is equally valuable," said Helen, trying to keep the peace.

Dr. Sanchez stared down at the floor. Helen was nervous that he was going to leave. Who could blame him? Whatever favor he owed Nicole it wasn't worth being attacked for.

"I hear you, and I agree. Too many doctors prescribe pills without giving their patients all the information that they need, but the demand is there, and patients these days feel they aren't being treated or taken seriously unless they leave with a test or prescription, which is why your work is so incredibly valuable. I mean, good health is not just an absence of disease."

Helen was not expecting that. Her respect for the doctor suddenly went up a notch.

"That's right," continued the doctor. "I have read the reports that show that women with reproductive mood disorders have a substantially greater history of anxiety, whether it's abuse, trauma, or something else. Their HPA axis is responding to a perceived life-threatening stress. And what is fascinating to me is, well, it has often been decades since their last abuse experience. The traumatic experiences were in their childhoods or teens, which means their physiological responses to stress are a maladaptation."

Helen and Kara looked at each other.

"When the brain continues to prepare the individual for

a severe stressor that no longer exists, this puts them into continuous activation of the HPA axis, the fight or flight response, which shows up as illnesses and disorders in my office. So, yes, it is a chemical imbalance, just not the one the drug companies want to peddle. It's an imbalance of stress hormones."

The ladies were silent for a moment as they realized they may have been too quick to judge this particular TV personality.

"Right, so what we are offering," said Kara, trying to keep the feeling in the room helpful, "is knowledge, explanations, and understanding instead of medications and bogus treatments. When I understood what was happening to me, it started to take the fear and anxiety away. And when I saw there was actually nothing wrong with me, my symptoms left, too. Knowing I didn't have to overreact to all my anxious, urgent, even suicidal thoughts meant my nervous system could calm down and the problems started to go away."

Dr. Sanchez smiled. "That makes perfect sense, and I'm glad it has helped you, all of you. I just don't know how you will convince the thousands of desperate women out there who are suffering that there is nothing wrong with them."

"We don't have to," said Helen confidently. "When they are ready, they will see it for themselves."

Dr. Sanchez wasn't sure, but he seemed curious.

"Can I ask one last question?" continued Helen. "I have had several callers ask me about histamines, as it seems to be the latest in-vogue answer for these reproductive mood

Very Well

disorders."

Dr. Sanchez nodded his head. "It's not just reproductive mood disorders, I hear it mentioned as the cause of so many conditions these days–food allergies, stomach problems, fatigue. They say that anxiety and depression and a myriad of other symptoms are the result of a histamine problem. But that is putting the cart before the horse, in my opinion. As I said, it's an imbalance or overload of stress chemicals and hormones, including histamine, and so many people are taking antihistamine medications and on all kinds of antihistamine diets trying to fix something that is really a symptom of a bigger problem."

"Oh, I tried all that!" exclaimed Alex. "My naturopath doctor had me on all kinds of supplements and had me completely change my diet. She said avocados and bananas are full of histamines, but I had been told by my nutritionist to eat avocados and bananas because they are healthy! The naturopath wouldn't even let me eat leftovers as she said the bacteria that accumulates has more histamines in it!"

"Did it help?" asked Sasha curiously.

"Well, I did feel better at first, but I'm wondering now that maybe it was because I was eating healthy, non-processed food instead of all that junk I ate when I was miserable. But then I started worrying about what foods and when and how much histamine was in this or that. And then she said it had to be organic, and I just got into such an anxious mess, paranoid about what I could and couldn't eat, that I was terrified to eat anything which caused more problems, and so my boyfriend banned me from all of it."

"So my question is this. If histamines are high in women with reproductive mood disorders, isn't that also the result of an overreaction to normal hormone changes and all the other of life's ups and downs? I mean, when I looked up the list of causes and symptoms of high histamines, it included everything! Isn't it all just the result of a prolonged, stressful overreaction to life?"

Dr. Sanchez nodded his head again. "Yes, I think you are on the right track. Histamine is a chemical created in the body that is released by white blood cells into the bloodstream when the immune system is defending against a potential allergen, like pollen or mold. This release can result in an allergic reaction, but as we all know, not everyone is allergic to these things, which means they are not inherently poisonous like...arsenic, for example. So, yes, something is overreacting in the immune system of these particular people."

"And could that be a history of stress?" asked Nicole. "I mean, I had terrible seasonal allergies when I was a kid, but my brother didn't, even though we were breathing the same air."

"Yes. I see it as the cause of so many physiological problems. In fact, histamine can also stimulate the ovaries to produce more estrogen, leading to a vicious cycle of these two compounds. It's as if prolonged stress 'trains' the stress response to be hyper-reactive, and because it wasn't designed to be activated for so long, people get sick, and too much histamine is one of those problems."

Kara started to laugh. "Meanwhile, the people who

Very Well

make antihistamine drugs must be laughing all the way to the bank!"

20
December

"I couldn't help thinking about what Sasha asked the doctor last night," said Kara as she sat down to breakfast with her mom.

"I can't believe that he was so open to our ideas!"

"I know!" replied Kara. "I can't get over how he didn't just get up and leave. Anyway, I looked up PME, and he was right; it's the worsening of the symptoms of another disorder, but not just major depressive disorder or generalized anxiety disorder. They say it includes eating disorders, bipolar, IBS, migraines–basically, everything we have seen that is made of stress in the first place! I watched a video, and they were saying that PME needs to be recognized as a diagnosis so more women can get help. But if it doesn't have any symptoms of its own, and is just coming from the worsening of other things that they are

Very Well

already trying to treat, what more do they think another label can do? It's like that whole Sarafem/Prozac nonsense. Just an excuse to sell more drugs."

"Helen, you won't believe the call I just got!" Sharona was on the phone calling Helen for support. "I just spoke with a woman from Malibu who had all the usual anxieties and agitations, and after we had chatted for a while, she mentioned her meds. I asked her what they were first prescribed for, and she said postpartum depression. I thought for a moment and asked her how old her kid was, and she said eight! I asked her if her doctor had ever reviewed her meds. I mean, why would a doctor keep prescribing for postpartum depression *for eight years?!* She said that she had changed doctors a few years ago and her new doctor wouldn't continue them, so now she has to get them from a pharmacist in a back alley down in San Pedro! I can just picture her driving away in her Mercedes SUV, looking down her nose at the junkies in the alley! I hope she begins to see that it doesn't have to be like this."[61]

IVF[62] was a topic that Helen had not even considered in her research and discussions until she met Leah on the Hotline. As she took her heartbreaking calls, she started to see that the experience of women struggling to have a child was all about hormones, too. Leah, a young woman desperate to

---
[61] True story.
[62] In vitro fertilization.

have a baby, had shared how she and her husband had been trying for several years to get pregnant and nothing had helped. There had been several heartbreaking miscarriages and many false alarms. Now they were trying IVF to see if that could bring them the child they so desperately longed for. The endless rounds of hormone injections and tests were taking their toll, and Leah was on the phone in tears, exhausted.

"*I can't find the prescription!* I'm at the pharmacy, I need the medicine, but they won't give it to me! They say it's not in the computer, and without the paperwork, they don't believe me! I have to get it today or my whole schedule will be off!"

Helen heard a loud thud as Leah dropped the phone. She could hear her crying, the noise of the pharmacy in the background, and what sounded like someone trying to help her. It sounded like they were saying, can you get up?

Oh no, thought Helen. *Did she collapse?*

"Leah, can you hear me? Are you okay?"

"Yes...I'm sorry, I...I dropped the phone, and then I almost passed out."

"Did you eat anything today? Can they give you a glass of water?" Helen felt helpless. She waited while the pharmacist gave her some water and helped Leah to a chair. They talked a bit more, and then Leah decided to go get something to eat. She was just exhausted from all the stress, worry, and overthinking.

Helen thought back to when Deborah had told them about the result of being in fight or flight all the time, about

Very Well

the effects it can have on the body. *When the brain thinks we are in life-threatening danger all the time, making babies is a luxury, and so it shuts down reproduction. I wonder if that's why Leah is having a hard time getting pregnant*, thought Helen to herself. And then she had an insight. A big one. She had been reading something from Sydney Banks, and suddenly, it hit her.

"I suddenly had one of those moments when my mind just opened up a little further," confided Helen to Deborah on the phone the next day. "I'm sure you've had them. It's like you are suspended in another dimension for a second, and then you come back to your chair, but not quite. Syd wrote:

> *The true workings of the mind is not to think.*
> *It's to be an open channel to the isness of all things.*[63]

"I had just been talking to this sweet girl who is desperate to have a baby when my mind opened up to see that the purpose of the mind is not just for thinking...*wow*! I suddenly saw that just using the mind for overthinking and anxiety is such a waste! Like...like driving a Ferrari sports car in first gear! I have seen for a while now that the creative energy of Thought shows up in many forms. You know, there are the usual thinky thoughts, and the stream or ticker tape of thought, and like we talked about before, images and music are made of that creative energy of Thought, too.

---

[63] S. Banks, *"Separate Realities"* (lecture).

But...what if...what if overthinking and anxiousness is just 'first gear' and there are other experiences to be had in the quiet beyond, before thoughts?"

"Yes! I see that!" agreed Deborah excitedly. "Syd often talked about a quiet mind, how when the noise of the personal mind quiets down, we can be at peace with what is, and nothing out there has to change. This is where the healing is. There are other experiences and realities for us to see. I think this is what he meant by the beauty and peace of all things."

"What if our purpose is to be that channel, and all that overthinking is just getting in the way, creating pain and the illusion of separation? When I woke up this morning," added Helen, "my mind was so quiet... I can't find any more words..."

"How do you make a hormone?"

Everyone looked at Geraldine, curious as to what she meant.

"You kick her in the knees!"

There was quiet for a second as it sank in. "Get it? Whore ... moan?!" Geraldine fell about laughing at her own joke as the others winced a little, enjoying her as much as the joke.

It was December, and the ladies had gathered at Patti's for a holiday party. The Colonial-style house was decorated in beautiful sage green and silver decorations to accommodate all the holidays. There was a tree and a menorah, candy canes, and Hanukkah donuts. It was a cool

Very Well

California winter's night, and the ladies were happy to be with friends who understood that just because it was the festive season, they might not be feeling so festive themselves. Lori had made it, but she was looking even more frail and withdrawn.

"I guess for me, knowing where I am in my cycle is really important as it helps give me more control when all these mad thoughts are popping up. I've got more awareness now, so I don't get caught up in them as much. The urgency behind the thoughts is my clue not to listen, and it really helps," offered Sasha as they all checked in.

"Twenty-six years into this, and it's just dawning on me that when I think *everything* sucks and it will *never* get better, my period will start in 48 hours!" laughed Katrina.

"I'm always ready to blow my entire life up three days before my period," cried Sofia, one of the new members. "I feel worthless, unmotivated, and that sets off my anxiety. It's a cocktail of disaster!"

"We are so glad you are here, Sofia," replied Helen as she welcomed three new ladies to the group. "What we have been discussing here is a new way to understand our experience. Sofia, when you said you feel worthless and unmotivated and that sets off your anxiety, I think everyone here can identify with that, but I would suggest that they are all made of the same thing, Thought. Thought is a creative energy that shows up in different forms, like anxiety, but it can also be creativity, thinking, images, even music. What I wanted to talk about tonight is something more, well, spiritual."

"Are we going to sing Christmas carols?" asked Geraldine.

"No, no, that's not what I meant by spiritual," insisted Helen, trying to keep the group focused.

"Oh good, because 'Jingle Bells' isn't gonna cut it tonight, I need a lot more than festive cheer to get me out of this mood. I feel more like the antichrist than Christmas tonight!" cried Geraldine as she slumped back in her chair.

Helen was beginning to see what Clarke was talking about, but she continued, "Okay...I want you to imagine a spectrum."

"A what?!" barked Geraldine. She was obviously in a low mood as her busy mind was making it hard for her to follow.

"A spectrum, you know, a sort of line, if you like." Helen stretched out her hands and motioned, as if going from one end of a spectrum to the other. "Our state of mind is always somewhere along this spectrum. At this end, we have us, well, me, the me that is up in my head and always thinking, all caught up in illusions, stories, and believing my low-mood, anxious thinking. Relying on myself to work everything out, so basically, frightened and feeling very alone and disconnected." Helen sensed Geraldine was going to interrupt again so she said quickly, "I'm not being down on myself or anyone else. We are human, and we all have our blind spots."

"You know how you talked about the, what did you call them, symptoms? No, characteristics of a low mood? Well, I saw it. I saw that when I get caught up in my thinking I feel bad, and then I get more and more anxious," offered Alex.

"I wanted to stick my head in the microwave last night!" cried Geraldine. "Is that low enough for you?"

Helen took a deep breath. "Yes, Alex! The more we believe our thinking, the more real it feels and so the more reactive we become. This is simply evidence that we are in a low mood. Now, on the other end, we have what you could call spirituality. You can call it God, Mind, Intelligence of the Universe...Higher Power, Loving Kindness, Buddha, Allah...Great Spirit, whatever you understand to be running the show. It doesn't have to be anything religious or anything that makes sense to anyone else, actually. Something loving and kind. Wisdom. That Source of Everything that is awe-inspiring to you. Think about how babies are born or even how a simple cut heals. There is kindness and intelligence in the system and so much Wisdom."

Kara smiled at her encouragingly.

"You see, when we rely on ourselves, we get anxious, insecure, and frightened. Deep down, we know that we are limited, and so it kind of makes sense that we get scared. But when we rely on this Loving Intelligence that is already making our hearts beat and the sun shine, well, we have no need to worry. We know that we are always taken care of. We relax. We can ride the hormonal waves and know that it will pass and that we are safe. The more our reliance comes from insight, a sight from within, the better we will feel because we are relying on the Infinite and there is no end to the Infinite."

The ladies were quiet for a moment. Even Geraldine had slowed down.

"I don't really understand what you mean," said Sophia, "but I feel very...calm right now."

"Wonderful," encouraged Helen. "That good feeling belongs on this end of the spectrum." She motioned her hand in the direction of the front door. "I can always tell where I'm holding on this spectrum at any time of the day. The lighter and calmer I feel, the more I know I'm on this end—trusting, present in the moment, and connected to the Intelligence of the Universe. But the more heavy and urgent my thinking is, the more I am on this end–relying on myself, up in my head, not present and listening to my busy, insecure thinking." She motioned her other hand toward the very grand, decorated fireplace. The silver tinsel fluttered in the warm air as the smell of fresh pine and cinnamon wafted around the room.

"I would have thought you would have pointed to the fire for the warm, peaceful end of your spectrum?" asked Nicole curiously.

Helen smiled. "The fire is fake. It's gas, I believe?"

Patti nodded with a grin.

"It's gorgeous, but it's an illusion. A very clever, seductive illusion, but it's made up. Sooner or later, illusions let us down or run out of gas, and if we don't understand that it was an illusion, our worlds fall apart. All our anxious and insecure thinking is an illusion, but out there, out there is an unlimited world of opportunity, possibility, and creativity."

Very Well

"Out there is terrifying," whispered Lori.

Sharona grabbed Lori's hand, and Georgia put her arm around her as they sat on the sofa.

Helen gave her a big, warm smile. "I know it can seem that way, but that's the low mood talking. From the basement, from our low moods each month, everything can look terrifying, but it's not true. It's listening to our low-mood thinking that is terrifying us, but we don't have to listen to it. What if you knew that you were always taken care of, that there is a Loving Intelligence already running the show? What if you could feel that love and support? You would know you can handle anything."

They talked some more about love and trust and how seeing it to be true melts away the fear.

Just as they were winding down, Patti asked a question. "You know how you explained to us that everything is made of Thought? You meant that how we *experience* everything is made of Thought, right?"

Helen nodded.

"I have been thinking about that. I don't know much about spirituality or anything about quantum physics, but...well, I get that hormones and brains are made out of chemicals, but..." Patti was struggling with something on a deeper level. "But I'm sure I heard Syd Banks say on one of those old tapes you gave me that all of life is...is one Divine Thought. I mean, and I am obviously no expert, but I'm wondering...well, does anything really exist outside of...spiritualness? I mean, is anything really real?"

"You mean, like if a hormone drops in the forest and no

one overreacts, does it really exist?" asked Georgia with a smile.

Helen was in awe of her friend, feeling a deep sense of love and connection as she listened. "Go on."

Patti smiled and continued, pointing towards the door, "Well, on this end of the spectrum, where we are trusting, we are feeling that connection deeply with the Loving Intelligence, Mind, as Syd called it. Maybe we are all just Divine Consciousness, and therefore everything *is* made of Thought, Divine Thought? Hormones and chemicals move, and bones and tissue grow, but everything can only exist by Divine Will."

The group sat in silence for a few moments, stunned slightly by Patti's insights.

"I get it," said Kara. "Anything that exists must be somewhere in that Divine Intelligence, in the Divine Plan, and therefore made of something…spiritual. Maybe hormones are little spiritual messengers? Maybe nothing really exists, except Divine Consciousness?"

Helen was captivated. She suddenly felt that gliding feeling again, supported and guided. She remembered Syd saying that the body is just a metaphor. Her understanding was unfolding like an exquisite white linen tablecloth. She could feel it go up in the air, the sunlight shining through as it floated down gracefully covering the surface of her mind, unfolding to welcome a fresh new experience. Helen wasn't driving her mind around in first gear anymore, she was seeing something new. Yes, we can innocently think our way into a mess of anxiety and hot flashes, but that is an innocent

Very Well

misunderstanding of what is real and what is illusion. Divine Mind has given us a way for our minds to heal, just like our bodies. A way to be in this physical world but not be consumed by it. How special to see that there is more to see. How beautiful to find the missing peace. "Wow, ladies, that was amazing! What a wonderful way to finish. Thank you."

Later as the ladies were leaving, Helen went to give Lori a big hug.

"I am terrified they will take my kids away from me."

"Why would they take them away?"

"When I go to the hospital and say I'm going to kill myself. I can't do this anymore. I need help and for the doctors to take me seriously. I want to get off these meds, but instead of helping, they just give me more."

Helen felt nervous. "I know it seems bad, but you really are very strong. Look how you showed up here again and how you are taking care of your children. You are one of the bravest people I know. If you feel that you are not safe, I mean, that you might hurt yourself, please, please let someone know. You can always call me, even if it's late. Please don't worry about bothering me. You are so special, and I want to help you. Do you feel safe to drive home?"

"Yes." Lori spoke so quietly that Helen wasn't sure if she should let her drive or be alone.

"Why don't you let me drive you home?" offered Kara. "It's no problem, and I can make sure you get home okay." She smiled knowingly at her mother, took Lori's arm, and gently guided her out to her car.

"I'm worried about that girl." Helen couldn't help

feeling concerned as she helped Patti to clean up after everyone had gone.

"I know. She seems so lost, and those meds aren't helping either."

"Sure, but if she wants to detox, I have heard you have to go very slow. If you come off too fast, there can be terrible side effects, and then the doctors put you on a higher dose because they say it's a relapse when really it's the brain adjusting to the detox!"

"Look at us," replied Patti. "Our lives have changed so much in the last year."

A week later, Helen's phone rang at 2 am. It was Patti.

"Helen! Lori just turned up on my doorstep! She says she wants to die! I think she might try! *What do I do?!*"

Helen was suddenly wide awake. "Keep her there. I'm coming." Helen ran into Kara's room and woke her up. "Get up, get up! I need your help. This is way beyond me. Whatever you have been studying in school all these years needs to work, *now*! No more rehearsing, no more books, get dressed!"

They drove over to Patti's house in Brentwood as fast as possible. The streets were empty and quiet, the night mist from the ocean gleaming in the light from the street lamps. They pulled into the driveway as Patti opened the door. She showed them into the family room where Lori was curled up on the sofa covered in a soft blanket.

"You poor thing, I'm so sorry," said Helen as Lori slowly opened her eyes.

Very Well

Lori stared into space like she wasn't quite there. Her skin was damp, the circles under her eyes darker. "Why does it have to be such...a struggle? Life, it's..." She took a deep sigh, as if getting the words out was like climbing a mountain. "If I could just go to sleep and...not wake up, it would be...over."

Patti and Helen continued to talk with her while Kara called some emergency services to find out the best thing to do. After a few phone calls, Kara found a bed for her at the hospital, and Helen arranged for Mateo, Lori's husband, to meet them there. Lori was not doing well at all. It was like she was trapped in a world of darkness she couldn't get out of.

21
January

As the weeks passed, the new volunteers settled in. Helen appreciated any time they could give and encouraged them to check in with her if they needed support. Sharona needed to discuss a call where the caller reported she was a year and a half into menopause and then started bleeding and having bad cramps.

"Helen, I suggested she go to the doctor, but why didn't she just do that? It's funny how some people are running to the doctor all the time, but others have to be pushed to go."

"Some people just need reassurance. They are scared and get up in their thinking, then just paralyze themselves, which scares them even more."

"You're right, I certainly did. She also said that she had a weird, very stingy, itchy rash under her arms. I asked if she was using the same deodorant, the same bath soap, and the

Very Well

same detergent. All we could figure out is that her body decided it didn't like something anymore. I'm also very allergic to store bought soaps; I've been lactose intolerant for most of my life. She wondered if it was celiac. Then we realized we were trying to figure it out before she had even made a doctor's appointment! We both started to laugh when we realized we were trying to do the doctor's job for him without any medical training! Dr. Sanchez would not have been impressed with me!"

Helen laughed with her. "Yes, it's amazing how low-mood thinking can show up as constructive thinking in disguise, but it's the heavy intense feeling that gives it away. When I feel the heaviness of trying to work things out and realize I'm really just overthinking, I learned to stop. It's amazing how fresh, new thoughts are always there. I'm sure you really helped her. If she was in a better mood by the time she got off the phone, you did her an amazing service. Well done!"

Then, Lily had a call that totally baffled her. "This woman said she was feeling so bad this month that it caused her to self-harm. I was nervous that I wouldn't know what to say, although I certainly had some terrible thoughts when I was suffering. Then she said it was shopping. I didn't understand at first until she said that her husband needs to take away her credit cards at that time of the month. *Mom, she was calling a shopping spree 'self-harm!'* What is the matter with people?!"

"What? Oh, wow. Well, as much as I think it is way too extreme to compare cutting yourself with spending money to get relief, I guess...I guess she is suffering, too. Actually, I really don't know what to say about that one, honey."

Patti, unfortunately, had gotten the brunt of someone's anger in one of her calls.

"Don't tell me to meditate or be mindful! If I could do that I wouldn't be calling for help! How is a hot bath with candles going to fix this demon in my head that wants me to throw myself off the roof!"

"I told her I agreed that none of that is going to fix it, at least not long-term. But she was so angry. I don't know if she heard anything I said."

"Maybe she was able to let off enough steam that she didn't take it out on her kids that night? You might never know how much you helped her. Remember, they are not angry with you. They don't know you. They are suffering and their wellbeing is a little covered up right now," offered Helen. "But it's always there and you are doing a great job!"

During Helen's shift on the phone that week, she had a curious conversation with a new caller who had seen Kara's interview with Nicole on Channel 7.

"I have a theory. PMDD is trauma stuck in the body. If we are unaware or unwilling to face trauma, it's forced out by that fluctuation in hormones, erupting like a volcano and spewing ugliness on our loved ones. It's like we need that spike to force it out."

Helen paused to collect her thoughts. "Tell me what you mean by stuck in the body."

"Well, they have to go somewhere, right? And all that

physical pain and suffering is proof that they are held deep in there. So now, I'm actively working on identifying and releasing traumas. I tell myself, I'm having these doubts, or starting these fights, because this stuff is actually important. So, being passive or polite in the moment of trauma is essentially me ignoring and pushing down feelings. So I store it away...and the pressure builds."

"Interesting. So why is that not called PTSD,[64] then?"

"Because it's connected to my cycle."

"Isn't it interesting that for some it happens with their cycle, for some it happens when they are 'triggered' by something like social situations, and others...well, it's just random and called generalized anxiety disorder."

"I guess."

"Do you see a common thread with all those examples?" asked Helen, hoping she was laying the ground for a shift in thinking.

"Trauma?"

"And what is trauma?"

"Well, it's some terrible thing that has happened, like abuse or the death of someone close or...or violence."

"Those are certainly very tragic things, but we all react differently to situations, don't we? For some, violence might be normal in their lives, like, say, a prison guard. They just get on with it, and others can get hysterical because their toast fell on the floor. We are all living in a thought-created world, and if we don't react to something, then it's not going

---

[64] Post-Traumatic Stress Disorder.

to bother us or our nervous systems. I don't mean denial or ignoring emotions. I agree that is not helpful, either. I mean understanding that we all have innate wellbeing, and it's the thoughts we have passing through our minds that are actually creating our experience. Therefore, trauma is made of thoughts; memories are thoughts brought into the now. The situation has passed, and because Thought is always moving, it can't get stuck."

"Not sure I get that, but as I face and release my trauma, I have fewer and fewer symptoms. It's not completely gone, but I have better control. My lows aren't as low," offered the caller.

"That's amazing. I'm so glad you are doing better. You have clearly had a shift in your thinking." Helen was wondering if she should go further and show her that insight had done that for her, and there was no need for all the analyzing and "processing." "We have a monthly women's group where we discuss what I'm pointing to. Maybe you would like to come and hear more about how thought works?"

The caller wasn't sure. She thanked Helen but said she was doing fine, which made Helen wonder why she'd called, and guessed she had just needed to be heard.

Helen had been checking in with Lori and her husband every few days to see how they were doing. Lori had been released with even more meds and was barely able to take care of herself, let alone her kids. Her mother had come to help, and several of her friends were doing what they could,

Very Well

but it was hard for everyone.

About two weeks after she had come home from the hospital, Lori's sister called. "I'm so sorry to tell you, but Lori tried to kill herself last night."

There was silence. Painful silence. The kind of silence that feels like falling. Falling down and down and you can't stop it. Helen couldn't breathe. There were times when she had worried about Kara and Lily hurting themselves, and times when she hadn't wanted to be here anymore herself. There were those times when she felt so trapped in those unrelenting, frightening thoughts, there was no way out. You are so very tired that you just wanted it to be over.

"Oh my gosh, is she okay?! I mean, is she injured, is she conscious?!"

"She's in the ICU at Cedars, but they say she is going to be okay. She just needs a lot of care right now. She's very fragile. I know how much you guys tried to help her, so I thought you should know."

Helen told Kara when she got home from class, and later she called Patti. They all cried at the thought of the unbearable pain Lori must have been going through.

"How are we going to tell the Women's Club?" asked Patti. "They will be devastated."

"I know. I think I'm going to ask Deborah to come and talk to the group. I don't think I can handle this one on my own."

Helen turned back to her books and opened her Siggy and Bertha file. It was pure escapism, but she also knew somehow that her wisdom was telling her, guiding her, to take care of herself.

1900–Freud publishes *The Interpretation of Dreams*.

Helen had never been interested in anything about dreams particularly, but something in the words caught her attention–the *Oedipus complex*. She remembered something about this from college.

Helen decided to look it up and, once again, found out there was a whole different story than the one Freud had presented, *literally*. She then found some quotes from Dr. Tomas Szasz, a psychologist and author in the 1970s. "Freud's use of the term Oedipus Complex is his insistence that it refers to something factual and that it must be taken literally rather than figuratively...Freud's error was in claiming that his own fantasies were factual findings."[65]

Well, he's not wrong there, thought Helen to herself. *We've all innocently thought ourselves into thinking some nonsense or other is real.* She got curious and looked up the original legend to understand more.

King Laius, grieved by childlessness, consults the Oracle[66] and learns that any child born to him will kill him. He therefore "puts" his wife away. Angry, she gets him drunk, seduces him, and bears a child. Laius immediately disposes of the baby, Oedipus, who is found by shepherds

---

[65] Thomas Szasz, *The Myth of Psychotherapy*, pp. 127-8.
[66] The Oracle of Delphi was famous throughout ancient Greece, and people from all the then-known world would flock to the area seeking answers--a bit like Google but more spooky!

Very Well

and taken to another childless king and queen to be brought up as their own. Oedipus is now a young prince, and one day, while traveling, gets into a very silly fight with a noble stranger and kills him, not knowing this was Laius, his birth father. Oedipus continues his journey to this new kingdom that had just lost its king and marries its queen, not knowing that she is his birth mother.

What a mess, thought Helen. It's *worse than a daytime soap opera!*

Helen then read a fascinating account of how Freud had gone to see a play based on the Oedipus legend by LaCoste, a French classical playwright. "As he was deeply in love with his own mother, who was a very great deal younger than his father, he (Freud) found a name to stick on his own feelings."[67]

Hmm, thought Helen. Dr. Szasz's reasons as to why Freud twisted the Oedipus legend to make it into his theory that children want to sleep with their parents now made total but weird sense.

"First, and most obvious, is that Oedipus didn't know he was killing his father or that he was sleeping with his mother!" cried Helen to Kara as she sat down later for dinner.

"Listen to you! You really should think about going back to school. It's like you are studying for a Ph.D.!" Helen ignored her and so Kara played along. "I think you will

---

[67] Quote from historian Edith Hall, "Natalie Haynes Stands Up for the Classics," BBC Radio 4.

probably find that Freud says it was subconscious."

"But how could it be, if he had no knowledge of them? Unless he was telepathic? How can something be repressed if he never had the knowledge of it in the first place? Freud took a conveniently well-known, not to mention bizarre legend, and then twisted it to suit his even more bizarre theory and presented it as scientific proof! As Dr. Szasz points out, if he wanted to get some juicy psychobabble theory out of the story, there is plenty of angry, maladaptive behavior going on without needing to rewrite it! Oh my gosh!" said Helen, suddenly realizing something. "It's a legend, a story, a...a made-up fable!"

"Yes, it's the Oedipus *legend*," agreed Kara sarcastically.

"He's not basing his theory on research or experiments. His theory is based on a made-up story. Can't you see that's, like, well, like me publishing a theory based on a popular movie, and calling it scientific evidence because it did well at the box office? *This isn't science*!"

Kara couldn't help laughing at her mother for getting so involved in her project, and then she suddenly thought of Lori.

"What is it, sweetheart?" Helen could see her daughter's face had changed.

"I just thought about poor Lori...and what a rotten deal she has been through."

Deborah was very sad when she heard the news about Lori and agreed to come and share what she could with the group. She had talked to many people who had

Very Well

contemplated suicide and had visited a few in the hospital as they fought the thoughts that wanted to take them out. When Helen broke the news to the group, they were stunned into silence. After a few moments, Alex spoke up.

"I am so sorry to hear this. She's such a sweet girl. I can't imagine what she must have been going through, is still going through. I...I...as a teenager and in college, I often thought about it. Never understood why. As an adult, I was extremely angry and always irritated by the people around me. I would cry, even scream. Then it got so bad that I took all the pills I could find in the house, but luckily my husband found me. I can't imagine what that put him and my parents through. They must have been so frightened." Sofia put her arm out and grabbed Alex's hand.

"Thank God you survived, and thank God Lori did too," offered Deborah with deep compassion. "I know it's a big shock and a reminder of what can happen when we get too far into the illusion of low-mood thinking. The stronger the illusion, the more our problems appear to be real and insurmountable. When I was in the depths of my despair after being mugged for the third time, I would wake up in the morning, cry for hours, and still not have a reason to get out of bed.[68] I never made any serious plans to end it, but I often woke up wishing I hadn't. When I look back, I can see just how much I was suffering, suffering innocently, because I didn't know any different."

She pulled a book by Sydney Banks out of her purse and

---

[68] Studley, The Myth of Low Self-Esteem.

read slowly:

> *"The trouble is you see this world as the only reality that exists. You have trapped yourself on a level of consciousness. You must learn to take the limitations of life and see there are more realities than meet the eye."*[69]

Deborah lowered the book and gazed at the women. "It's easy to see when others have thought themselves into a corner, trapped themselves in a level of consciousness and can't see any way out, but it's much harder when it happens to ourselves. I had a client call me in a terrible panic recently. She said, 'Either I go into work and get sick from all the stress from my toxic boss, or I hand in my notice, but as no one is going to hire a 50-year-old woman, I will lose my house and be out on the street! *Either I die from work or I die on the street!*'" Everyone smiled a little, as they all knew they had thought themselves into similar dark corners.

"I could have said it's just your thinking, but that wouldn't have been helpful. It's true, but she was in such an anxious state, it wouldn't have been kind. I agreed with her that this 'seemed' to be a really tough situation, like she was caught between a rock and a hard place. She agreed emphatically. So I suggested that if both are a disaster, why not take the one with salary and benefits? She paused, and I could almost hear her thinking shift. It was just enough to open up the conversation that maybe there were some other

---

[69] Sydney Banks, *Second Chance* (Ballantine Books, 1983).

Very Well

ways to see this. Maybe it wasn't as hopeless as she had thought.

"As we continued talking, she saw that her boss was doing the best he could with his really lousy thinking, and she was only ever experiencing her thoughts about him. Also, how did she know she would never be hired again? Maybe she could teach or be a consultant with all that experience. Her mind started to open up to fresh, new thoughts. She started to see that she had trapped herself in some kind of hell by listening to her own thoughts."

"So how can we help Lori?" Georgia was clearly concerned.

"Well, it seems she is surrounded by people who love her and care about her, but sadly, unless she is ready to see something different, there isn't much we can do except love and accept her. Remember she has innate health; we all do. She has all the courage, resilience, and wisdom she needs to get through this. She isn't broken and doesn't need fixing. All she needs is to be pointed in the right direction, to her own wellbeing."

The group nodded. They understood, even though the concern was very present.

"The trauma of what happened isn't going to...well, I mean, won't she have PTSD from it?" asked Julie hesitantly. "Won't she need some serious therapy now?"

"When I used to look back at some of the terrible things that happened to me from a low mood, I was devastated. I felt stuck in it and couldn't see a way out, and the psychiatrist I was sent to just kept getting me to relive the terrifying events. I could never get well that way. 'Real therapy' as you call it actually kept the pain alive. Syd says, 'Going back into the past to fix yesterday's negative memories is like trying to blow out an electric light bulb!' In fact, he said it is 'psychological suicide!'[70]

"When I look back now, from a better state of mind, what happened to me is just a part of my history, like growing up in the UK or working in Hollywood. It was a long time ago, and I am not that person anymore. Now I can look back in full detail and see it with understanding, even love, and compassion. We are not our traumas or our stories. We are not our thoughts about the past. We can observe those passing thoughts, and because we are the observer, it means we are not what we observe. I am as healthy and whole as I think I am and Lori can be, too."

"So if we are not our thoughts, who are we?"

Deborah paused. "We are the blue sky."

---

[70] Ibid.

22
February, March, and April

The weather was still cool as the new year faded into February. It was always Helen's favorite time of the year; it meant sunglasses and boots for a few days before the southern California sun came back with a vengeance. Things were getting back to normal after the holidays, and now that the volunteers were helping out with the hotline, Helen felt things falling into place.

Lori had asked to see her and so she drove over to her home in Los Feliz, a beautiful 1930s neighborhood not far from the Hollywood sign. Mateo showed her into the back room where Lori was resting. She still had dark circles around her eyes and was a little bloated from the side effects of all the pills, but she had already been taken off many of them and was eating and sleeping well.

After some hugs and how are yous, Lori opened up

about what had happened. "It was all too much. My mind was literally telling me to either hurt my kids or hurt myself. It was terrifying. I was hallucinating to the point where...well, I just couldn't shut it out anymore."[71]

It was upsetting for Helen to hear, knowing that the snowball of distress had been started by innocence and pushed down the hill by ignorance.

"You seem so much better, though."

"I am. This amazing doctor came in and reviewed my case and halved the number of meds I was on straight away. He said it was criminal the amount they were giving me, that they clearly weren't necessary and were making me sicker. It wasn't the PMDD. I was hallucinating from the medications." Lori was talking slowly, but she was much clearer than she had been. "But it's okay. Mateo was furious at first when he realized it was the side effects of the meds that were making me suicidal. He wanted to scream and shout at them, but... this doctor managed to calm him down and get him to look at the bright side, I guess. I don't know what they talked about but...but he seems like a different person."

"You seem like a different person." Helen was very relieved but curious about what could have happened.

Lori grinned. "I think I am. Something 'shifted,' as you say. I don't know if it was changing the meds... or maybe an

---

[71] If you are having difficulties with the side effects of medications please do not stop abruptly, please consult a medical professional. For more information go to https://medicatingnormal.com/ and watch the documentary, *Medicating Normal*.

Very Well

insight, but... I just don't feel the pressure of those thoughts anymore."

Even though her speech was slow, Helen felt like there was someone home for the first time since they had met. It was like she was reflecting carefully to choose the right words instead of searching helplessly in the dark for them as she had before.

"I mean, the crazy thoughts still come. I worry about what I have put Matty through, and how the kids might be affected. How will I get back on my feet, and what if it happens again? When you would talk about Innate Happiness, I felt... guilty that I couldn't be happy. I didn't know what it was to feel happy anymore." She took a deep sigh. "But now it's almost like I'm watching those thoughts go by, like that ticker tape you always talk about. I'm not my thoughts. What happened, that wasn't me."

Helen was so happy, impressed, and relieved to hear her talking like this. She seemed almost content. "Right. You are not your thoughts, not even the good ones. They are just spiritual energy passing by, and the more you see that, the better you are going to feel."

"I still get tired pretty quickly, but I feel better every day. It was so nice of you to come, Helen."

"Of course, my sweet."

"I feel like...like I have come home. I mean, I know I'm home with Matty and the kids, but I mean home here." Lori placed her hand on her heart.

"I think so, too."

Helen was so thrilled to share the good news with the others at the next Women's Club. They were excited that Lori was strong enough to take calls now. They couldn't wait to see her again. The two women had arranged to meet every week to help get Lori back on her feet. As part of the discharge protocol, hospital management had insisted on mandatory appointments with a psychiatrist and a therapist, so they always had plenty to talk about.

"How are the appointments going?" asked Helen on her next visit.

"Okay. I have to go twice a week to the therapist for now, and once a month to the shrink. It's quite a challenge, but I guess I can't get out of it. Jess, my therapist, makes me talk about what happened over and over, about coping skills and living with limitations, which is no fun."

"Why do they think that helps? They say that they have new ideas these days of how to help, but it seems to be the same old thing to me. I'm reading an amazing book right now by Dr. George Pransky, and he calls it '*low mood therapy.*'[72]

"That's exactly what it is. I go in feeling fairly okay and come out feeling worse. How can talking about the past, all that painful stuff, make anyone feel better?" She hesitated. "But you know what, she never asks me to talk about what *it* was like."

Helen didn't understand.

---

[72] George S. Pransky Ph.D., *The Relationship Handbook* (Pransky & Associates, 2014).

Very Well

"When I was unconscious. I mean, she asks me about before and after, but not what it was like during."

Helen was curious. "Do you remember what it was like?"

"Yes. I can remember being in the bathroom where I took the pills. Everyone was out, and although my head was really fuzzy, I can remember this voice saying 'it's for the best' and 'take more.' Like it was forcing me to do it. I started to get woozy, and everything was spinning. I lay down on the floor so that the cold tiles would cool my face, and then I...I was floating."

Lori looked at Helen with deep compassion as if she needed to take care of her, her big brown eyes full of understanding for what she was describing. "I was free. Free of the pain in my head and my heart. I don't know how to describe it, but there was light, a wave of white light. It's such a cliche, but there was just...beautiful light, and there was room, so much room. I felt fluid, as if I could take up all the room there was. I didn't know where I ended and where anything else was. It was... sweet, I mean, it smelled sweet, and it was warm, like sunshine and .... I was floating."

Lori reached out her hand and Helen took it gladly. "I know it sounds crazy, but I don't know how else to describe it."

"It sounds...beautiful."

Lori paused for a while and then said, "It was like I was hovering above me. I could see myself on the bathroom floor, but it was okay. I knew I was okay; I knew I was just sleeping. I was so tired, I just needed to sleep. When Matty came in and saw me there, I could feel his panic, and I wanted to let him know I was okay, but he couldn't hear me. He picked me up and shook me, trying to get me to wake up, to throw up. He rushed me to the hospital, and then I kinda left it all for a while. I think…I think I went away, somewhere safe."

Helen stroked her arm and listened intently, with nothing else on her mind. There was nothing else in that moment, just the two of them, nothing else in the world. Helen was so present she didn't realize an hour had passed already.

"I know I'm not crazy. I feel saner than I have in a long time," Lori said confidently.

"I don't think you are crazy at all. I think that was your innate wellbeing. You saw it, you 'saw' the feeling. It sounds like peace. I think it sounds beautiful, and well, I don't blame you for not telling the therapist. This is precious."

They sat peacefully in the quiet for a few minutes. "I was thinking, maybe you could help the therapist by sharing what you see to be true about how experience is created? About innate health and how everyone has it? Maybe she will see something different, that we are never damaged, and there is always hope."

Lori continued to make great progress. By the next month, she felt well enough to come to the Women's Club. Kara picked her up, and the ladies were so pleased to see her.

"Thank you all so much. Thank you for your kindness, the flowers, and the calls. Thank you to Sharona for taking

Very Well

my kids out so many times. They love being with your kids and have so much fun. It really means so much to Matty and me."

"It's our pleasure. We are so happy you are with us and doing so well."

It was a wonderful evening, everyone sharing where they were holding and what they were seeing that was new. Lori joined in and gave the women so much to think about. She was still weak physically, but her spirit was as strong as anyone in the room.

Helen drove her home after the meeting. Lori stayed in her seat for a few minutes after they arrived, deep in reflection.

"You know what? I'm starting to remember it differently now," said Lori.

"What? The night it happened?" Helen switched off the engine and turned to listen.

"Yes. Remember how I said I was up there, watching what was happening to me?"

Helen nodded.

"Well, recently I have been remembering it, feeling it...differently. I feel now like I was deep inside of me. Like, you know, like deep inside a beach ball? Like I was surrounded by a cushion of air, soft and safe. When Matty was shaking me, trying to get me to wake up and get me to puke, I knew he was trying to help me, but he wasn't holding *me*. I mean, I know he was holding my body, but I was deep inside me, safe inside. I know that sounds weird, a little strange maybe, but I wasn't my body."

Helen smiled. "It's okay. It doesn't matter if I don't understand, but I think I kind of do. Syd said we should go past the physical to the spiritual, right?"

Lori smiled in acknowledgment. "When we got to the hospital and they were putting a tube down my throat and my body was jerking around, I could feel it, but it wasn't...touching ...*me*. I don't know how else to say it, but I felt safe."

Helen thought for a moment. "Before it sounded like you were having an out-of-body experience, but this sounds like...awareness?"

"I thought that, and then I realized I was unconscious so I wasn't really there. I don't know what I'm saying, but that feeling of safety was so warm and secure. It was like I was surrounded by...by love."

The two women sat still for a few moments.

"That's beautiful," said Helen. "I think this is why we cannot be broken. The love you felt then, that is who we really are, all the time. It's our essence before what Syd Banks called the contamination of personal thought. You were seeing your life from that place before thoughts come into our minds and get all mixed up into illusions and misunderstandings. Thought, the spiritual essence of Thought, is fluid and mystical; it moves and flows. It's love and is unlimited.

"When Thought comes into our consciousness, it takes a form like thinky thoughts and images and sounds and sensations. Probably other things, too, but that's how I see it right now. It's like when it's going across our 'screen of

Very Well

consciousness,' it takes one of those forms, and depending on our state of mind, we either have nothing on it or we get sucked into the illusion of it."

Lori was taking it all in.

"Which is why we cannot ever be broken or damaged, because a formless loving energy has no form to break!" continued Helen.

"I think I get what you're saying. That light and big 'roominess' feeling, the space, the endless space I was feeling and filling up is love, pure, unconditional love, and unconditional love can't be broken."

"Yes, you are the blue sky!"

The next time Lori called, she was crying. Helen was scared she had taken a step backward, but she wasn't crying for herself. She was crying for Jess, her therapist.

"Helen, I tried to tell her about the love and how it was uncontaminated by thoughts, and she told me I was wrong! That I was dreaming and needed to get back to real life! She actually got frustrated with me when I said I was doing fine, because she thinks I'm not! Oh my God, I wanted to yell at her for being so negative all the time, but I knew one of us had to stay calm."

"Oh no! I'm so sorry you have to go through this. Look, it sounds like she is in a low mood, and from that low mood, she can only see what's wrong. She is doing the best she can with the thinking she has at the moment. Can you see that?"

"Yes! It's so obvious! I just want to hug her and tell her it's going to be okay. She is where I was–all stuck in the negative, seeing only limitations–and, Helen, I'm beginning to see just how lost I was, how anxious and afraid I was all the time. I *knew* the world was scary and that my kids were in danger, so I was right to be thinking and thinking and thinking about how to fix and change things. I never saw that as anxiety before! I just thought I was being a responsible mother!"

A few days later Lori called again. "Helen, you won't believe what happened this time. Jess apologized! She said she went home and thought about what I said about unconditional love and how it's who we really are, and she said she felt a calm come over her. We had the most beautiful talk, and she is recommending my meds be taken down again, and that I only need therapy once a week now!"

"Oh wow! That's such good news! See? I knew you would be able to point her in the right direction. She is lucky to have you as a patient."

The two women laughed at how ridiculous it all was and agreed to meet in a few days.

"Lori, I learned this great analogy recently about medications from one of my Principles teachers, Dr. Bill Pettit.[73] He said when our minds get all speeded up with anxiety and overthinking, it's like we have our foot on the accelerator. And then when we are given psychiatric

---

[73] My teacher and friend, Dr. William Pettit, Jr. M.D., retired psychiatrist, who was mentored by Sydney Banks for many years.

Very Well

medications, it's like putting the other foot on the brake. You can kinda live like that for a while, but it's not the best way to live. If you come off the meds without anything changing, it's like taking the brakes off, but your other foot is still on the accelerator! And that's how people relapse. Either it's the side effects of coming off the meds too quickly or they are still going 100 miles an hour with their thinking and crash and burn again."

"I get that. I feel like my accelerator is slowing down big time with your help, and Dr. Sanchez says I can come off all the meds now, but like you said, slowly so as not to crash and burn."

"Dr. Sanchez?! Dr. Richard Sanchez?" asked Helen in amazement.

"Yes, why? Do you know him? He's the one who came to the ICU when I was at Cedars and checked my charts. He's been overseeing my case ever since."

"Tall, handsome, kind of overconfident?"

"Yes, he's tall and handsome, but he's always been really kind to me and Matty. Why?"

Helen was buzzing with how he could have known about her case and why he would have taken such an interest.

"He came to speak at the Women's Club when you weren't there! You know he's a TV doctor? I mean, he's a real doctor, but he's on the Channel 7 news."

Lori shook her head. "I've been so out of it recently I haven't watched TV in ages. All I know is he's been amazing and he's getting me off these pills, which I can't wait to be done with. I can feel that I just don't need them anymore."

"And what do they say about your postpartum and PMDD now?" asked Helen, intrigued. "I mean, it's been three months since you were in the hospital."

"I know. Well, it seems to have melted away. My monthly cycle is happening, but I just don't feel that huge drop in my emotions like I used to. In fact, I have stopped worrying about it at all. So I feel a bit low sometimes, but I just watch those thoughts go by. Anything crazy, I just tell my husband, and we laugh it off together. It's completely different now."

"Wow, that's amazing. Insight can change everything!"

That night, Nicole called. "You beat me to it!" cried Helen. "I was going to call you. Did you send Dr. Sanchez to the hospital to see Lori when she overdosed? It must have been you!"

"Uh, yeah. I was so frightened when I heard what happened; I knew they needed an independent medical mind to look over everything. She was on so many medications, I knew it couldn't be right."

"Thank you. Thank you. Thank you! You may have saved her life, Nicole. She is doing so well now, and it's all thanks to you and Dr. Sanchez for getting her off that stuff."

"I know he can come across as all showbiz, but he's a really nice guy underneath, and he was really impressed with your group. It got him thinking, so you never know."

"You never know..."

"Anyway, that's not why I called. I called because I have

Very Well

some news, some very sweet and sad news."

"What?" Helen was intrigued.

"Well, I'm leaving L.A., that's the sad part. But...drumroll...I have been offered a senior producer job at NBC's *Today Show* in New York, and Helen, they want me to write content, too!"

"Oh my goodness, Nicole, that's amazing!"

"I know, I can't believe it. It doesn't start for another month, so I have time to pack up and finish my contract here, but, yeah! I couldn't have done it without you."

"Oh, you are going to do so *very well*!"

23
Beverly Hills

A few weeks later, Nicole was on the phone asking Helen a curious favor. "Can I ask you to be my date? I have to go to this event and I need a friend to come with me. It will be like our last chance to have some fun together before I leave."

"Me? Really? You must have lots of younger, trendier friends you want to hang out with."

"I want to thank you for everything you have done for me before I leave for New York. Helping me with my own stuff and that news piece we did, it really did push my career in an amazing direction. It's a Lifetime Achievement Award thing for Jay Leno, you know, an industry thing, but there will be a lot of stars there, and we get to dress up. It'll be fun, so will you be my date, please, please?"

Helen chuckled, shaking her head in bemusement. "I guess, but there is no need to thank me. You have already

Very Well

done so much to help us."

Helen had thought a lot about Lori's description of her near-death experience. She had heard other people talk about the light at the end of the tunnel and how there was limitless glory and magnificence on the other side. As she was reflecting, she remembered that Freud described human beings as dark, untamed beasts, and that he believed at our core we are conflict. But the two ideas just didn't fit together. How could he believe that, and yet, everyone who has a near-death experience always seems to talk about seeing light and love? Helen turned back to her books. She was much more inclined to believe Lori. *Follow the good feeling,* she thought to herself.

1901–Freud begins the analysis of his eighteen-year-old daughter, Anna.

Helen paused. *He did what now? If analysis is all about digging into sexual dreams and neurosis, what business did he have doing this with his own daughter?* Helen was disgusted. *That is it,* she thought. *I can't take reading any more about this man.* Where *is that book on Bertha?*

In the same year, Bertha had been addressing charitable organizations, and in 1902, she had founded her own organization called Care by Women, stressing that social work was the "duty of the donor, not the right of the recipient." She had taught casework techniques, how to find foster homes, and helped immigrants with their needs. It was at this time she had taken on the mission of fighting the white slave trade, what we call sex trafficking today, campaigning and helping young displaced women and girls.

That same year, she'd been described as a "lady of sharp powers of observation and thorough training in social problems." She had been sent as a representative of the National Conference on White Slavery to Galacia, what is now western Ukraine. Ironically, her unique ability with words, speaking, and storytelling that Breuer and Freud turned into psychoanalysis was what helped her in her work with the orphans and displaced women who came to her for help. Bertha had made an incredible recovery from a bedridden hysteric to a powerful leader and prolific author.

In 1905, when Bertha was 46, her mother passed away. She fell into a depression, but there were no accounts of her falling back into the hysterical darkness of her youth. *Maybe she was just grieving?* thought Helen to herself. Later that year, Bertha traveled to Russia to report on the atrocities of the pogroms.[74] The barbarous slaughter of Russian Jews foreshadowed what was to come in the Holocaust. Bertha had continued her social work, fundraising, and campaigning. She built a home for unwed mothers and never hesitated to say what she saw to be true even if it offended the status quo. By 1909, there were nine wards in her Home, and in 1910, more land had been donated by Baroness Rothschild so that Bertha could continue her

---

[74] Pogrom - an organized massacre of Jewish people in Russia and eastern Europe.

Very Well

incredible work. In 1909, she traveled to London, Toronto, New York, and Washington, D.C.

Helen paused again. The only thing Helen knew about this time in history was the movie *Titanic*. She thought about the tight corsets and the gas lamps, the horses and carriages and the big hats. Traveling to all those places all in one year, even today with airline travel, would have been exhausting. How had Bertha done it all, on her own, in 1909? Helen was deeply moved and inspired. She couldn't believe how courageous Bertha had been.

In 1910, Bertha delivered a speech to the first international conference on white slavery, and in 1911, she continued to travel for her work–Budapest, Saloniki, Constantinople, Jaffa, Jerusalem, Alexandria–and on into 1912–Lodz, Warsaw, and Moscow.

In 1913, she published another play, and in 1914, when World War I broke out, she had been overwhelmed with people to help, but she'd done it. Freud, on the other hand, had been busy meeting with the military officers of several countries, selling his ideas about "shell shock," what we now call PTSD. After the end of the most horrific war in history, he wrote:

> *Our psychoanalysis has had bad luck. No sooner had it begun to interest the world because of the war neuroses then the war came to an end.* [75]

---

[75] Ernest Jones, *Sigmund Freud: Life and Work. Vol 2: The Years of Maturity* 1901–1919 (Hogarth Press, 1955).

Chana Studley

What?! He's annoyed that the war ended?! thought Helen to herself. *Does the man have any morals?*

In 1917, Bertha started a correspondence with the famous philosopher, Martin Buber, which continued until her death. They had become great admirers of each other's work. Although Bertha challenged him openly, their always formal relationship had remained strong.

During and after the war, funding for her work had become a daily struggle. Hitler was gaining power, and as a Jewish woman from another age, Bertha's life had become increasingly difficult. It was the roaring 20s, but the persecution of the Jews was becoming the norm in Germany. "How will we survive? How will we bear the hatred and misery?[76]" wrote Bertha.

As the Nazis gained strength and then power, in 1933, the Gestapo ransacked and destroyed their way through millions of lives. Bertha stepped up and took leadership roles wherever she could, even though her own health was failing. She had rheumatism and painful gallbladder attacks, but she kept writing and working for others, and in 1934, at the age of 74, took a group of Jewish children from Germany to Glasgow in Scotland.

In 1936, at eighty years old, suffering and bedridden with a tumor in her liver, Bertha was summoned by the Gestapo. Standing up to their interrogation had been her last defiant act. Following this, her pain had become so

---

[76] Guttman, *The Enigma of Anna O.*, p. 275.

Very Well

extreme that she needed morphine, the drug that had enslaved her as a young woman. Right until the end, she continued talking, telling stories, and on May 28 she passed away, surrounded by her friends and the women and girls she had spent her life helping.

On November 10, 1936, Nazis and people from the local village came with torches and forced themselves into the orphanage. The "screaming and wailing of the children was horrifying and heartbreaking as the barbarians chased them out."[77] Many of the children were sent to Auschwitz; only a handful survived.

Helen was silent, her mind subdued by the cruelty, her spirit awe-struck by Bertha's resilient love and courage. She sat back in her chair as she read Bertha's eulogy from Martin Buber:

I not only admired her but loved her, and will love her until I die. There are people of spirit and there are people of passion, both less common than one might think. Rarer still are the people of spirit and passion. But rarest of all is a passionate spirit.
Bertha Pappenheim was a woman with just such a spirit. Pass on her memory. Be witnesses that it still exists.[78]

In Bertha's will, she requested that whoever visits her

---

[77] Guttman, *The Enigma of Anna O.*, p. 325.
[78] Judith Herman, *Trauma and Recovery* (Basic Books, 1992), p. 19.

grave should place a small stone "as a quiet promise…to serve the mission of women's duties and women's joy…unflinchingly and courageously."[79]

That is who we really are, thought Helen. Joy, courage, love, and passion. Under all the stinky thinking and misunderstandings we are…love.

Helen was almost ready when Nicole came to pick her up. "Tonight's the night for our big night out! I know I'm early, but let's go to the Beverly Hills Hotel and have drinks first. We look so good, we might as well make the most of it!" Nicole was in a crazy mood and very excited about their evening together. She looked even more spectacular than usual.

They drove across town and rolled up the famous driveway to the big pink hotel on Sunset Boulevard, where so many stars had come and gone in the 100 years since it had been built. The valet drove away their car as they glided inside.

"I came here once with my husband, Gary, when he made his first big real estate deal. We thought we had arrived. We were young and naive, but it was fun. Seems so long ago now," reminisced Helen as she sipped her cocktail.

They enjoyed their drinks and the admiring looks from the waiters and guests and then drove the short distance to the smaller hotel for the Leno event. The valet took the car keys as Nicole looked at the tickets.

---

[79] Ibid., p. 20.

Very Well

"Oh no! I thought it said 8 pm, but it was really 7 pm for dinner, and the show started at 8!"

"But it's 8:15!" cried Helen nervously. "Maybe they won't let us in?"

"I'm so sorry, I'm such an idiot! Quick! Follow me!" She grabbed Helen's hand and rushed her through a side door. Suddenly, they were in a passageway that looked like it was leading to the kitchen.

"Where are we going?" cried Helen, as she tried not to slip in her new Manolo Blahnik heels.

"I've been here before. I think there is a side door here somewhere where we can slip in and not disturb the show. Quickly, through here!"

She pushed through a swing door that a waiter had just come out of, and they walked discreetly into a very, very dark event room. Helen's eyes couldn't see where they were going as Nicole led her to a table and they sat down. A spotlight came up on the stage as Patti walked on, looking stunning. What was she doing? How did she know Jay Leno?

As her eyes adjusted, Helen saw Kara, Deborah, Joe, Lily, and Carl sitting around the large banquet table, grinning madly. Why was Dr. Alice here?! She was so confused. Were they invited, too? Kara never said anything!

"Good evening, ladies and gentlemen. I would like to welcome you all to the Second Unsung Heroes Foundation Gala Event!" announced Patti as she took the microphone. There was applause and so Helen joined in, hoping it wasn't what she thought might be happening.

Helen's heart started to pound as the full room started directing their applause toward her! She looked around and in the darkness, Sharona, Georgia, Sasha, and Alex were all grinning at her. They were all dressed up so beautifully. Geraldine and Clarke and Julie and Katrina and other staff from Neiman's, all applauding her. Nicole gave her a huge hug as Helen glared back at her.

"As you know, we are all about celebrating those amongst us who do so much for others and ask little for themselves. Tonight, we are here to honor and celebrate Helen Vargus and her work with the Hormone Hotline. Helen is courageous, kind, and selfless. A woman of grace and dignity, and I am privileged to call her my friend."

Everyone clapped. Helen was in shock.

As the crowd settled, Patti continued, "I'd like to start our wonderful evening by welcoming back our honoree from our last event, Ayeesha, to tell us what she has been up to! Please welcome the amazing Ayeesha Washington!"

Patti stretched out her arm as Ayeesha, now a confident young college sophomore, stepped up onto the stage. She was dressed so elegantly and told everyone how well she was doing, that she was getting top marks in all her subjects and was already enrolled in a master's program in social work. And the car they had given her was being put to good use, taking her grandparents to hospital appointments and continuing to help with the homeless. The audience clapped and cheered as she left the stage.

"You are an inspiration, Ayeesha. We know you will go far. Next, I would like to invite one of the courageous

Very Well

women who have been helped by Helen and her work. Ladies and gentlemen, Mrs. Lori Ruiz!"

Out of the dark stepped Lori, strong and confident, her eyes sparkling as she walked towards Patti's outstretched arms.

"Helen, what can I say? Your kindness and wisdom touched my heart. Even when I couldn't respond, even in the depths of my despair, you knew I was okay. I can't tell you how much it meant to me when you would talk to me like I was well, even when I felt so awful inside. In my ugliest and most frightening moments, you showed me respect and unconditional love. You just knew I was okay underneath all that suffering. When all the doctors and therapists doubted I would ever get well, you knew I could.

"Your love and confidence in my wellbeing inspired me to be my best self, and I know many of the women here will join me in thanking you for reaching out and being there when we needed you. I know my job now is to share that love with others, to help them fall in love with life, like you helped me to do. You have given us all more than your time. You have given us your heart. On their behalf and on behalf of our very grateful families, thank you from the bottom of my heart." Lori blew Helen a big kiss, her wellbeing and health lighting up the room.

Patti was choking up and had to fight back the tears. She put her hand on her heart as she continued with the show. "Thank you, Lori, you truly are an inspiration. Next, I would like to ask Kara and Lily, Helen's daughters, to come up and join me." The two girls kissed their mother as they passed to take their places next to Patti on the stage. Kara took the microphone first.

"Mom, you are the bomb!" Everyone laughed and clapped. "You have no idea how many women you have helped and the lives that they, in turn, have affected for the good. When I was in my teens, and I'm sure driving you both crazy, you stood by me with such love and understanding. I don't think I would have made it through without you. I love you, and am so proud of the work you are doing and where this will go, but most of all so proud to call you my mom!" There was more clapping as she passed the microphone to Lily.

"After the birth of my baby, I was in the darkest depression. I *knew* there was no way out. As many of the ladies here will know, it feels like you are down a deep, dark well, and you are going to drown. Mom, you reached in and saved me. You showed me that it was not real and that I had all the courage and resilience I needed to get through it, and I did. Your strength and wisdom are amazing. How you took care of us after Daddy died when you must have been suffering so much yourself is unbelievable. On behalf of my sister and all the other women you have helped, we thank you so very much for being you!"

Everyone stood and applauded the girls and Helen. Tears were streaming down her face by now, happy, joyful tears.

Lily handed the mike back to Patti. "As you all know, we have been collecting donations to help support this wonderful work that Helen and her volunteers do, to pay

Very Well

for the phone bill and the advertising so that it can continue. To present the Unsung Hero donation gift this year, please help me welcome ... *the Governor of California!*"

The crowd applauded Governor Campbell as he walked onto the stage. Helen was really in shock now. Nicole stood and guided her to the steps, and Lily took her hand as she joined them on stage.

"Good evening, ladies and gentlemen. It really is a privilege to be here tonight." Governor Campbell took the microphone and addressed the crowd. "First, I need to make a public apology. I was invited to present the check at the first Unsung Heroes event and had to cancel at the last minute." He turned to Helen and paused for a second. "I know that put you in a terrible situation, and I am deeply, deeply sorry."

Helen could tell he was apologizing for much more than just bailing on their charity event; his words were sincere and heartfelt.

"So, I am extremely delighted to be able to be here tonight to celebrate with you and your wonderful family, and present to you this check for $10,000."

There was more applause, but he put up his hand to the crowd so that he could continue. "I have been so touched by the work you are doing and the incredible help you are bringing to women and their families that I have created an endowment from the state of California to support your work."

Everyone gasped.

"In memory of your late husband, I have created the

Gary Vargus Memorial Fund to support two full-time members of staff."

The crowd jumped up. Kara, Lily, and Patti were now in shock.

The governor handed the mike to Helen as she nervously stepped forward. She paused, looking out at all the beautiful faces of the women she had helped. Helen thought about her husband, Gary, and their life before. It was a very nice life, and she had been very happy, but now, she felt alive. She remembered how she used to be so down on herself for being stupid and how nervous and insecure she felt going to the conference in San Diego. But where did all those insecure thoughts go? They had vanished, and she hadn't even needed to work on them, just like Deborah had promised. A loving confidence filled her heart as she took a moment before addressing the audience.

"When my husband died, I thought my life was over. There was such sadness that I felt I would be swallowed up by it. But I had two daughters to raise, two beautiful girls who needed a home and someone to guide and teach them. Well, as it turns out, they have been my teachers–the best, most amazing teachers I could have wished for. They have taught me never to give up, that we all have innate wellbeing and courage, all of us. There are no exceptions, no matter what you have been through or how you feel right now. We all have all the resilience and wisdom that we need to face life's challenges.

"Sydney Banks, who has inspired so many of us here, said that 'life is a contact sport,' and some truly awful things

Very Well

can happen to us, but we have a choice in how we see it. We can either see it as Wisdom, telling us something, pointing us back home to what we already know, or we can see it as tragedy and sink under the pain."

Looking toward Patti and then out to Deborah, Nicole, and her family, she closed with words of deep gratitude and love. "So, with amazing friends and the support of people who truly care, we all have everything we need. Thank you, everyone. I am so truly blessed. And as Syd so eloquently said,

A mind full of love and good feelings can never go wrong."[80]

---

[80] Banks, *The Missing Link*, p. 117.

Acknowledgments

Thank you to everyone who supported and encouraged me in writing this novel. Especially to all the women who shared their stories and insights; Marina Fuchs, Kelley Dulio, Chayelle Rose, Shifra Chesler, Catrine Strothers, Jennifer Wooldridge, Nicole Cohen Yechezkel, Wendy Williams, Hadassah Johanna Hazan, and Carol Banayan.

So much gratitude to Jack Pransky, Pallavi Schniering, Jennifer Wooldridge, and Chayelle Rose for reading the manuscript and for their great feedback.

Thank you to Dr. James Davies for permission to reprint the story about Prozac and Sarafem.

A big thank you to my wonderful editor Heather Osborne who has saved the day for me several times and Rochel Leah Fox for her excellent proofreading.

To Christine Heath, thank you for your gracious and generous forward. And my deepest gratitude to all the amazing women who took the time out of their busy schedules to read and write reviews; Dr. Amy Johnson, Natasha Swerdloff, Rohini Ross, Vikki Ede, Jacquie Forde, and Dr. Rani Bora.

Chana Studley

And finally to Mr. Sydney Banks. Thank you for sharing your wisdom, love, and understanding that still guides us to look within and change the world.

With Love, Chana

About the Author

Chana Studley is a sought-after coach, mentor, and teacher. She leads Wellness programs and retreats about the Three Principles and the Mindbody Connection, book clubs, and one-on-one coaching in person and online.

If you are looking for help with any hormonal problem or other chronic physical issues including pain, migraines, skin and gut problems, allergies, and asthma please reach out and we can find the right program for you.

Chana has also opened a private membership group. This is a safe community space for sharing and support: weekly Q&A, webinars with guest speakers, a book club, and a resident health and fitness expert. Go to her website to find out more and sign up.

Chana speaks at conferences worldwide and is available for consultations for organizations, businesses, clinics, and universities.

You can contact her at:
chanastudley.com

Resources

Facebook Groups:
PMS, PMDD, Postpartum Depression, Menopause, and The Three Principles
Stress, Wellbeing, and The Three Principles

Other books by Chana Studley:
The Myth of Low Self-Esteem
Painless

Recommended reading by Sydney Banks:
The Missing Link
In Quest of the Pearl
The Enlightened Gardener

Three Principles resources:
Sydbanks.com
3PGC.org
3PUK.org
Chana Studley - Youtube Channel

Printed in Great Britain
by Amazon